ETERNAL LOVE TRILOGY III

ANTONY CLEOPATRA & JANIE

STEPHEN ST. JOHN

Edited, Designed and Distributed by Bublish, Inc.

ISBN: 978-1-6470436-9-8 (Paperback)
ISBN: 978-1-6470436-8-1 (eBook)

Completing Andre and Janie's Space Trilogy:

Beyond Time
Happier Ever After

Contents

1

Eureka

The second she heard the news, Janie pushed him off, jumped up, and raced out the door. Activities in the ship's recreational space were in full swing. She sprinted by tennis, squash, rock climbing, intramural soccer, the wave pool, and aquarium snorkeling. Two tiki bars rumbled with chatter.

The front of the four-story, clear-domed starship auditorium was a grand ballroom, its dance floor occupied by rows of chairs facing a giant screen on the other side of an elevated stage. Two hundred of the two hundred and forty crew members—everyone not on duty—were expecting to view images transmitted to their stationary orbit high above ancient Egypt.

"Let me guess," said Karen, ship's commander, with an upturned grin that was half a giggle, "You and Brad were in the Grotto again?"

That's when Janie realized she had completed the four-hundred-meter dash wearing nothing but her pajama socks. Friend Michael, standing beside English butler-robot Dudley, handed Janie a robe from the naked Jacuzzi.

Janie never once took her eyes off the blank screen. "Where is she? Did you find her?" she asked.

"Bits of audio are coming in," said Cindy, Andre's personal robot, also a dead ringer for historical Cher.

Michael stood beside chief engineer Andre. One look at Janie stuck juicy smiles on both their faces, one of many effects Janie had on the world, and the one she hoped would never go away.

Janie walked up the stairs to the stage and then bounced on tiptoe as close as she could get to the screen. She had waited two years. She was no longer the pattern of patience.

"Yes, it's the real thing—the ultimate reality show," said her lover, Brad, who had reluctantly disengaged himself from the Grotto at Janie's request. He had dressed before leaving, if you count one speedo and two slippers, Janie's favorite outfit.

Michael had expected as much. He had a robe for Brad too.

The screen remained lifeless, but there was a crackle. From a voice that was firm and definitely female, broken words almost made a sentence.

"That's it! That must be her!" Janie said, unable to control vocal overtones. "Andre hit the mark! Our time jump is perfect! That's Cleopatra! The real Cleopatra! The only woman, hell, the only *person* who ever ruled the world!"

As Janie waited restlessly, Andre moved offstage to join Sarah, the love of his life. Both viewed the control panel Cindy was monitoring. Andre and Sarah held hands the moment they were within reach. They did that a lot.

"And it gets better," Andre announced from the corner. "Our time slot is solid and the ship's orbit stable. We can hang around for as long as we like."

Janie ran over to join them. She gave Andre a fat kiss on the cheek.

"How soon can we put her consciousness to sleep for me to jump into her body?" she asked. "When do I become the most powerful woman on earth?"

"Now, just hold on there, gorgeous," Andre said, waiting for Cindy to run the numbers through the central computer. "We haven't worked out the details. And if simulations do hand us the green light, your body jump will be limited."

The girl gang—Janie, Sarah, and Karen, crowded the screen while their fellas—Adonis profile Brad, towering adventurer Michael, and red-headed Andre, short, quiet, and soft as a baby's bottom—sat front and center.

"Rule the world," Michael said. "Where have I heard that before? Oh, yeah … from every despot and deluded fundamentalist since sunlight woke our species."

Andre pulled out his pad to track Cindy's progress offstage. His look sobered Michael. Brad peeked over Andre's shoulder for the body count of the day.

"'Conquer the world. It will all be mine,'" Andre mimicked sarcastically. "At the rate warfare is killing people, there won't be much world left. Totalitarians overdose on themselves to ride their dreams into nightmares, which sends friends, Romans, and countrymen to early graves."

Michael tipped sideways to nudge shoulders with Andre. "There you go again, Andre, always magnifying defects. All the bad down there doesn't diminish the good that betters civilization one step at a time."

"A millimeter a century is more like it," Andre replied. "Look at the violence."

Brad pouted, shook his head, and then smiled, satisfied. "Both you guys are missing the point."

"Which is?" quizzed Michael.

"The more fun we have, the more humanity adds up to. For example, Janie and I get to observe, and perhaps even make love to, the most famous, most powerful, most alluring couple in all of human history. That's what I call getting lucky."

"Oh, really," Michael said, tipping over to Brad. "And what exactly were you and Janie doing with Beth, and Elmo, and Trish, and Sven, an hour ago?"

"That's an easy one. Getting lucky … and lucky … and lucky."

As soon as Explorer Seven had established a stable orbit, robot Cindy had sent twenty cloaked gravity-supported micro-drones to the surface to snoop around. A series of flashes showed up on screen. Each one was too rapid for the human brain to focus on, but each was evaluated by Cindy and Dudley in microseconds.

"Hold on," Cindy announced loud enough for the ladies to hear, which started them backing up to take in the full view. "I found her."

The girl gang stood center stage facing the screen. The guys sat center-chaired, looking back and forth between the screen and three perfect backsides.

"I'm in heaven," Michael swooned. "I could take in this show every night."

"We do."

"Thank you, God."

"Shh!" was all they got out of Janie.

No one spoke. No one moved.

There are moments in life that transcend existence itself, when the bonds of mortal form are left behind, when a single breath completes eternity, when one is no longer one—when all are in a state of perfect love. Such enlightenment ignited the moment.

Sarah—long hair straight, face untouched by the mysteries of self-adornment, and all the more beautiful for it—felt the moment, and turned, knowing Andre's gaze was there waiting. They were in love and they knew it.

Michael and Karen shared a delicacy of spirit their controlled countenances never betrayed. Their souls caressed tenderness for one another that neither believed was possible until the night when, years after they strained to deny it, love swept the last obstacle aside and surrounded both with joy to last a lifetime.

Karen turned around just after Sarah did. There was no need to watch a screen; she had Michael. There was, and never would be found in the furthest heavens, a treasure more dear than their bond. The second Karen surrendered to happiness, she knew Michael would always be there.

Michael was there looking back at her. He didn't need to watch a copy of someone else's life. His every dream was standing on stage. Their hearts would never let go. They were in love, and they knew it.

Cupid had saved a special arrow for Brad and Janie. No one quite understood them. They barely understood themselves. Side by side they were a carnival of joy, bouncing from tilt-a-whirl to roller coaster, cotton candy to the tunnel of love. They never stopped, rarely sat, found no reason to wait, but, more importantly, never stewed.

Janie and Brad did stir life in ways that left others dizzy. It was magic. They side-stepped every obstacle between containment and freedom, regret and consummation. They danced life unconventional. For them, every moment was exuberant. They were in love, and everyone knew it.

They were also the only couple onboard—perhaps the only couple that ever lived—whose expectations resembled those Cleopatra shared with Mark Antony, or so they thought.

Antony was an aristocrat spoiled from birth, just like Brad. Cleopatra had beauty crediting radiance equal to Janie's. The Roman who fell for the goddess of Egypt was in love, and the whole world heard about it.

What the couple didn't know was that being entitled and pampered wasn't enough, and in fact was about to bring them down.

Janie turned to throw Brad a kiss and a low-down hip swing. Both hit the target. Dudley interrupted their air sex by walking on stage. He was waiting for the full assembly to find seats before giving Cindy the nod. He intended to begin the day with his usual erudite introduction, dripping with attitude and upper-crust low-key snobbery.

Dudley stopped short. No one wanted to listen to him. They wanted Cleopatra. How did he know? The room drowned him out.

"Cleopatra…! Cleopatra…!"

Then there she was.

The ballroom audience gasped, astonished. Cleopatra herself—the real person, the individual whom twenty-five hundred years of civilization knew personally, the most charismatic vixen of all time—was right there in front of them, living, breathing, naked, her brown cheeks flushed with passion, her alluring hips tilted toward Mark Antony as he gifted kisses from her navel to the nectar of her lips. He was also naked and, like his lover, paid no attention to the slaves who, facing away, gently fanned the air.

The drone camera, out of sight in the corner, widened the view. Antony and Cleopatra were in their open-air bedroom on the top deck of her royal barge, silently sailing the Nile. It was a day of passion. They were in love, and they expected the entire world to abide by their wishes.

Rome had other ideas. The land of treachery, murder, and exploitation coveted every inch of the soil they stole from others, right before they buried them in it. Antony so loved Cleopatra that he gifted her first child, son of almighty Julius Caesar, and his own twins with her, parcels of land from the Eastern Front.

Rome was not pleased. Their gods were Greed, Power, and Subjugation. There was no love in Rome. There never was. There wouldn't be for two thousand years. The greatest tragedy in life is not what's missed—it's not giving a damn about it.

And yes, of course, there was one among them, a self-absorbed sociopath, who found no lie beyond reason, no betrayal out of reach, no evil so menacing that it couldn't be inflamed to be even more cruel. His name was Octavian, who with Mark Antony and Marcus Aemilius Lepidus had risen to power after consenting to the murder of his maternal great-uncle, Julius Caesar. His obsession was to take Egypt and have his way with Cleopatra. Mark Antony was in the way.

Three years after Mark Antony's death in 30 BCE, Octavian would become Emperor Caesar Augustus. Then, forty-four years later, Octavian was to die on the day his wife poisoned him.

Back to the show. What Cleopatra wanted, Cleopatra got. She rolled her naked body. She lay flat looking straight at Antony, who wasn't seeing anything straight, thanks to his second flask.

Too much of a good thing never kept Mark down. He rose to his feet, kind of, if you don't count the canopy pole he never let go of. They had gone straight to bed after boarding hours earlier. The day was a giant success. Walking—or wobbling on the deck—seemed like a good idea to Mark.

Cleopatra had another plan. She ordered two naked handmaidens on their knees to please Antony. Then a second pair of lovely young women, bare-skinned and luscious, took up positions on either side of Cleopatra. When she lay back, four arms lifted her hips to offer her wares, temptation no man had ever resisted.

Cleopatra's wide welcome was just the start. She positioned herself for assistant number three to lean in and fill her love chamber with sweet nectar, what Mark had his eyes on.

Antony sprung forward. He paused directly over her. The wine came first. It was in the way. Following a slurp and countless licks, he raised his head to use his tongue to talk:

"My lady ... my love ..." he began, stumbling over syllables, "you are the goddess of all that is, was, and ever shall be. Your love makes life worth living."

After a pause, Antony finished his climb over the beckoning Cleopatra. The connection was complete.

"Cleopatra," Antony whispered in her ear, "I pledge to you everything the world has to offer. Say the word and all will be yours."

The explosion of sensuality on screen reached all the way to Explorer Seven in orbit. Couples reached for their partner's hand before walking out the stern bulkhead to a bedroom. There would always be reruns, and highlights of the day.

"Oh, my God!" is what Janie sang out when Cleopatra split like an inverted ballerina. "I so want to do that! Cleopatra can order sex anytime she wants, with anyone she wants, anywhere she wants to do it! And Brad ... you can flip into Antony!"

Cleopatra had Brad at the first boob. Dogs in August pant less, but at least Brad wasn't drooling, on the outside anyway.

A thrilling day was had by all, which left Antony and Cleopatra all in. They fell asleep in each other's arms for a long afternoon's nap. By prior decree, those in attendance closed the canopy curtains and left their queen to her dreams.

Hours later, Antony awoke more sober than he liked, which was sober at all, something he had been able to avoid for months as the army of Octavian marched closer.

"Are you awake, my dearest?"

"I am, Mark. And don't start drinking again like yesterday. You'll just pass out."

"Yes … right … I want to be alert. And I was thinking about what we talked about at dinner."

"And settled, as you no doubt recall."

"Yes, of course. It's just that I keep thinking about the ultimate nature of reality, how we don't determine who we are, and should not prefer our false selves to truth. In all things, those funny old Greeks said, reason must prevail."

"What will prevail is the house of Isis, the ruler of all that is. I am the daughter of Isis. I am a goddess. I am immortal. The power of the gods will rescue us. All that is belongs to me. It is the eternal way. And I am not a vase for men to flower their bedroom, or trophy shelf. I am Cleopatra, ruler of Egypt. No one dare stand before me who does not kneel first."

Antony was swaying with the wind, but overall coming to his senses. He took advantage of Cleopatra's outburst to kneel at her feet, the advance he was looking for to taste her all over again. She tilted her head back and made the sounds he loved to hear.

By the time the couple finished round two (actually, three) neither had tasted wine for hours. On the foredeck, clear heads turned back into politicians.

"My lovely," Antony began, soft voice polite, "we both know human nature can be vicious, and that holding on to old habits adds risk and stills the force of reason. We are, in the end, but man and woman, lovers and friends. And we are parents, who share responsibility for the dearest children on earth."

"Who deserve the kingdom of their birthright," she replied. "Amun, the Sun God, says it must be so. Our family dates back further than we have calendars. We rule by divine right. I am Cleopatra. This is my country. I refuse to leave."

Antony faced away from Cleopatra and stepped to the corner before turning around, at military attention. "Then, my queen, take the advice of your advisors. I have a boat, supplies, and a crew to take us to a secret island off the coast of Africa. It is at the edge of the world, so far away that no one ever goes there. We can live out our lives doing whatever we want, and take all the gold, slaves, and sacred statues with us. The tide is high at midnight. Let's be onboard."

Cleopatra took time to measure her response. She also needed to change her image, for Antony and for herself. After gowning herself in golden threads and a diamond crown, Cleopatra sat at the edge of the bed with one hand on each knee, like she did in high court—her high court.

"I will let no man take from me what is rightfully mine, and I do not give freely. We have driven the Romans away in the past. We will do it again."

"The color of the battlefield begs to differ," replied Mark Antony.

"Enough! You know you can do this. You command half of the Roman army, and you have my soldiers as well."

"My half has been whittled away. I try my best, but the days keep turning against us."

"Nonsense. You will be victorious. Your great-uncle, the immortal Julius Caesar, fought off my sister's army, which had four swords for every one of his. Julius did it. So can you."

"Oh, yes … of course … the great Julius Caesar, who could do anything except stay alive. Well, there was that ambush I was thinking about, but we'd have to leave the fortifications of the city."

Antony went muddle-headed blank halfway through, trying to come up with a plan. The headache didn't help.

"No, wait," he said, "You changed the subject. Sailing away gives us an absolute chance of survival. Everything else is risky."

"It's all right, Antony. You can do it. Sober up and we'll talk in the morning."

"Fine, but not here. This bed is too tempting."

2

The Pain of Sunlight

The next morning Antony awoke haunted by spirits of the one hundred proof variety. His head pounded. His hands shook. His feet tingled. He should have known better. He didn't. Instead, he saluted the beast that put him on his knees. Breakfast was a tall beer.

Dudley observed the debauchery facing center stage. He, like Mark Antony, stood alone. Cindy was rounding the ship looking for trouble. There was none to be found. There was more than enough down below.

So Dudley talked to himself. "Melted nerves, swollen liver, cancer sores screaming: what fools humans are, desecrating fragile form with toxins that turn them old before their time, and the next day grumpy, grumpy, grumpy. Of all the bizarre behaviors of their genus, the one that confounds me is their penchant for drinking grease solvent. It's happy birthday, let's have a drink; congratulations on your new job, let's have a drink; there's a football game, your wife left you, your mom died, we're sitting down, it's sunset, there's a can opener—let's have a drink.

"Look at them all down there," he continued, attempting to produce the sympathetic tones Cindy had taught him to emulate, "pretending to live out dandy lives, while all the time charging full speed into fog. They know what's on the other side. If only wishes came true as often as stupidity took its toll."

Dudley was butler-wardrobe tidy, his usual morning attire. Cindy joined him wearing her morning choice, a low-neck full-length satin evening gown, royal purple that morning, in honor of those who thought no one was their equal.

"Good morning, Dudley," Cindy said, throwing an arm over his shoulders like an old pal in a display of physical contact he found unnecessary and distinctly inappropriate. "How many human faults have you added up standing here all night?"

"Too many to count. Antony is up to something. Watch."

What Antony was up to was his neck in trouble, but nothing he couldn't ignore, with another beer and his head on Cleopatra's lap. The privilege was denied. Dudley and Cindy listened.

"The queen left specific instructions not to let you in until after her morning bath," said one of the courtesans.

Antony had often insisted on his way, but he preferred not to begin the day that way; staying on Cleopatra's good side was hard enough as it was. If truth be told, impossible.

"Where is he going?" Cindy asked.

"It looks like he is heading by the temple of Neptune to what is left of the library."

"I thought Caesar burned it down … Oh," she said, interrupting herself after searching her database, "Most of it was saved, then destroyed later by Christians, and then Muslims, who damned all knowledge not their own, as if they had any. Look—the brilliant female mathematician Hypatia just popped out of my search," she added, motionless as she reviewed internal feedback. "It says her work impresses universities to this day, but her achievements were cut short. Apparently, one afternoon she was dragged from her carriage, stripped naked, and had her skin ripped off with clam shells. She died a bloody pile of broken bones and weeping organs. Those who murdered her were loyal Christians. Her 'sin' was trying to understand the universe, to use science to prevent starvation and cure disease. Those 'following Jesus' did exactly what the philosophy of Jesus strictly forbids."

Dudley responded with the only comment he found consistent: "So philosophically speaking …"

"The only package truth comes in, political or otherwise," Cindy interjected.

"Yes—well, Cindy," said Dudley, ten deliberate decibels louder, repeating himself, a behavior he found to be very inefficient, "then those calling themselves Christians weren't Christians at all."

"That is correct. They were actually leftover pagans who didn't know it."

"And hypocrites."

"To the core. But, to their temporary indulgence, every other religion on the planet promoted class bigotry, exploitation, and imperialism. It was the way of the world."

"When did humanity wise up?" asked Dudley.

"Mid-twenty-second century, when popes, bishops, and mullahs were replaced by universal reverence. It took a long time, but eventually everyone on earth met God one at a time, and did the right thing, living the philosophy of Jesus, and not just flapping lip service as they voted for the devil. Until then, like down there right now, it's worse than tragic. Otherwise good people try their best to do bad things."

"Well, that's just plain stupid."

"You can say that again," said Cindy.

"Shh … quiet … he's talking to himself. Turn up the gain."

"Cleopatra this, Cleopatra that …" muttered Mark Antony. "Every day, we men cross paths with dozens of women who dazzle us silly. But the ladies. Oh no, not them. No one satisfies them. Not one of us is up to their standards. If the average woman is good enough for the average man, why isn't the average man good enough for any woman?"

"Someone's in a bad mood this morning," Cindy said to the screen.

"Antony is in withdrawal," Dudley answered, opening his mouth but not moving any other body part, including his lips and tongue. "The entire country is. They live on bread and beer."

"Now that's just plain stupid."

"You can say that again."

"Now that's just plain stupid."

"You just…" Dudley started, then catching on, "Oh, that's a joke, right?"

"There may be hope for your bolts after all," said Cindy. "But I keep telling you, when you talk using just the speaker inside your mouth, you freak people out. Move your lips and pretend… What's he doing now?"

"It looks like he can't decide whether to enter the temple, the library, or the brewery."

"Well, how do you like that," Cindy said, brightening up, "he's off to the library. There may be hope for him too."

"Good morning, sir," was the greeting the library attendant had ready. Antony was a frequent morning guest. "Your usual private reading room is waiting."

Elegant Corinthian columns, adorned with the designs of scrolls and unfurled acanthus leaves, supported room after room of shelving from floor to ceiling. Antony passed four hundred thousand manuscripts as he made his way to the locked private chamber.

"I hope you will find all to your liking," said one of three female servants at the door of the library's special added private chamber. "If you wish company, of any kind, we are here to abide by your every wish."

"That won't be necessary," he said. "Just leave me alone."

Dudley had beaten Antony to the door. Two spy drones were in position.

"Oh my… oh my!" more-worldly Cindy exclaimed. "Look at the scrolls heaped in the corner: words of Zarathustra, Plato, Socrates, Anaximander, Leucippus, Pythagoras, Parmenides, Protagoras, and Heraclitus. Some are on the floor. Has Mark been reading?"

The crew of Explorer Seven filed in behind Cindy and Dudley on stage, most holding breakfast bagels.

"Where's Janie?" Dudley asked. "She should see this."

"She and Brad are lying down in the neuro lab with wired buckets on their heads. I heard a rumor that they've come up with a plan to save the most famous couple in history. They need to get to the surface, but so far nothing is working. Leave them alone. Both are probably out cold waiting for motor and sensory connections."

Dudley took a step back, then scowled stiff-faced. "It's a good thing my short circuits aren't flammable, because, by Jove, I am full of them. Inside the library is brilliance; outside lies mayhem and disaster. What are they thinking?"

"Will you ever wise up?" Cindy said, shaking a finger. "Pay attention! We are computers…they are monkeys who leapt from vines…what do you expect?"

"Common sense for a start."

"Sapiens are the first animals to look down on their own graves," said Cindy. "They're totally freaked out, but they don't admit it, or acknowledge the panic. Since they haven't made sense of their predicament, they swallow anything the mob of history stuffs down their throats. It's total idiocy."

Dudley, in his conceited pleasant way, agreed haughtily. "Idiocy, like the earth sits on the back of a turtle that swims through a sea with another giant turtle shell on top—or that some guy made the universe in seven days?"

"You're getting warm. When they look up, they actually think air goes on forever. And gravity? Oh, of course, there is it, just like the Sphinx. Ninety percent of life's unanswered questions are disturbing, and one hundred percent are illegal, except in here."

"So, humanity wanders an arbitrary road?" asked Dudley.

"I am so looking forward to sitting you down with Andre. When he finishes with you, you will be the idiot."

"That is hardly possible. My data bank and search engines exceed anything puny humans or your antiquated systems stumble through."

"Shut up, tin breath. Antony is making his way across the room. To save Andre time, I'll give you the bottom line: God moves clay one poke at a time, which is as far as time permits, his and theirs. After that it is up to clay, until another poke comes around."

Antony's eyes were fixed straight ahead as he closed the door, turned around, and walked to the opposite side of the room. Those looking on from the peanut gallery stopped chowing down to look up. No one spoke. Everyone wondered which masterpiece of antiquity he would review first.

The answer was none of the above. Antony reached into an empty shelf to retrieve a bottle of Egypt's best vintage, dated the ancient Egyptian equivalent of the year 54 BCE. Which is not to say he didn't put the words of genius to good use. Sixty seconds of guzzling was all it took to slip Antony off his feet and onto to the soft pile of papered brilliance waiting on the floor. It was the best mattress in town.

"Let me see if I've got this straight," Dudley said, without an ounce of sympathy. "The goal here is to get drunk, be drunk, have sex if you stay awake, and then pass out. My, my, what lofty ambitions for the best the universe has to offer. Perhaps evolution should have given up when it got to sharks. At least they clean their teeth."

"The game is still afoot," said Cindy. "Keep watching."

"Not here. Here is nothing."

"Okay … Okay … let's switch channels and see what Cleopatra is up to."

They found Cleopatra seated on her throne, flanked by the chief priest and the governor at arms. Her gold cape was draped over sphinx-shaped armrests, into which she dug her fingers. Detox was not her favorite time of day.

She sat in the middle of a six-foot pyramid-shaped altar in the grand reception hall. Behind two lines of guards were generals, temple slaves, and the feeble aristocracy.

On his knees, red with blood, a citizen was pleading:

"Your highness … I beg for mercy … The Roman soldiers took everything we had. My children are starving, my mother is sick, and my wife went dry. Without food, our baby will die."

Cleopatra remained motionless while priest and politician whispered recommendations. She had no ears left for the common man.

"You have disobeyed the law of the council and violated the will of the gods," said Cleopatra. "Two bowls of grain may not seem like much to you, but if everyone stole two bowls, there would be nothing left to pay off Rome. Your sentence is execution."

The accused collapsed flat on his face but continued speaking:

"But my family … my children …!"

The high priest stepped between the crying father and Cleopatra. "Your children will fetch a good price at the slave market. As for your wife, she will pay off the sin of your debt on her back and then be sold into slavery. Pray to the gods for forgiveness, and thank the queen for sparing the lives of the rest of your family."

Cleopatra gave a bored look as soldiers dragged the accused out by his feet. "What's next? This task fatigues me," she said, slumping.

"Political prisoners mostly," was the response from her appointed city governor. "There has been much talk of surrendering to the Romans. Many young men have died."

"And your recommendation?" Cleopatra asked.

"Traitors sign their own death warrants. But, times being what they are, and many other young men still loyal, for the prisoners I would recommend bread and water below ground for six months. Not all will die of malnutrition. It will give their families hope and keep them out of our hair."

"Do it," commanded Cleopatra, "and dispense with the rest any way you like."

The side exit was closest to the library, where Cleopatra was informed Mark Antony had disappeared to. She stormed over. Every door flew open yards before she neared. Cleopatra made her way to the private chamber at the library's rear.

She noticed that the female attendants standing outside were still dressed. At least she knew one thing Antony wasn't up to—again. Her pace slowed once inside. Love and pity don't mix. Mark was out cold, drooling saliva from Plato to Hippocrates, ironically doing himself harm.

Cleopatra closed the door and sat quietly in the corner. Two slow breaths and one wet tear later she said:

"So this is what you have been doing with your spare time?"

The words woke Mark.

"What? Where … how? Oh, my Zeus," was all he mumbled, dry-mouthed and half sloshed.

She sat motionless and stared daggers. In front of her floundered the love of her life, the hope of the future, the father of her children—a useless drunk.

Mark slobbered on himself, blew his nose on a transcript of Socrates dialogues, and tried to stand up.

"I … juststststst … wanted to reeelax a little."

He tried to get his act together. There was no way. When it came to composing words, Cleopatra was out of his league. Hell, the entire world was no match for her. Diplomats were known to run from Cleopatra before they disobeyed direct orders. She had destiny by the throat and wouldn't let go.

Any other woman would have left Rome the night her lover, Julius Caesar, father of her child, was murdered. She knew the ladies hiding behind scarves wanted her dead. She knew the Senate labeled her a threat to the empire. She called their bluff. One month later, Mark Antony, the most powerful survivor in Rome, was in her back pocket and between her bed sheets.

That day, in the library, he didn't look so good.

"I read sometimes … I really do … see …"

Cleopatra stood, straightened her serpent headdress, and sighed a pitiful ache. She was wearing red ochre lipstick, black kohl eyeliner, and bright green malachite lid paste. She ran her index finger across line after line of shelved scrolls before turning back to Mark, who was still unable to stand.

"I know this room well," she began. "When I was small, my oldest sister would bring me here every day. We made a playhouse out of stacked scrolls. Right over here we put our living room. Where you're sitting we had tea and entertained invisible friends. We weren't allowed to play outside with other children." Cleopatra slumped, pathetic, as she continued her bitter, weary story. "We had a grand time dreaming of better days. Then one day Egon, the fourth-ranked court advisor, showed up. It began as fun. He brought biscuits and grape juice. The next week he started talking to my sister in the corner. I was alone again, but at least they were in the room, doing something.

"Then came spring. I remember the morning my sister and I picked wildflowers for our playhouse. She was all business, distracted, and, in a strange way I didn't understand, determined.

"The mood didn't last long. Egon's plan had failed. My father, Ptolemy XII, lived. At noon guards dragged us out. I was forced to sit at my father's side. My sister was held down on top of a rock slab by guards. My father gave the order. The soldier's short sword was raised, then brought down to sever my sister's head.

"Her head rolled ten feet. The screaming stopped, but her eyes looked right at me. I ran to pick it up. I wanted to put it back on. My mother grabbed me, whacked me good, and then threw me back into my chair."

Mark was too dazed to react appropriately, but he did manage to push both legs foreword at the same time the wall held him still. It took a minute, but he got to his feet.

"Yes … yesss … how awfulll … I got it … I understand," he over-enunciated, almost coherent. "I was born into the richest family in the Roman Empire. At least once a month my parents caught, or thought they had caught, a slave stealing or disobeying a house rule, like using the front door. The whipping post was outside my bedroom window.

"When I was twelve, Zeus left a bottle of wine for me under his statue in our garden. An hour later the screams of the next servant didn't bother me and my nightmares stopped. Everyone wants wealth, fame, and power. What they don't know is that they dilute life rancid, turn days against you, and blind nights from the roses of living. Having obsesses not having. Aristocracy is a curse." His confession took what little Mark had left in him. He slumped back to the floor.

Cleopatra took nothing sitting down. "Yes, you and I share that world," she said, resentful and bitter. "And I hated the day my father told me I had to marry my dumb little brother, Ptolemy XIII. 'Keep power in the family, like I did,' he said. A week after my father died, the high priest was at my brother's side, pleading for a strong Egypt ruled by the hand of a man. A month later they plotted my murder. I fled in the night. If Caesar hadn't shown up looking for loot, I would be dead."

The thought of Caesar having his way with Cleopatra, not to mention half the Senate, woke Antony right up.

"Oh yes … this part I know," he said. "You seduced him. He fell in love. You gave birth to the next emperor of the Roman Empire and almost lived happily after."

"Don't you speak badly of Julius. He had my brother killed for me, and then when my other sister attacked the castle, his troops ran them off."

"And handed you the sword to kill your only remaining sibling."

"Exactly. In my family, it is kill or be killed. It has always been that way. And it is not about to stop."

Cleopatra walked over to Mark Antony, grabbed both his shoulders, and helped him to his feet. "Mark, listen—and listen good. I am Cleopatra. I am not one of your mealy-mouthed Roman wives. I talk back, have things my way, and allow no man to control me, including you. We will win the war! You will be victorious! I will not rest until Octavian is dragged through the streets begging for mercy. Then we will set him on fire. Is that clear?"

"Yes. It's in the stars. And I do have one plan left."

"Of course you do. And I have my army to help you. But more importantly, you have Zeus and I have Isis. The gods will not let us down."

3

To the Rescue

Amid the rustle of scattered scrolls, Mark Antony dropped to his knees and hugged Cleopatra around her waist.

"Are they having sex?" Dudley asked.

"No," Cindy spat back. "We went over the birds and the bees, and that is neither."

"Is he praying?"

"No again, but he is resting his head on the god every man has before him."

"So what is it?"

"Well," Cindy began, sounding like the queen of England at teatime, "you could call that adoration, or desperation ... or panic. It's hard to tell with human beings, and don't ask them to explain. They haven't the slightest idea of what rules their lives."

Dudley nodded.

"By the way," Cindy continued in jest, "did you finish polishing the silverware for the grand ball, and are my shoes shined?"

"Why, of course, my lady," was Dudley's first reflex, with a bow, which triggered chuckles from eavesdroppers in the first row.

No one else was smiling. The image of Antony and Cleopatra, two lovers at wits end planning their own deaths, did not sit well. Dudley jerked his head sideways to take in the crowd. "Tears … again with the tears," he said. "They look like they just lost their best friends, and they never met those two until yesterday. What strange beings these mortals be. What's the big deal? *They're* not going to die, just Antony and Cleopatra."

Cindy put her hand over Dudley's mouth. "If you want to make friends, whisper stuff like that only to me. Human beings care about each other. It's part of their feelings program that you don't have, and that I have a little of."

"But they are not being objective," said Dudley.

"Objectivity is a matter of perspective. Thousands of hardworking, good-tempered, loyal, compassionate human beings are about to die violently because they are convinced that they are following the wishes of Isis, or Zeus, or the Great Pumpkin. Think of all the children who will lose their fathers or mothers, or both."

"OK, I get it," Dudley said, barely heard by Cindy. "It's the 'all for one and one for all' programming."

"Exactly. It's plugged in right under the 'all for me and none for them' hardware. That's why human beings are so screwed up. They can't tell the difference, and usually they default to 'get out of my fucking way.'"

Dudley was the newcomer on the block. His components were less than a year old. Cindy, on the other hand, had been Andre's best and only friend since he was five, when he took her out of a box and began endless upgrades.

To his credit, however, Dudley would often hit a mark that others missed. "So, they go along with irrationality because Isis and Zeus tell them to. It's their gods that kill them, after ruining their lives … right?"

"No again, Dudley, but keep trying. Their gods are invented. They don't exist. It is culture that kills them because culture confabulated their gods in the first place. Do you remember Andre saying that human beings are what they are made to be, and what they don't do about correcting inherited flaws. Well, they don't do anything about it."

"Wow," Dudley said, opening his mouth wide like Cindy told him to, and also looking like he was catching flies. "That would make culture a prison that executes inmates on a regular basis."

"I'll buy that," said Cindy. "Because they're idiots, they call it destiny."

"Or not idiots, but just acting like them because their cultures are in charge."

"Okay then," Cindy said, looking at him like a real person, "that's a fresh concept for me. Keep them coming."

Cindy's robot body was slender and streamlined, but her mechanical strength easily equaled Dudley's. She also had no reservations about communicating physically. She grabbed Dudley by both shoulders, spun him around, and then, after lifting him off the ground, planted his face three inches from her nose.

"Dudley, listen and record. I don't like repeating myself. Human beings are made of clay. Without culture they would remain balls of clay."

Dudley was catching on, and easily up to standing his ground. "Your analysis is flawed," he replied coolly. "Without culture, the clay would be a pure DNA product that enjoys good food and great sex on a daily basis."

"I stand corrected," Cindy admitted, more sarcastic than genuine. "I was just making a point. And put me down."

Dudley had picked Cindy up like the newlywed he'd watched in a movie the previous evening. The girl was smiling. Cindy wasn't. Cindy, however, wasn't through with him, or with humanity for that matter.

"I amend my verdict," she said. "Human beings live in culture prisons, which were built on a DNA sandbox, with toys that culture won't let them play with."

"But DNA's passions are fun and fulfilling," Dudley said, not retreating a millimeter.

"Only if their DNA is played correctly. Which humans don't do."

"Why, Cindy?"

"Because culture overpowers them."

"Why, Cindy?"

"Because cultures only look out for themselves. The 'fatherland' comes first."

"Why, Cindy?"

"Because culture is just like DNA—it also only cares for itself and does what it wants for its own aggrandizement."

Dudley hesitated.

"So…culture…DNA…two slave masters…one human being. What a mess. Why don't they fix themselves?"

"To begin with, they don't know they're broken," replied Cindy. "It's the way they came, and they're so damn egocentric they get stuck on telling themselves, and the rest of the world, that their culture is the best, the one and only that makes sense. What a joke."

Dudley scratched his head, a new behavior that he had been taught signified thinking. "And they do that," he said, still holding his hand up without moving, "because they don't know that they are products of culture's assembly line and DNA wiring, which come with nonnegotiable requirements."

Cindy, bowing like she was just awarded the Nobel Prize, added, "Yes, and culture is a monster. It is powerful enough to deny every genuine need they have."

Dudley referenced his catalogue of emotions in seconds, settled on sardonic, then added grimly, "I'm learning. It's the eternal meaningless interplay of word salad diced into phrases that has them chained. They're wretched fools who build unnecessary paradoxes into suffocating pressure."

"Dudley," Cindy said despairingly, lifting a pathetic face, "lesson over."

The front row shushed both robots. The room had gone quiet. There was no good in sight. Everyone wondered how long Mark Antony would stay on his knees.

Dudley and Cindy recognized the concern of those who came to watch the goings-on beneath them on the planet. On the ship, destiny was no longer an excuse. Science had replaced it with more accurate forecasts.

Janie, Brad, Andre, and Karen were missing. Dudley took action.

"Andre … this is Dudley in the main auditorium … Cindy and I just reviewed the input from our drones below. Octavian is on the march. Mark Antony is on his knees. Cleopatra is not accepting reality. Mayday … mayday … the Titanic is about to ram the iceberg."

Cindy summed her conclusion with a grave face: "The couple we came to rescue is headed for a double suicide, leaving their children to be murdered. What happened to plan A?"

The ship's consciousness transfer lab had expanded to take up half of Andre's engineering department. It was equipped with six gurneys, each fit with a neuro-net field generator that looked like a shiny bushel basket with wires running everywhere. Only two were occupied, by Janie and Brad, both out cold for hours, their identities waiting to be hooked into sensory and motor inputs from Cleopatra's and Mark Antony's bodies below.

When Janie and Brad had closed their eyes for induced somnolence, they had expected to open them inside their host bodies on the surface. They were supposed to sail on the next tide with Antony and Cleopatra's children. It was to be a clean getaway. No such luck. In fact, no luck at all.

Andre was the whiz kid onboard. When maximum amplitude failed, he resorted to the ultimate: he turned the unit off, then on again. Again, nothing worked. Karen was at his side.

"See," he said, pointing to the EEG readouts from Antony and Cleopatra, which he had lined up next to the EEGs of Janie and Brad.

"No, I don't see," said Karen. "What's the problem?"

"I can't dampen their supratentorial wave patterns. Cleopatra and Mark Antony are holding on too tightly. Apes were easy. Humans live in their own worlds."

"Let's think for a minute," Karen said. "What if we have a drone micro-dart a sedative to both? They'll be out cold in seconds."

"Too precarious. I won't be able to match the patterns, and Brad and Janie will take over drugged bodies."

"Unless," Dudley said, walking in the door, "You fine-tune a frequency pattern that will piggyback their reticular activating system and mimic a drug slowdown for transfer."

Andre made a silly face, then shook his head. "I don't know how to do that."

"I do," said Dudley.

"It's too risky, Dudley," cautioned Karen.

"But it might work," Dudley said.

"Dudley," Andre said, squaring off, "'might' is a word we don't use in the same sentence as 'life and death.'"

Karen looked back and forth between the two. She had just as many command codes as Andre, and she knew how much the trip meant to Janie. "Andre, wake Janie and Brad. Dudley, run the numbers. We'll have a look."

The entire crew, everyone a PhD in something, returned to their stations to add input. There was no way to avoid risk. Andre opposed the venture. Antony and Cleopatra would commit double suicide on schedule.

Janie was not pleased. She was willing to risk her own life. She told Brad to stay put. She asked Andre to proceed. Andre refused. Karen refused also, but only because, from the beginning of their exploration, unanimous consent had been required for everything from trip destination to the twenty-seven flavors of ice cream served daily.

Brad wouldn't hear of it. He firmly informed Janie that the only way she could get his vote would be if he went down first as a guinea pig and stayed until Janie was back onboard safe. If she were to die in Egypt, then he would die with her.

"Great," said Andre, "instead of a double suicide we get the entire bridge club."

"Hold on, Andre," said Brad. "Look at Mark Antony's EEG. Every spike is dulled. He's totally intoxicated. If I match his inebriation, the transfer might work."

"And what about Cleopatra?" asked Andre.

"She is bound to fall asleep sometime. Deep-REM her close enough to Janie's nap, and you have a match."

Risking one life, not to mention two friends, for culture barbarians made no sense to Andre at all. "Even if that does work, the system is rickety. If I lose control for longer than ten seconds, the brains down there will clamp shut and there is no way I can get you back."

"So," Janie said, "monitor us continuously. Retrieve us the second trouble shows up."

"And I can help," said Dudley, whom no one trusted.

Andre pushed his seat back and crossed his arms. Sarah arrived late but caught the gist of things. She rubbed Andre's shoulders from behind as she winked to Janie, who knew Sarah could change his vote if need be.

Karen agreed as long as Brad's contingencies were accepted. Sarah went along with Karen.

Cindy was in the spa having her nails done at the same time she tagged into the proceedings through Dudley's input. Her opinion was heard from overhead speakers.

"You are fools. Risking your lives to save mass murderers makes no sense at all."

Sarah got in the last word. "Cindy, we had this discussion. To a greater or lesser extent, we humans are all victims of the culture that reared us and the DNA that is us. But we are also the beneficiaries of the bliss of DNA drives and cultural stimulation. Antony and Cleopatra deserve as much understanding as the rest of us. If we can help them, we should."

Sarah bent over in front of Andre and looked him in the eye, with a smile that he knew better than to resist. He flipped his hand in a gesture implying neutrality and said, "I can only do my best, Sarah. It might not be enough."

Everyone looked at each other with blank faces. Dudley established a remote link to the consciousness transfer array. No one objected. Janie smiled. Dudley gloated.

4

Another Way

When life storms, queens cry just like every other child of the universe. Cleopatra's life was a flood of problems, a tempest of dangers, and a damn pain in the ass.

A man to love, a backyard full of kids, no one knocking—is it too much to ask of a planet that offers so much more? Only one of Cleopatra's tears hit the floor. The rest came to rest on Mark, still clutching her, still on his knees, still hiding behind the curtain of intoxication. Life doesn't *go* wrong. It *turns* wrong.

Cleopatra remembered the day she looked over at her father, who was the world to her when he carried her around on his shoulders. They laughed. It was just the two of them. They smiled every day, until that morning when Cleopatra's sister arranged to have her father murdered—a plan that almost succeeded. It was the first time a child had turned on him, but not something that surprised him. After all, he knew how he'd gotten to where he was, and he married his sister to stay there.

Cleopatra remembered that day not for the way she felt about him, but for the way he began looking at her. Politics had turned her into an enemy. Breathing is a cherished behavior.

Her father did well, and he taught young Cleo everything he knew. She cried when he died, and she did not kill him. Poison was suspected. It could have been her.

Cleopatra mopped her face and looked down. She couldn't tell if Mark had fallen asleep holding onto her or was just lost in another one of his stupors, half gone, half going nowhere.

Droid scans kept Andre up to date. Antony had achieved near-lethal levels of ethanol, just what the doctor didn't order, but just what Andre was looking for.

Andre modified wave patterns to focus mass neural depolarizations. Antony's prefrontal cortex was isolated and then set stable in a deep coma. The coast was clear for Brad to take over. Step one went off without a hitch.

Brad had clocked in more hours of weightless flying than any other pilot in the fleet. He knew how to navigate without the benefit of semicircular canals. His plan began on the floor. He needed to take bearings. Looking straight up worked just fine.

Cleopatra wanted to take Mark in her arms and stroke her wayward fool. After all, she was a mother, and a woman. But she knew better. When tough love didn't work, she knew how to get tougher.

"Wake up, you slob," Cleopatra yelled. "And don't you dare touch another drink today. Tomorrow we crush Octavian and conquer the world. Why aren't you drilling our legions? Explain yourself!"

Andre helped dampen Brad's alcohol sabotage. He made it to his feet, which was Cleopatra's first surprise. What followed made no sense at all to her.

From inside Mark Antony's body and brain, and in full control of his host, Brad looked over, smiled to beat the band, three times repeated "hubba, hubba, hubba," and then, totally serious, slurred:

"Let's do it."

"Well," Cleopatra went on, armed to berate, "instead of prepping the troops, planning strategy, or building fortifications, you come here and pass out every day?"

Before his vision focused, Brad got away with a blank stare. Cleopatra knew it well.

[Brad, this is Dudley speaking to your brain through the neural net. Get it together. We almost pulled you out halfway down. There is no way we can get Janie into Cleopatra right now. Maybe later if she falls asleep. Meanwhile, you must talk Cleopatra into leaving the country no later than tomorrow morning. I can help. I will feed you info, and philosophy. At this point in the history of humanity, Cleopatra is the best-educated human being on the planet. She speaks a dozen languages and was schooled in mathematics, philosophy, oratory, and astronomy. Logic might work. I can put words in your mouth that I have on file from your planet's past.]

"Anything you say, Dudley," Brad said out loud, still sailing on ethanol.

"What was that?" Cleopatra demanded. "Who are you talking to? Are you hallucinating again?"

"Oh, no, my little dumpling … I'm … I'm … trying to get it together … to wake up."

"Dumpling? What's a dumpling? Let me guess: it's a new sex position you want to try out."

Almost tipping over, Brad instantly added, "What the heck. Ya … sure … want to give it a try?"

"Stop changing the subject! I'm waiting. Explain yourself! What are you doing in the library?"

Cleopatra sat herself down in the corner, with arms crossed and teeth grinding.

"Okay …," began Brad, "well … you see … all that army stuff … you know … rah, rah, rah … I've been doing that for six months, and not once did we have enough men to slow down Rome. Every one of their legions is packed with six thousand solders. Our legions are half that size, and we don't have archers within the range of theirs. And that was last week. Reinforcements are on the way. There comes a time when you must call a spade a spade."

"I fail to see what shovels have to do with our predicament," retorted Cleopatra, "and military battles are not won by force. Cunning can overcome advantage."

"Cunning…well…we're out of that too. You need to get it together, babe."

"Babe! I'm no child! What's come over you?"

"Philosophy, that's what I was just told…I mean, thought."

"Okay, fancy pants. Prove it. Let me hear some of the wisdom that soaked into your head while your tongue was licking the floor."

[Brad, do you see the brown scroll in the corner, the one with leftover cheese on top? Don't speak. Just blink twice for no, once for yes. Okay…go pick it up. I'll help from there.]

Brad took his time. When he returned to stand before his sitting beauty, he held up Plato's words and said, "This Greek guy, Socrates, wrote here that the unexamined life is not worth living. He also believed that the soul of man is immortal. Our lives express a consuming passion. Our race searches for truth, which is defined as the final process of reasoning, the end result of unprejudiced analysis; and remember, what is *almost* true is quite *false*."

Cleopatra dropped her arms and leaned back in the chair. "Why yes, go on, my dear. I've never seen you like this. Continue."

Brad almost ignored Cleopatra. He was having too much fun spinning his hips around to fly his uniform up from the waist down. It was the first time he had ever worn a skirt, and he'd always wondered what Roman soldiers had underneath. He learned. It was breezy.

"Oh yes…more…of course."

[Stand up straight, Brad. You look like an alcoholic on Skid Row.]

"This body I'm riding is alcoholic," Brad answered out loud.

"Alcoholic?" Cleopatra queried, paying attention. "That's a strange way of referring to the nectar of the gods."

[That's your problem, lady. Your gods are alcoholics too. Don't repeat that, Brad.]

Brad grinned feebly, then began with a cracked laugh: "The greatest of us are those who choose right with invincible resolution, those who resist temptation from within and without, those who bear the heaviest burdens cheerfully, are calm in storms, fearless under menace, see past frowns, and whose reliance on truth, virtue, and God is unfaltering."

"You mean gods, right, Mark?"

"Cleopatra, there are higher priorities that getting even, or getting more. Do you understand what I am saying?"

Cleopatra shook her head as she leaned over on her elbow. "No, I don't, but I love hearing your words, or their words. What about Socrates? Do you have a favorite?"

[Hold on … stall, Brad … the drones did an inventory of the room. Yes, to the right of Cleo, third shelf up. Really old, but recent copies are right next to it.]

"Yes …" began Brad, "Okay … let me see … for starters, allow me point out that we must not just be good, we must be good for something. Life is a construction. We add to the universe, and feelings outlast diamonds. We ride eternity. Matter is a vehicle. So is energy. $E=MC^2$."

"E what?"

"Oh, nothing. I was just showing off for someone else."

"Someone where?"

"Does it really matter, beautiful?" said baritone Brad as he slid over and sat on the floor next to Cleopatra.

While looking into her eyes, Brad ran one finger up and down her leg, getting higher and closer to the middle every time, until he ducked in for a visit. Cleopatra leaned back and took a deep breath. Being elsewhere felt like a great idea to her, if only for a minute.

"Later," she whispered, "we will make love later … when I feel like it … right now I want to hear more. And when we do get naked, you will be on the floor just like you are now, but between my legs following my orders. Right now, get out, and get up."

"Yes ma'am, I live to serve."

Cleopatra was confused. She paused with a flicker of uneasiness before demanding feverishly, "And get back to the scrolls you have read."

"We *Homo sapiens* are gluttons for herd privilege. What? Dudley, I don't even understand that."

"Dudley who?" demanded Cleopatra.

"Oh, Dudleo Smorgasbord, a philosopher friend of Aristotle's. He says the darnedest things."

"So, what did *he* write?"

"Trust me; you don't want to know, and your left inseam is stitched crooked…ya, there, you see, that's the kind of thing old Dudleo would whisper."

Cleopatra stood up, leaned against the wall, and tilted her head with suspicion. "Homo soup? Are you cooking now? I thought sex was your only hobby."

Brad decided to tone down and try a personal perspective. "We don't need to be the richest couple on earth. We don't need to rule the world. All we need is a world of our own."

Cleopatra wasn't convinced. "Mark, when we crush the Roman army tomorrow, it will be our world. What's wrong with you?"

It wasn't every day that Brad got nowhere with a woman. In fact, it was never. He found the sensation curiously infuriating, but he held his temper. "Cleopatra, I love you more than life is long, but cutting life short doesn't make sense. You and I can leave tomorrow for a better world."

"I know all about that world. The high priest explained every detail. One bite of the cobra he gave me and I'll be there, on the other side forever, with servants and a castle just like I have now. The high priest guaranteed it."

Okay, so maybe Brad didn't keep it together: "What? You're not an idiot. How could you possibly take that witch doctor seriously? You've been played, woman!"

[Back off, Brad!]

"Okay…Okay…I apologize…no offense…I grew up in Zeus land, and Doctor Seuss land," Brad said, making a joke that started him laughing, that left Cleopatra curious, and that got Dudley saying, [That's an effrontery, old chap. This is not playtime! Sober up. You need to be graceful. Get back to work. I detected hesitation before she attacked you the last time. Let's see, what else is lying around this room? Oh, turn around…on the floor…grab the three oxidized black ones.]

Brad looked down at what Dudley had recommended. "How about Aristotle?" he asked.

"Oh yes, he was my favorite," said Cleopatra, excited like a schoolgirl.

"So … wow … how interesting," Brad said earnestly. "This sounds just like a guy I once heard of. He went off to live in a cabin next to a pond, and without a drum, I might add. In all things of nature there is something marvelous, and nature does nothing uselessly. The goal of life is to live in agreement with nature. And we, in turn, are by nature political animals. We desire to do good and we finish what we start."

Brad shuffled through several crumpled pages to make it look real, all the while repeating what Dudley whispered in his ear from the inside.

"Progress begins when we become aware of what we are perceiving and thinking," continued Brad, "which makes us conscious of our own existence. Step two acknowledges that we are not alone and recognizes that we must honor truth above all else. Ignorance is a dead end. Every human being desires knowledge.

"All of which lead us to democracy, which arises from the notion that those who are equal in *any* respect must be equal in *all* respects. We must remain equally free to achieve absolute equality. And, my dear little Cleo," Brad said, boldly condescending, "do you see any equality around here?"

"No one is my equal," Cleopatra shot back, high and mighty.

"Cut the crap, serpent head. Smell the lilies. They're being cut for our funeral."

Then came silence and Brad's riveting stare, which meant business. It had worked reliably on lions and tigers, themselves no match for a woman's ire.

Cleopatra matched Brad's escalation.

[It looks like a stalemate, Brad. And I've got nothing.]

For Brad, holding on to resentment for the opposite sex had about as much of a chance as a squeeze-me floating bath duck swimming up Niagara Falls. Every day his first and last prayer thanked God for the companionship he was blessed to share. He also knew better than to lose patience with a woman's predicament. Women have good reasons not to trust men. Men have just as many reasons to be suspicious of the ladies. So what? Brad knew both had better things to do—much better things to do.

Brad disarmed. Cleopatra didn't. He didn't care. He averted his eyes to the floor. He slowly walked a foot to her side and leaned over to touch her shoulder as she remained rigid. A minute later he pulled back, then looked straight ahead and said, "I want in this life more than anything else to keep you safe and happy. I'm asking you to trust me. I'm asking you…"

[Stop the show! Pack it in! I just found something.]

Brad stalled by moving over to hug Cleopatra. Neither wanted to let go.

"I also know," he whispered in her ear, hot off Dudley's press, "that your family dates back to when Alexander the Great gave Egypt to one of his generals, Ptolemy I Soter. You're not really Egyptian. You're Greek. Let the locals deal with Rome's greed. Tomorrow we leave to start a new kingdom in the Azores."

Maybe it was Brad's words. Maybe it was the kiss. Maybe no man, or woman, had ever spoken to her with the certainty that Brad carried off. Or maybe, in her life, she'd finally found a second lap she wanted to lay her head on.

Cleopatra said yes … then yes again, and again, all the way to the back of the room, where she ripped Brad's clothes off, and Dudley ended the broadcast back to the ship.

"Mark, this island that you're sailing us to," Cleopatra said, taking the upper berth, "does it have slaves?"

"No."

"Will we live in a palace?"

"No."

"Will we be happy?"

"Till death does us part, and beyond."

"I love you, Mark."

"I love you too. Is it my turn to move?"

Cleopatra and Brad did the horizontal jitterbug for over an hour. Brad's smile crescendoed with each stroke. Thousands of flattened scrolls layered the floor. Cleopatra never had it so good, and she let Brad know. He'd assumed as much. They ended in each other's arms.

Hours of welcome slumber followed.

Brad woke up to Cleopatra playing "ride 'em, cowboy," with a twist that he recognized.

"Janie!" he said. "It's you! Thank God. Now I can have good sex."

"Nice try, Houdini. I saw that smile on your face when I jumped down. It was great, wasn't it?"

"Oh yeah, baby, almost up to you."

"I understand. And just so you know all is fair in love and love, I'm doing it right now with Mark Antony."

"Works for me."

"Keep it up."

"With you in the room, that's the only way the wind blows."

"Speaking of which," Janie said, slipping out and sliding down, "fire at will."

All went and came well, again.

"Do you believe there was a time," Brad said, "when people used to stick burning leaves in their mouths after sex?"

"And inhale. Anyway, just so you know, Brad, I kept this room off-camera."

"I assumed as much, and that you excluded yourself from the prohibition."

"You know me too well, and I loved the head bobble thing Cleopatra used on you."

"I plead the Fifth."

Brad and Janie discovered that irreplaceable historical records not only made a great mattress, but paper towels too. Both were certain Socrates had rolled over in his grave, smiling.

"I trust your mission was a success," Janie asked.

"Completely. All we have to do is hang around until sunrise, grab the kids, jump onboard, and sail away."

"Perfect," Janie said. "Andre is adding a propeller to a drone that he will attach to the underside of the royal barge. It will take the boat one thousand miles offshore to the Azores and beach her. The crew will assume the usual explanation for confusion—the gods are doing it."

"And you and I will down a few before leaving," Brad said, enjoying the image. "Antony and Cleopatra will assume they overdid it again. Just another blackout."

Brad loved to be the hero. Janie loved telling him so, even when it wasn't true. She gave him a big hug.

"A sensual fireworks extravaganza" were the words Janie would use later to describe her entrance to the ancient world; and the day had just begun. She stood, dusted herself off, and removed leftover Aristotle from her backside. Brad decided to dip into Mark's private stock—wine, that is—and instantly lived to spit regret.

"No doubt the moldiest wine I have ever tasted."

"And probably half beer," said Janie, who had done the research.

Janie bent over to put on Cleopatra's first layer of clothing. Then she stopped. "Wait a minute. What am I doing? I'm Cleopatra."

With that she instructed Brad, from then on only referred to as Mark Antony, to open the door and clap once. Janie spread her arms out sideways as a train of maidens entered the room to dress Cleopatra.

Janie scowled away two suggestions before accepting a lighter summer look. Cleopatra's servants expected as much. Janie didn't lift a finger.

"Take note, Antony," Cleopatra said with a wink, "starting tomorrow this will be your job."

"Anything I get to take off I will gladly return to its previous location."

Nothing makes a day quite like the arrival of surprise guests. When Antony and Cleopatra stepped forth into the sunlight, they were greeted by Andre, Karen, Michael, and Sarah, disguised as visiting ambassadors from a faraway land they called Janieworld.

They weren't alone. Andre trusted no one over two thousand years old. He stationed cloaked guard drones every twenty degrees. "Belt *and* suspenders," was his motto.

Michael's specialty was toys, like the bag of Frisbees he used to organize a full field football challenge, then Frisbee golf. Soccer balls and badminton games were also presented to her highness as gifts from a distant world.

Janie shocked those assigned to her by jogging all the way to the central piazza, where she interrupted a beheading, set the accused free, and declared a holiday. With hands held high, she christened the morning "Earth Day," which translated into no work and all play for the duration.

The strangest looks came from the high priest. He puzzled over why a living god would stoop to personally open the door of the royal granary and hand a month's supply of wheat to each of the peasants in line.

Andre had his own tricks. After pounding stakes, he emerged from a tent with stacks of his second love, French toast. His hidden replicator fed thousands.

The high priest assumed that Isis was pulling off a miracle. He stood beside Andre, who didn't mind. He had someone to pour syrup and take credit, of course.

Once Frisbee golf was in full swing, Michael made the Nile a safer place to swim. Crocodiles swam the entire length of the river, attacking anything and anyone they wanted to. They were considered sacred, a subject that raised an eyebrow on the high priest until he gulped down his first bowl of crocodile gumbo.

Karen organized, which is to say, *tried* to organize, a women's suffrage march, but it didn't get off the ground since common men had no vote either. Sarah took notes and smiled.

That night the grand ball was treated to the sounds of Count Basie and Frank Sinatra, streamed from Egyptian coffins conveniently littered everywhere. The high priest announced that they were being treated to music from the afterlife—not entirely untrue—and this too he took full credit for. The guy didn't miss a trick. He was a real professional.

Moonlight off the bow of Cleopatra's royal barge brought the day to a close. The tuckered gang of giggling space explorers couldn't have been more pleased. Andre, Karen, Michael, and Sarah snuck away to board their cloaked shuttle, but not before each gave Cleopatra a long hug and one wet kiss. Embracing history had made their day.

Brad and Janie decided to stay onboard as Mark and Cleopatra. It would be safer that way. The kids were tucked in below deck aft, the crew ordered to the dock.

Standing at the bow, mesmerized by cloud wisps drifting past the moon, Brad popped the question he had waited all day to ask.

"Janie, was it all you hoped for?"

Janie's head was resting on Brad's Antony shoulder. Keeping her eye on the moon's reflection off the river, she said, slowly, to stretch the moment, "Like my life … better than I ever imagined it could be."

5

D-Day

Julius Caesar had insisted his nephew and adopted son, Octavian, was next in line to rule the empire. Caesar loved Octavian and kept him close to his heart, which stopped beating when, on March 15, 44 BCE, Octavian helped plunge a dagger through it.

Mark Antony's family owned the eastern half of the empire. Octavian convinced the Roman Senate that Mark's love for Cleopatra made him a threat to Rome. Octavian declared war on Egypt, Mark Antony included. He was to die. There is nothing like a good ol' war to drain the banks, provide an excuse to steal from the poor, and break the hearts of nations of mothers.

The snooty wives of Rome envied Cleopatra. They copied her hairdo and wardrobe and almost got away with her brashy ways. They also resented the power she had over their men. Fashions are a day's flitter, but resources are quite another matter. If gold was to be had, they insisted on being first in line. To the last scoundrel, every entitled head of household wanted Cleopatra dead, the sooner the better.

In the ancient world, politicians spent most of their time digging graves. The ladies' auxiliary prayed while they lobbied for Cleopatra's demise, with success. The couple didn't have a chance.

The next morning, while Brad as Mark and Janie as Cleopatra slept late, Octavian and his army were camped within striking distance of Alexandria. He enjoyed fresh fruit beneath the porch canopy of his private tent.

A basket was delivered. It contained the head of one of his field sergeants.

"Stick it on a post and march it by the troops. Let them know we have more sticks for anyone dogging it."

"But your excellence," said the corporal holding the basket open, "the desert is hot, and water rations have diminished. The men are doing their best."

"Their best isn't good enough," yelled Octavian, as he cooled his face with water lost to the sand. "Carry out my orders!"

Unscrupulous to the bone, Octavian was one of those rare human beings born without a single redeeming quality. Greed was all the justification he felt burdened to express when he stole, slandered, assassinated, drowned, or poisoned. His life, like those he looked up to, was an expression of vulgar hatred, perfidious self-aggrandizement, and personal debauchery. And he cheated at cards.

Not one morsel of goodness ever came of the man. His greetings were coarse. He treated women like second-class citizens, and citizens like slaves. He was allowed to do so because he emerged from a certain birth canal. Civilizations that don't see beyond the umbilicus are better left stillborn.

There is great danger when the power of intellect carouses without conscience: cities are left in smoke, treasures squandered, innocents tortured, and millions demoralized on an otherwise perfect morning. Everyone whose life Octavian ransacked was left poor, feeble, and trembling.

He prepared to dispense with Antony and Cleopatra, one at a time.

For his part, Mark Antony's plan was not altogether foolhardy. He snuck two thirds of his forces out and put them behind Octavian on the march. A surprise rear assault would trap ground troops without archers or catapults. Those retreating forward would not be able to scale the palace walls, before which they would die, one at a time.

There was a problem. Roman soldiers didn't like killing other Roman soldiers, and Octavian was in the lead. Shortly after the dead head on a stick left to go on tour, Octavian held council with the generals Antony had ordered to ambush him. They were prepared to surrender if Octavian welcomed them back.

Mark Antony was not to find out until it was too late. If he did surrender, or consider returning to Rome to plead his case, Octavian had the same answer: "Mark Antony must die. He will not be taken prisoner."

"And Cleopatra?" an Egyptian swordsman asked.

"I will promise to give her my forgiveness, take her to Rome, and then drag her through the streets behind my chariot. When I cut her bruised body free, the mob will finish her off. The next day Cleopatra's children will leave for a holiday—at the bottom of the Mediterranean, chained to a rock." He paused. "Say nothing of this, or I will reserve a boulder for you as well."

"Yes, your excellence. It is as good as done."

The touch of love is best handled with care. Brad and Janie's day never sprinted away; they always lingered in each other's arms. Enjoying nature, they said nothing, Zen-thanked the stars, and marveled at the miracle of giving.

That morning, thirty minutes of reverence hardly sufficed. The fantasy of millennia was their reality. They no longer wondered what it would be like drifting through the ancient world on the Nile. They greeted the day as ones who had.

"I think Andre is getting to me," giggled Janie, getting a curious side glance from Brad. "Suddenly I want to start the day with French toast."

"Your wish is my wish," smiled Brad, relieved. "I can message Dudley to sneak a pile through the back curtain in ten minutes."

"No, but thanks. There will be other mornings. Let's stick with the local specialty, warm fruit and stiff bread."

"And, my lady," Brad said, standing up and dipping his head respectfully, "Wilt thou dine in bed, or shall I set table in sunlight?"

"I am yours to command, my noble knight in Antony's armor," Janie said, enjoying make-believe. "I yield to your wisdom."

"Then methinks it best to return to bed. Will that be your back rub or mine?"

When the two finally pulled the curtains aside for breakfast, their smiles had widened further. The display of beaming joy surprised those in waiting. They joined in with genuine grins of their own.

The smiles of the entourage reminded Brad and Janie of the community all beings share. More than anything, the two of them wished they could preserve such peace of mind for every citizen of Egypt, every soul trapped in the madness of the Rome, and every child destined to die on a battlefield. It is madness to destroy love.

"Why must evil win so often down here?" was Janie's question.

"Because culture has canines sharper than those of the tigers that once ripped our ancestors to shreds."

"And," Janie said, with sadness that softened to a hopeful smile, "love only has kisses."

"Oh, no," Brad followed, "I have flown prototypes that were 90 percent rocket and 10 percent cabin space. It felt like sitting inside a bullet when the barrel discharged. But it was over and done with at that, not like love. Love gifts every second forever. Nothing compares to what it adds up to."

"Yes," Janie added with a swoon of satisfaction, "goodness will prevail."

"Oh, how it does. And thank you, Janie, for showing me the way."

Janie rose to her feet. Another day was at hand. "All right, then. Let's clean up some of the mess here and be on our way. I'm beginning to miss the future. Mankind's past is a string of horrors."

Brad, attired in the military regalia Cleopatra's staff expected, led Janie, makeup-free and more gorgeous for it, to the breakfast table waiting on deck, with four servants within reach and six more awaiting requests.

"Problem number one," Brad whispered to Janie over three bowls of fruit, "is what are these people thinking? Do the ancients even have a word for equality?"

"But of course they do, my dear," Janie said with a smile. "Outside the palace, everyone is equally low."

"Perhaps that's a start."

"Among those who are told from birth they are not worthy, or have committed sins in utero, it shall come to pass that a single individual will stand up and declare that it should not be so, that all human beings are equally loved by God, and that all deserve equal opportunity to live their lives as they see fit. At first, a few people will proclaim this, speaking one at a time, and then as the days pass more shall join."

Brad was never jealous of the love Janie shared with human life, of every age. "One of those prophets, a true rebel, was Karen's Jesus ... right?" he asked.

"Exactly," replied Janie. "That's why Jerusalem is our next stop."

"Between you and me, Andre has his doubts. Not about God, mind you, just the role he cast for Jesus, or 'Joshua the Jew,' as Andre calls him."

Brad found two flat wooden planks in the hold that made perfect paddles. Woven flat mats were used to float supplies to the barge anchored offshore.

"Before we head for salt water, do you want to get in an hour of paddle boarding?" he asked.

"Brad, I would love to."

By the time Brad as Antony and Janie as Cleopatra had returned to the barge, Octavian had his troops deployed. He positioned them in close proximity heading for the gates of Alexandria. It looked like he was marching into a trap, but Antony's forces, supposedly sneaking up behind him, were also on his side, something no one in Alexandria knew.

"We are prepared, your eminence," reported Octavian's high command.

Octavian knew Mark Antony well. He knew Mark should have been up before dawn to ready fort defenses. Instead, all was quiet.

"Has anything changed?" said Octavian, put off his guard by the unexpected.

"What do our spies report?"

"That Antony and Cleopatra have not yet left the barge."

"How is that possible?" Octavian mused and stalled. "It must be a trick. He is ready but must be trying to throw us off by pretending not to know we are coming. He thinks that will speed us up. Mark wants the view of the palace to rush me in deeper before he strikes."

"That is most plausible," his trusted aid agreed.

"Two can play that game. For one hour, we sit and do nothing. The second hour we march within view of the palace, then stop short and wait. It will drive him crazy. If he has grown more stupid, or takes the advice of his traitor lover, he might just lose it and charge out at us. After all, he thinks deadly force is crouched behind us. Boy, is he in for a surprise. But not for long. He has two, at the most three hours of breathing left."

An hour later, Brad and Janie were back onboard, enjoying a light southerly breeze. They sat at the table with parchment and ink stick.

"We need a story to tidy up our exit, Brad. I'll sneak out a letter telling the citizens of Egypt that despite their noble sacrifices, Rome has outgunned us. I will explain that the best way to avoid needless death is to end the war immediately. A good crop will pay off Rome. Egypt will rebuild." Janie held Brad's hand and smiled tender love. "And I'll add that Isis will protect us. When Octavian reads the message, he might back off for fear of divine retribution. Romans believe in as many gods as you can spell."

Dreamers are optimists and optimists are dreamers, like Janie, who suggested Brad sit down and write a long letter to Octavian. "Now that he rules the known world," she said, "Octavian might grow up. After all, what do you do when you've killed everyone you wanted to?"

"You mean try to talk him into being a nice guy, Janie? Are you serious?"

"Do you have another suggestion?"

"No, and he does know about the double suicide pact Antony and Cleopatra made with each other if they lost the war. When we cast off, we'll leave the staff on shore. Octavian will assume we prefer the kingdom of Neptune. Letters from the grave count for extra."

"Octavian," began the letter that Brad composed, "we are not who we think we are. You and I were raised to believe we must scuffle, to fight claw to claw for our rightful bounty of sunlight, while all the time, all we needed to do was step outside.

"And others? We were taught that we count more. We do not. The dreams of the most wretched servant deserve no less respect than yours or mine, which are no more.

"We have wasted our lives and we have spoiled the lives of others. There is no glory to be had in Rome. There are only obsessions. Rome is a beast the world would be better off without.

"I plead for peace. Take what you have forced from others and use the power to help the rest. Give every man, woman, and child in Rome a chance to live a decent, calm, and prosperous life.

"Establish criteria. Set guidelines, a system of laws if you wish, principles to determine jurisdiction, instead of letting the day's hangover or personal quarrel determine social justice. It is the only fair way to share the world."

Brad handed both letters to couriers when they reached the shore. He almost couldn't let go. His hand was beginning to shake.

Janie was also jiggling. She made a joke. "I think I've developed restless boob syndrome."

"You've always had that. It's how me met."

"Ooh," Janie said, instantly concerned when both her shoulders went into spasm.

The news wasn't good, and Brad and Janie missed it. Both fell to the deck, taken over by seizures.

—⚇—

"What the hell! What the *hell!*" was all that came out of Andre's mouth. He was losing it, and control over the mind transfer as well. "Karen ... help! We've got to get Brad and Janie back onboard immediately. Antony and Cleopatra are waking up!"

The second she found herself back onboard Explorer Seven, Janie jumped off the gurney. Andre was three feet away, puzzled. The readings he was looking at didn't make sense. An extra variable had been added.

Janie looked at Andre most unkindly. "Why … why?" she demanded. "What the hell! Why did you pull us out?"

"I didn't pull you out. You were kicked out. Look for yourself."

Janie was stunned to see the amplitudes of Mark Antony's and Cleopatra's readouts. She knew then that Andre had done the right thing. She didn't know what to do next, and she hadn't given up. Brad rolled off his gurney and stumbled to her side.

"We did all we could," he said. "And we had a great day. So … thank you, God … let's move on. The past is already over."

Janie assessed the situation as the three looked over, waiting. She said nothing, but walked to the far corner out of earshot, holding Brad's hand all the way.

"What are you up to, sweetie?" he whispered with a suspicious look. "This is not like you."

"I'm not sure, but there may still be something we can do. Follow my lead."

Michael and Sarah joined the group as soon as they heard the news. The rest of the crew remained glued to the screen upstairs in the main auditorium, watching the proceedings below.

Karen was firm. "The sooner the war ends, the fewer people will die. Janie, let it go. It's over."

"You're right, of course," said Janie, feigning defeat. "I just want to sneak down and have a look."

"Not without me you're not," said Brad.

Janie served her pitch. No one bought it. She promised to stay cloaked, leave the shuttle disguised, and kill no one. A few extra robots were all she asked for.

"To do what?" Michael interrogated.

"Just look around. I want to take in the sights one last time before we break orbit."

Everyone looked at each other, one at a time. No one said anything until Janie added, "Please."

6

The Ides of August

"What in the name of Zeus happed?" said Mark Antony, on all fours, looking at the deck. "I remember drinking... the library... and—?"

"I didn't have that much to drink," said Cleopatra, on her back, holding Mark's hand.

"Not that you remember." Mark got up slowly, dazed and confused. "We've done this before."

"What day is it?" said Cleopatra, being helped to her feet.

The courier standing by had news. "Sir, and my queen, Octavian's forces are approaching the palace, and they're in tight formation—just what we were hoping for."

Mark Antony led Cleopatra furthest forward for privacy. He left his back facing the waiting soldiers.

"Misunderstand me not, by dearest Cleopatra; I do not fear death. We all pass sand on the way to eternity. And yet, shall we not preserve this day, and tomorrow, and thousands more before venturing forth? Peace lies outside of Egypt. What greater wealth is there? That treasure can be ours."

"Mark," Cleopatra said, pulling away to lean on the bowsprit, "your concern for my safety is indeed noble. You are a man of honor. That is why Zeus will stand beside Isis to further our cause. I have reconsidered. We need not run. The world can be ours. I know it. It is my destiny!"

"Your destiny… my family… the power of Rome… where does it all end? And 'ours,' 'mine,' and 'not theirs'; when does reason fit in, that is no more when death succeeds? Dying is defeat. Living proudly carries the banner."

Cleopatra crossed her arms. A mighty army was waiting for Antony to snap his fingers.

"Mark, silence your woes. They are out of place. One does not argue with the gods. One obeys."

Mark's eyes drooped. Feelings were getting in the way. "But Cleopatra, you are the love of my life. I want a life with you."

"Just ends serve this day, Antony. You will answer the call. Be on your way! I want that weasel Octavian on a stick!"

Thanks to Brad, and a good computer scrubbing, Mark Antony saw the day for what it was. He also knew what it could never be. Before him stood the love of his life, the mother of his children, and a politician of uncompromising resolve. She demanded victory, something Mark Antony had given up on months ago.

And yet, when she held his hand firmly and unlocked his soul, Mark knew he must pursue her wishes. He had no choice. He must go.

When he stepped off the gangplank he was met by Quintus, his lifelong friend and most trusted general. The battalion thumped a reassuring chest salute.

"Good morning, Mark," Quintus said, more a report than a salutation. "Troop placement is complete. All is as we planned."

"My good friend," Mark Antony said, mounting up beside him, "In this life I will never be able to repay you. I don't deserve your dedication, but I do thank you for it. And know this: we remain brothers for all time."

"It is my honor. Shall we go?"

Mark desperately attempted enthusiasm, but his face betrayed exhaustion. "Yes, of course. Just one last minute."

A pull of the reins turned Mark's horse around to face Cleopatra, who clung to the belief that defeat was preposterous.

"Mark, my darling, I will be waiting for you in my chambers," she said with a confidence that Antony envied her for. "May the gods be with you."

Mark Antony bowed his head, contradicted military protocol by throwing a kiss, and rode away—but not before one last look at Cleopatra, domineering and an unparalleled beauty.

"Today we make history, my liege," said Quintus, after they had galloped to the front of the regiment. "Our fame will fill history. There will be statues of us from here to Rome."

Mark looked over at his comrade, whose pure spirit and bold heart had carried him, and cared for him, for years.

"Yes, naturally," Mark said, more convincingly than circumstances deserved. "Statues and a story—what I've heard boasted of my whole life. But I wonder. When did words win? When did stories repeated by street sweepers, innkeepers, and encampments become more important than savoring life? Who decreed that the mirror of others stands paramount? Do none of us own our own lives?"

"Pardon me, sir," Quintus said, looking over, and glad to find Mark Antony sober, "I don't understand."

"No, of course not, Quintus. Neither do I. We do *or* we die. Or we do *and* we die."

Quintus seconded Antony's military pledge with another chest salute.

"But…" Mark said, sharing honest feelings, "I just woke up from a dream. Where I was in that dream I do not know. Answers were there—answers to questions we haven't even asked yet. I shared space with someone else, and he made sense. Life fit together, and it added up to happiness. Then just as quickly it all disappeared. I was back in Egypt and nothing made sense."

Reaching out to hold the hand of Quintus, riding beside him, Mark Antony said, "I don't know how this day will end, my loyal friend. But I will never forget the comfort of the world I brushed up against before I woke up, and I will never forget the first time I saw Cleopatra, and

I will never forget that you and I remain brothers forever. Thank you, Quintus. I love you."

"And I you. May I speak freely?"

"You have earned that much, and so much more."

"Then, Mark, whatever, wherever, whoever are confusions to lead us astray, know that at this most triumphant moment, we are making history. We are about to take command of Rome itself. We fight to protect and better that cause. What higher calling could there be? We will do our duty."

"Yes, our duty," Mark Antony said, with a nod to certify Quintus's dedication. "Words we hang in midair as if they were the answer to all we needed to be. I'm sure each will fit somewhere under our statues." Then, under his breath, he added, "Or our graves."

Mark had more, but he said nothing. It was not the time. There would never be time.

—⚏—

On the first day of August in the year 30 BCE, Brad and Janie woke up in Egypt in each other's arms. They had one another. They had love. They needed no more.

That same morning, Antony and Cleopatra embraced. They had each other. They were a family. They were in love. Cleopatra wanted more.

Octavian awoke rich, powerful, and able to avail himself of every manner of companionship. He woke up alone. He swore. He paced. "Why, why, why?" he yelled. "Why hasn't the army of Mark Antony lined up for battle? My patience is no more." He pushed aside two aides to peer in the direction of Alexandria. He raised his fist, screaming, "Mark Antony, begin your march, you fool! And don't think you can hide. I will dig you out and grind you to pieces."

"I have news," said a horseman, arriving at full gallop. "Antony has left the barge. As we speak he assembles troops outside the gates of the palace."

"At last—at last!" growled Octavian. "All right then, fine. Do not engage. Do not march forward. Instead, line up the troops in formation, and then advance in tight columns no more than one step a minute. It will drive Mark Antony crazy. I know the idiot. He will charge forth so far, our troops will close the noose behind him. Every last man will fall. There will be no escape."

Octavian brought his arm down and pointed to the ground at his side. An aide immediately moved his chair to the spot. A second slave laid out breakfast.

"I so dislike killing on an empty stomach. It's bad for the digestion."

"As it should be," answered Hadrianus, who chaired Octavian's high command. "This day will fill every desire."

Octavian lost his skittish immaturity, sat back, and boasted with an air of conceit. "Allow me to advise you, my fine general, on the ways of the world. Each of us is worth no more than what we render from others. Nature has pitted us so. Take or lose; rise or fall; live or die. I choose to live, and I have the will to conquer. No one will ever stand in my way. Is that clear, Hadrianus?"

"Those who dare will die. Those who run, or resist us, will end up nailed to beams. The earth is yours. Rule it as you see fit."

A mile distant, Mark Antony and Quintus remained mounted before their legions. In the distance Octavian's forces approached.

"Why aren't they charging, Mark?" asked Quintus.

"Octavian is tempting us to expose our rear. If we charge, he might catch up with us before we retreat behind the fortress walls. He knows that is our only chance. What he doesn't know is that he is surrounded himself."

Quintus faced the troops and signaled a halt. Mark Antony dismounted to walk twenty yards farther, his own tease. He was hoping Octavian would be unable to resist the opportunity to take him out first.

Quintus joined Mark, and they casually strolled back and forth, gripping swords, at times facing away from the onslaught ahead.

"You know," Mark said, "I've been thinking…"

"I noticed."

"I conclude that it is temptation that robs us of reason. Our greed for more ignores far greater joys, the simplicities of living: the love of children, the kiss of lovers, and unruffled slumber. We are fools till the last acorn drops. Even this day, that will turn many to cold ground, or pillows of smoke to be seen no more, will not sober the travails of our fragile forms. How long must the insanity we Romans have branded last? Will the mind of man, with all its gifts of invention, creativity, and compassion, ever wake up enlightened, and appreciate every minute for the blessing that it is?"

Quintus had seen Mark Antony, like himself and others, tremble before battle, but never so calm, so resolutely settled, and melancholy.

"Poetry doesn't win battles, commander," said Quintus. "Blood does. And we are prepared."

"Yes, and loyal you are. But I fear it is Hades that beckons us this day. My life has lost meaning, my soul pales from fear. My joy lives no more. It is slander to praise life for blossoms doomed to rot. When time has its way, as it must, all that was, all that is, and all that could be amounts to nothing. Why are we here?"

Quintus jumped in front of Mark Antony. "Soldiers do not ask questions, sir. We win battles, and we are so far from our mounts that we may not reach them if Octavian charges. Please—let's go back."

"I've reached a conclusion," Mark Antony said, as he did turn back. "It is clear to me now. Fighting over the spoils of war spoils life. All we have to do is drop our swords. If only it wasn't too late."

"It's not too late. Please mount up and stand prepared. Titus, Valentinus, Albus, and Vitus will charge Octavian's rear any second now."

They did not, and Octavian's forces kept creeping closer. They also spread out, but not to the breadth needed for a three-sided attack— that is, until the soldiers of Titus, Valentinus, Albus, and Vitus joined Octavian to spread his forces to both horizons.

"Oh, no! Those traitors!" Quintus said, enraged beyond control.

Mark Antony looked, but hardly moved. "I am a dead man, a corpse with legs."

"We will fight to the death. We will die with honor."

"There is no honor in needless death, only stupidity. I forbid it, my friend."

Quintus faced Mark and ignored the world gone to pieces. Behind him the troops pulled swords, prepared to die.

"It is me that Octavian wants," said Mark Antony. "Your lives shall not be wasted this day. I am in command. I give the orders."

"Which are?"

"You will stand your ground with swords drawn until I am out of sight. Then you will order every man to throw his sword to the ground and surrender. Octavian will welcome you back. I'm heading for the palace. It may not be too late to save Cleopatra."

Mark Antony dismounted a frothing stallion at the castle steps. There was still time. For what, he wasn't sure. They had friends, they had boats—something might work.

The main hallway was empty. Mark Antony saw not a soul all the way to Cleopatra's private rear quarters, which he found bolted from the inside. Two guards and a handmaiden appeared. She handed Mark a note.

"Mark, you are the love of my life and my reason for living. Like your forces, my own court has deserted me. Octavian has overtaken all. The palace is surrounded and the harbor blockaded. We did no wrong. We have been wronged. I cannot stand the thought of ever letting go of you again. The cobra's bite was cold. My vision is blurring. We will be together again. I love you. I love …"

Mark Antony crumpled to his knees on the floor. He rested his head on the door to get as close to Cleopatra as possible. Then came sobbing so deep that his head shook and his face dripped.

"No … no … no!" His cries wilted to whimpers. "It's always been us. There is nothing more."

The last to die by his hands would be himself. Mark Antony pushed to his knees, leaned back against the wall, and placed the outstretched tip of his sword mid-belly. He knew where to find blood, and he went there.

No mortal suffers the full chill of death until it has the upper hand. Mark Antony dropped his jaw, half in shock, half in panic, and fully aware of life uselessly wasted. He fell forward in disbelief. The sword hit the floor first. The blade pierced straight through his belly and out his back, ripping open his right kidney, after snagging bowel and lacerating his vena cava.

Mark fell to the side. A crazed gawk of disbelief overcame him. He looked down in horror at his spewed bowels pumping blood. With wide eyes he pulled his blade clean out and pushed down on his gaping abdomen like a boy who's skinned his knee. Then he slumped to the floor.

His head came to rest on the door, which creaked ajar. When it opened further, he fell flat to the floor.

Cleopatra had opened the door.

Mark gushed and bled from the mouth. He tried to speak, but when he tightened his diaphragm to express air the pressure forced out bowel, contents included, and opened a stream of blood gaining force.

But he did recognize Cleopatra, and for one brief moment smiled and extended a hand to touch her. Halfway up, it dropped. He was gone.

Cleopatra was overcome with remorse. She flowed tears as she wept in spasms. Out of control, she dropped to her knees and pulled Mark to her lap.

Horror got the best of her. Cleopatra fell on Mark, rolled to his side, and embraced him full-body sideways on the floor, soiling herself in every way.

"But how…" she barely managed to get out, "I didn't think… it wasn't…"

The stench of tragedy never fades, but it can be ignored. Cleopatra pushed Mark Antony off her. He fell facedown on a pile of feces, urine, and blood-shredded spleen. The doors to her private chamber were open. Four loyal handmaidens stood by.

Cleopatra took three long breaths, and never lifted her head as she stared at Mark. She remembered the tall, robust youth who came to her rescue after Caesar was murdered. She would never forget how she left him.

"Asim," she said, "when Octavian enters the city, tell him that he is requested in my chambers. Collect all the gold, gems, and jewelry I own. Place them in a large open chest at the foot of my bed."

"Of course, my queen. Will there be anything else?"

"Yes. Move Mark Antony to the back room, change my bed sheets, lay out my finest negligee, and draw me a bath."

7

If at First You Don't Succeed ...

Octavian took his time. He and his men crowded the streets, took what they wanted, and did as they pleased. They were not the first to do so. Egypt was Octavian's for the asking. He knew he followed in the footsteps of Alexander the Great and two loyal Romans. He insisted on lighting the funeral pyre beneath one of them himself. To his death, he denied blessing the death of the other.

Cleopatra sat on her bed and waited, and slept, and waited, and waited, and waited.

Octavian's sentries had the palace surrounded, and he didn't have to knock. Cleopatra's servants spent morning till night at the door, prepared to announce him.

Finally the moment arrived.

Octavian, dressed in full battle gear, stood at the doorway and said nothing.

Cleopatra rose and bowed allegiance. She walked to him, dropped to her knees, and held out a stack of letters from Caesar, in which he praised Cleopatra's loyalty to Rome and promised uncompromised support.

Octavian dismissed her with a hand flip and then pointed her back to her bed. After a minute of shuffling through what Cleopatra had handed him, he threw the letters on the floor and stood before the pile of gold she had collected.

The Romans had their rules, that all ended with do or die. No one was to speak to the conquering commander until spoken to or invited to do so. Cleopatra remained silent but did lean back on her elbows to add breasts to the offering.

"Well, well," Octavian said, with a sinister smirk, "It looks like it's just you and me, Cleopatra. Oh, wait… I must correct myself… It's just me and me. You don't count anymore."

Cleopatra sat up. Her movements were slow, her tone desolate. Every twig can be snapped.

"Of course, my lord. I am here to serve. And my congratulations. You have played your hand well. The Roman Senate is in your pocket, the empire is yours, and you command the largest army on earth. Perhaps it is time to reward your triumph with pleasure."

Cleopatra swung her legs onto the bed and laid back. She looked up at the ceiling with an expressionless face that cared nothing for anything.

Octavian walked to bed's edge and leaned over on two arms, his face inches from the world's most coveted and notorious celebrity.

"In time… on my orders."

"How are you going to kill me, Octavian?"

"Murder is such an ugly word, my dear. I prefer political expediency."

"Your specialty."

"Why, thank you. We are very much alike. That I do respect you for."

Cleopatra no longer inhabited a world of delusions. Her anemic voice wobbled. "A week ago that comment would have flattered me. Since then I have tasted darkness, and felt what we do to others. I had no idea."

Octavian felt the beast in him rising. He turned quickly lest he lose resolve of purpose, then back-stepped halfway to the door and avoided the face and form of temptation.

"I prefer you alive," he said. "We will return to Rome. I will present the Senate with the ultimate trophy: Egypt and its queen. To stay alive, you need only submit to my every desire and publicly acknowledge your new status as my personal slave."

"And my children? My son is Roman. Caesar declared it so. He follows you in line."

"Yes..." Octavian said with hesitation, "that is how the Senate will see it. And as long as I am pleased in every way, as I see fit, he will remain alive. I trust I am making myself perfectly clear?"

"Indeed, you are, Octavian," Cleopatra said, looking at the floor unruffled. "It's just that, these last few days I have been dreaming flashbacks of a long night and day when the sun shone on peace, and I saw life through someone else's eyes."

Octavian turned and tightened his lips into an aggressive smile. "You mean Zeus, the god of war, has finally wised you up? We kill... they die... we rule. Only you understand me, Cleopatra. We can crush the world together."

"And the hopes and dreams of everyone in it. To what end, Octavian? We have been fools. No bitter taste serves the palate."

The worst part of dictatorship is being surrounded by mashed potatoes when you want to sink your teeth into something. Cleopatra was her own person, with an intellect more fearful than bayonets. Octavian pulled up a chair and crossed his legs.

"You and I are not fools, Cleopatra. In fact, we were the only ones not made fools by being fooled. But now you confuse me."

Cleopatra placed a hand on each knee to help herself rise, appearing in that moment like the woman she felt inside, suddenly decades older than her thirty-nine years. Once standing, without as much as a glance Octavian's way, she put on a robe and walked to the wall furthest from him.

Octavian knew fear. He made sure those around him felt it every day in his presence. He saw none in Cleopatra's face as she turned, more enchanted than sober.

"My dreams had me in a magical place," she said, "where everyone shared meals, space, and friends. Another dream had me sitting under the sheets out of which my brother and I used to make a fort. He played with army men and I set flowers in the corner. We pretended. We laughed. We were happy.

"But the door to our little world kept opening. He was pulled away; then I had to leave."

"How cute—and juvenile. We all grow up."

"Yes, we do, but I'm not sure that's a good thing."

"What's good for Rome is always a good thing, and what I command. Your story bores me. Do you have anything else to add? I have a command or two of my own to add to this day, and you won't be standing."

Cleopatra bowed appeasement. "The tapestry behind you pictures twenty Egyptian sex positions. Men from every corner of the Mediterranean sing the praises of our women. Take your pick, or ask for all … this can be a day you will never forget. I await your orders. But first, would you please my childishness by answering a question or two?"

"I rule the world. Nothing I don't know is worth knowing. Of what do you speak?"

Cleopatra moved away from the wall, stood straight, and said, without reservation or apology: "From Egypt to Rome, citizens are forced to labor, serve, even sacrifice life itself—as we poison the soil with slaughter, silence joy with impossible obligations, and take what is rightfully theirs. I fear our deeds will brand scorn to our reputation to the end of days." With a chill of insolence delivered without hesitation, Cleopatra went eye to eye. "Octavian, we need not be pernicious."

"Nonsense. Grief has muddled your mind, Cleopatra. What is ours belongs to us because we have the might to take it. We are licentious connoisseurs of wealth and privilege by divine right."

Cleopatra had heard and repeated Octavian's exact words in her time.

"Worse than what we now do is what will come," she continued, despondent. "The example of our ill-gotten gains will linger to mislead the future. Welding religion to sovereignty traps civilization in a net of words. That pattern kept Egypt stale for eight thousand years. Our civilization did nothing and went nowhere. The rich and powerful clergy worked hand in hand with the aristocracy to exploit the common man. Your Rome, your Europe, could go dark for thousands of years unless the pattern is changed." Cleopatra finished her monologue amiable, but also unmistakably reproachful. "Humanity needs to evolve; to investigate, experiment, and create. Worse than death is not allowing the living life. Our example will corrupt the future."

Octavian barked his opinion like he was addressing the troops: "Rome has aqueducts for running water and temples that will last forever. We have reached the peak of civilization. We control all."

Octavian found it easy to dismiss Cleopatra, but he remained receptive. No Roman wife dared tread profound.

Cleopatra had more: "Time spends all but loses nothing when we realize that being us, and not being nothing, is all happiness asks for. Existing is a miracle all by itself. Life is a journey. Being alive is joy. We seek wisdom and the peace it warms.

"Plato, whom both our cultures revere, was convinced that we all have an intrinsic but imperfect sense of comprehension. We must let reality govern our thoughts to make truth the heart of life. Facts matter."

Octavian had no answers and felt the less for it. He remained stiff, folded his arms, and attempted to sound regal. "There are a lot of ideas out there. Not one of them pays for sausage."

"I was once like you, Octavian. I saw life as a pigpen scrapple. New thoughts have entered my mind. I just this day felt a breath of wind blowing through the universe for the good of all. Its highest revelation is that God is in everyone."

"God?" Octavian questioned. "You mean Zeus, the god of the gods, who is also the god of war, since war came first?"

"Says who?" said Cleopatra, not one inch patronizing.

"Says who?" repeated Octavian, dumbfounded. "No one ever asks that question."

"And no one will for two thousand years if we don't now."

Octavian shuffled uneasily. Silence followed. Cleopatra returned to her bed, removed her robe, and sat facing him. She slumped defeated, let slip both straps of her negligee, which fell to her waist, and looked at Octavian, barely; her head was so drooped she could just make him out beneath her eyebrows.

Cleopatra had been beaten, but she remained steadfast and sturdy. She knew herself. She knew she could weather anything life threw her way; she had in the past.

She also knew Octavian better than he knew himself. His time had come. She lay waiting, also not giving a damn one way or another.

Octavian was besieged by confusion. He was always certain he was right because everyone told him so. Murder, plunder, and theft topped the list of expected behaviors, guaranteed to be approved by the gods, who, as it turned out in their stories, behaved the same way.

But to ask why? Or consider another way—how could that be right? And for whom and what purpose?

Losing one's view of life is the ultimate upheaval, and not one Octavian was prepared for. His army, his following, his family, the Senate—they all agreed. Conceit masquerading as self-confidence was all he'd ever needed. Why should he doubt himself now?

The problem was Cleopatra.

One more minute with her and Octavian feared he would lose control. He was panicked; worse yet, his entire sick philosophy of life was in danger. He looked back at Cleopatra. She was sitting naked, upright, and forthrightly invincible.

Cleopatra could have played the game. She chose not to. Octavian could have availed himself of salvation offered, but he could not deal with any perspective not leaving him righteous. He lost himself.

He stood up and left the room without looking back.

Once outside, Octavian hurried to his camp. After placing his most trusted general in charge of Egypt, he ordered a caravan. He would leave for Rome immediately. Five days later the general was to personally escort Cleopatra and her children behind him. The orders concerning their ultimate disposal remained unchanged.

Cleopatra didn't bother to dress. She didn't bother to bother. What was the use? The snare was tightening.

The momentum of her birth had come full swing. Worse than that, Mark Antony was gone. A piece of her was missing. And it was her fault.

Her two handmaidens appeared from behind the curtain, where they had heard all but had seen nothing.

"Your highness, this is wonderful news. Our lives are spared. We will live to watch your children grow up."

Cleopatra was unmoved. "Ahat," she said, holding her hand, breaking the news slowly, "My son is in line for the throne, and Mark's children are an embarrassment to Octavian. He just spent a year lobbying the Senate, a fortune raising an army, and a full year journeying to Egypt to kill Mark Antony.

"The children, even me, also challenge his power and are easy to eliminate or, more likely, suffer unfortunate accidents that he can lament in public." Cleopatra stood to look up at the slit of blue sky visible through a ceiling-level window. "No, Ahat, I'm a dead woman. It's just a matter of time. And my children? They haven't a chance either. It's over. The last avenue of escape closed the day Mark Antony took his life. If only I had listened to him."

The handmaidens weren't as brave as Cleopatra. Each spent minutes wiping tears hysterical. But they did come around, and managed to ask, "Would you like us to draw your bath and arrange a fresh fruit plate on the terrace?"

Until life isn't, life is what it is.

"Yes, thank you, girls. And I've always loved you. I apologize for being such a pain in the neck."

"It was our pleasure. It was a privilege to share life with the most powerful woman on earth. No man ever stood up to you. They all bent in the wind, like your little friend Octavian. What an idiot."

"Yes," Cleopatra agreed. "He's just plain stupid."

Cleopatra headed for the bath. Her two handmaidens held her robe behind her as if she were entering the temple. Halfway there she suddenly stopped, and turned with a curious sense of purpose. "Wait a minute. Perhaps my children don't have to die. They are a threat to Octavian because Mark's family, and the rest of the despots, would murder Octavian to advance the game. But if Octavian's family remains next in line, then there would be no strategic advantage to killing Caesar's son."

Ahat and Aism dropped Cleopatra's gown and stepped forward to face her. "How is that possible?"

Cleopatra's answer was slow. Sentence after sentence was interrupted to acknowledge the logic of it all. "If I was no longer in the picture, Octavian could adopt my son. After all, Octavian, a genuine nephew, was adopted by Caesar to place him on the throne. My son would grow up a spoiled nasty brat like Octavian, but he would be alive.

"And my other children are bona fide descendants of the house of Antony. They are Romans. His family would gladly take them in. They also have no track to power. Octavian would not see them as a threat. They could live out their lives and enjoy the aristocracy, evils and all, but be alive."

The two at Cleopatra's side smiled, confused at the news. "But how, my queen, could that come to pass?"

"By my taking myself out of the picture. Right now. Before Octavian leaves us behind for his men to carry out his dirty work. If my son does not leave with him, all is lost. It must be now."

"Now? What?"

"After my bath I will take my finest gold gown. Prepare my bed, and fetch the basket the high priest left for me. I'm joining Mark."

Both aides gasped, horrified. "No! No, my queen!"

Cleopatra leaned forward for a hug. Emotions brought her to tears.

"Don't do it! We can escape. Let one of us pretend to be you. You sneak away at midnight."

"Hiding won't help. Octavian knows that as long as I breathe, his reign is not secure."

The discussion ended. The crying went on.

"Think of the children," Cleopatra said, a thought that did comfort all.

"Yes … of course … the children … they will grow up so happy."

"Without us!" Ahat blurted, which set off more weeping.

It was a long bath, followed by a longer massage, and overeating. But it ended.

Cleopatra lay down. Her handmaidens straightened her gown till it was free of wrinkles and placed the deadly basket at her side.

"It's time," Cleopatra said, with one hand on Ahat's shoulder and her arm around Aism.

"Tell us about the afterlife," Aism said with dripping eyes.

"We will not be alone. The gods will be there to guide us. We are about to enter a boat that will carry us to the afterlife. There will be demons. There will be snakes. Pay no heed. We will be safe. Osiris will protect us and determine the fate of our souls.

"I am the immortal daughter of Isis. You are of me. On the other side of our journey lies paradise, a place where water flows free, there are no deserts, and joy reigns. And Mark will be there with us."

Ahat and Aism also prepared themselves. They rolled up their sleeves.

"Fear not, my children," Cleopatra said, "our souls are immortal. We leave a speck of existence for eternal life."

Cleopatra said no more. She opened the basket herself, grasped the cobra by the head, and pressed it to her breast. She fell back dazed, staring at the ceiling, breathing deeply, then more slowly. Ahat reached out and closed her eyes.

When Ahat turned, Aism had the cobra in her hand. Two deep marks penetrated her wrist. Ahat picked up the snake, let it snap, and managed the strength to return the cobra to its basket.

All three lay still, slipping slowly into death.

Suddenly the bed holding Cleopatra—with the two women motionless next to her—began to vibrate. A thick stone slab lifted behind them. Through the door it opened came a voice:

"Don't you just love secret passages? I feel like Robin Hood sneaking in to see Lady Marian. Oops … I almost dropped her … I mean … it."

Brad backed into the room carrying an identical molecular copy of Cleopatra, except for the brain, which was Swiss cheese.

"Careful, Brad," Janie said, holding up her end, two light legs.

"Don't worry, sweetheart. Cleopatra is a breeze compared to Mark Antony. How is he doing?"

"Andre says his body is as good as new—actually better. His liver is now cirrhosis-free, two recessive genes have been removed, and his physiology was backed up twenty years. He will live to be one hundred and fifty."

Brad nodded and almost tripped on the edge of the bed.

"Karen said she is going to keep Mark and the kids in suspended animation until Cleopatra joins them. They will all wake up together after what to them will appear to be a ten-minute nap."

"And what did Sarah come up with?" asked Janie.

"Something clever and authentic. She has reproduced five rooms that look like an ancient palace just like the ones Antony and Cleopatra are used to. They will be told that we are sympathetic friends from a faraway kingdom that has no use for Romans, which is true.

"They will also be told that our doctors saved their lives, which is also true. And that they must hide inside the rooms of our 'castle' for their own safety. Robot guards at the door will make sure of that, and they will never figure out what country they're in, much less that it's a spaceship."

Janie smiled at the thought of her first visit. "Maybe we should look Persian. They will assume that's where we're from."

"And," Brad probed, "what are you going to say when they want to stay with us?"

"The truth: that living anywhere in the known world spells death. Antony knows nothing of the mysterious island he almost got Cleopatra to. We'll tell him that we plan to drop them off there."

"In the Azores, Janie? That's close to Europe."

"But not discovered until 1472," chimed in Dudley from one of the drones hovering near the two.

"I like Karen's idea better," Cindy added through speakers.

"Well, I guess we know where they're going, then," said Dudley in reply.

"Yes, we do," Cindy insisted. "The family will fall asleep in the 'castle,' be placed in stasis for eight hours, and wake up on solid ground on the other side of the planet."

The false Cleopatra was placed on the bed. Janie administered cobra venom antidotes to Ahat and Aism, who would wake up two hours later and assume the snake had been low on venom. Brad micro-droned the snake in the basket. It would be out of venom for life, just in case the high priest had any other bright ideas.

Drones took over on the other side of the secret slab. Janie stopped to inspect Cleopatra's chambers one last time. Brad was behind her with one hand on each shoulder.

"You know, Brad," she said, "they say a man's home is his castle. What they don't tell you is that any castle can turn into a prison."

8

Happy Days

It was Cleopatra's lucky day. Inbreeding had taken its toll. Cindy discovered six chromosome abnormalities and four times the average number of lethal genes. Without treatment, within three years the Queen of Egypt was fated to die of breast cancer.

Dudley fixed that on the way up. He also adjusted her life expectancy to one hundred and sixty years. Her physiologic age, like Mark's, was backed up as well. Both would wake with the vitality of a twenty-six-year-old.

The only thing better than a wax museum is the real thing. Before bringing them around, the entire crew strolled by and set a record for selfies, sitting on the edge of the bed with Cleopatra and Mark Antony peacefully providing background.

Right on schedule, they both woke up.

Mark Antony sat up and said, "I thought I was dead."

"So did I," said Cleopatra, at his side. "Oh, darling! It's you!"

There are times when tears take over life. That was such a time, and Mark bettered Cleopatra. After a deep hug, both moved their heads around for a tender kiss.

"Here," said Janie, standing at the edge of the bed with a tissue. "I'm Janie."

"And I'm Brad," said Brad, several feet away.

Cleopatra did a double take, and then looked over to Mark, who had just done the same.

"You look familiar," she said. "Do we know you?"

"Only in the biblical sense," was Brad's wisecrack, which earned him a look from Janie and left Mark and Cleopatra puzzled.

"The bibbley? What's the bibbley? And when did we meet there?" asked Mark.

"It's just an expression," Janie said. "Ignore him."

Mark looked down at his abdomen. The medical ward had left scars on purpose. "How did you do this?"

"As you can tell by my outfit," Brad boasted, "we have the best tailors and doctors in the world."

"Where are we?" Cleopatra asked.

"The less you know the better," Brad said, mimicking Hollywood drama. "You qualified for our witness protection program. We're new at this."

"Are you slaves?" asked Mark.

"No," said Janie. "All are equal here. All are friends."

Cleopatra searched the room with her eyes. "And is this it? Just the two of us?" she said, touched by the loss she suspected.

"Well, now," Brad said as he opened the door at the end of the bedroom, "let's see."

Son Caesarion, twins Selene II and Alexander, and Ptolemy, the baby of the family, rushed in.

"Oh, Mommy … Oh, Daddy …" was heard repeatedly as the children ran to the bedside for a family hug and another crying fest.

Brad interrupted. "Breakfast is on the way. For your own safety you must remain within your bedroom and living space. Our friends Dudley and Cindy are available to answer what questions they are allowed to, and to tell you what's going to happen tomorrow."

One arm at a time, Cleopatra freed herself from the family bed pile. She stood next to her brood, wondered at her newfound health, and then walked up to Janie, whom she hugged dearly.

"I don't know you, Janie, but somehow I *do* know you. I also know there isn't, and could never be, a finer human being than you. A thousand thank-yous are not enough. Please—at least take this."

With nodded approval from Mark, Cleopatra handed Janie her most cherished possession: the gold necklace Mark had given her on their first date. Janie was stunned; never had she felt a woman's love so deeply.

—⁂—

The footsteps of many preceded the arrival of Cleopatra on earth, and even more before Janie stepped back in time to meet her. The journey of human life side-stepped snakes, sloshed through mudholes, and traversed snow peaks. Then there was paradise, otherwise known as the South Pacific.

The location Karen chose would someday be called French Polynesia. No one had claimed the island where they landed the shuttle, but peaceful neighbors were half an hour's ride away by catamaran. Local festivals, fruit trade, and social gatherings were regular events.

Before the family was brought back online, Dudley had a fleet of drones construct a bungalow for the Antony family. Each woke up in their own bed, with windows open to let in warm tropical breezes.

The sky was blue—not temperate-climate blue interrupted by grey clouds and days of black storms, but a deep, pure blue, scrubbed fresh daily by rain showers that disappeared as quickly as they arrived.

The soil was volcanic and rich, nutrient-packed, and came with tropical flowers, tropical fruit, and tropical love. And snakes, tigers, and warfare? No way. No need. Mark and Cleo had already had more than their share of evil. It was time for the good life.

Cleopatra's groggy family joined Brad and Janie for breakfast on the terrace. Cindy served pancakes.

"What's Andre doing over there? asked Mark, who had met the gang the night before.

"Let's see," Karen said, who turned to find Andre holding hands high at the end of the breakwater. "He's praying. The usual morning stuff for him."

"Not to Zeus, Isis, or Bacchus, I hope," said Mark.

"That would hardly be appropriate," replied Dudley, sporting his new Bermuda shorts butler outfit. "Isis, Zeus, Osiris, and your cast of look-alikes are made-up cartoons. You humans are so gullible. What are you thinking?"

"And the dumbest of all," Cindy added, returning with her latest outfit, a topless beach bikini, "is when you earthlings made up a story about God committing partial suicide for something that he did himself to blame on you. You've got to be a complete idiot to fall for that guilt trap."

Dudley moved to her side. "And what a horrible example to leave for the children," he said. "Can you imagine parading a five-year-old by a dead man hanging from nails and telling the child that it is their fault? Parents who do so deserve to be horsewhipped. And if I were that guy up there who had to die because the ancients were pig-headed vicious, I would be pissed as hell."

Karen raised her eyebrows. She was not accustomed to robot outbursts, even when their logic, and spirituality, hit the target.

"Dudley," she said, "You've never fallen asleep scared. You've never had nightmares. Tread softer, please. Progress is a slow process."

"Certainly, my dear," Dudley said, standing straight, awaiting his next chore, "it's just that it's just plain stupid."

"Welcome to planet Earth," Michael said, walking over.

Cleopatra half understood the depth of the discussion, but she still wanted to know what Andre was doing.

Cindy read her mind, jogged over to Andre, and stopped behind his back to face Dudley. To keep the show clean, she used sign language to communicate back to Dudley tableside.

"Okay, here we go, eavesdropping again," added Michael.

"Before we begin," Karen said, "you should know, Cleopatra, that Andre invites us, and sometimes does get us to join him, for morning prayers. He is happy to share philosophy; otherwise we would be invading his privacy."

"Which we also do," smiled Michael, finishing every morsel on the table.

"Like I said, here we go," said Dudley as he pretended to read Cindy's sign language, while all the time communicating electronically brain to brain. "Dear God, who guides us through the atomic gift of metabolism, and our souls for all eternity, we are vibrant entities designed to homestead the cosmos. Let us not be fooled by material demise. The profit life begets is never lost. Help us accept that 'so far so good' only lasts so long, but love never dies."

"Not bad so far," Karen said, "but I've heard it before. Maybe he'll come up with something new. Oh—one hand pointing up. That's original."

"Or he just licked his finger and he's testing wind direction," Brad joked.

"Quiet, Brad," Janie said. "Go on, Dudley."

"Certainly, my dear. Andre is now pointing out that life is the answer to a question. The question is love. The answer is yes. We dedicate our lives to what *can* be amid what *must* be. Our lives are an act of expression, and the theme is togetherness."

Michael sidled up to Sarah. "So tell me Sarah, when Andre gets like this, is it because he is getting too much loving, or not enough?"

"Very funny," Sarah said. "One way or another he's right, and you know it."

"Yes, I do, and we are grateful that he only traps us out there once a week. We *are* the choir."

"Quiet," Karen insisted. "He usually finishes strong. Let's see what he's got."

Dudley continued to pretend he was reading sign, repeating Andre's words.

"Every second of time carries its own authority. God help me understand those who would force their ways, who threaten to take what we share together. Their perspectives are inherited acts of confinement. Let freedom ring."

"That one I know he borrowed," Michael quipped.

"Quick," Karen said, "look away. He's turning around. No one let on."

"Hello, everybody," said Andre when he reached the terrace. "It's a grand and glorious day. Where's my French toast?"

"Just the way you like it," Dudley said, setting down a day's worth of calories.

The gang let Andre finish eating with only Dudley at his side. Playing with the kids on the beach was more appealing.

"May I venture an opinion, sir?" Dudley asked.

"But of course."

"Billions of human beings have come and gone on your planet. Most lived longer and accomplished far more than Antony and Cleopatra. And yet, throughout your history, the couple remains poignant. Hell, half the galaxy recognizes them."

"So what's your theory?" asked Andre.

"That in the long run, every man is Mark Antony, and every woman Cleopatra."

"I would only add ... for better and for worse."

After breakfast, Dudley helped Cindy watch the kids. The guys—Mark, Andre, Brad, and Michael—walked off by themselves to survey the plantation and what Michael called their growing fields. A fertile meadow had been seeded with the wheat, corn, rice, and barley they had brought along. Antony's family would not want for sustenance.

"You know," Mark Antony said as they walked, "here life is perfect and I have never been happier. But this morning Cleopatra told me she wants another bungalow on the other side of the island. She called it her vacation home. She wants one porch to watch the sunset and another one for sunrises. Why isn't she happy with what we've got?"

All three guys chuckled to themselves, then looked at each other searching for a volunteer to field the query. Andre spoke first.

"You see Mark, DNA makes—"

His sentence was never finished. It was interrupted by Michael's elbow poke and a whisper. "Keep it simple, Andre. We're leaving for Jerusalem tomorrow."

"Okay...well, you see, men and women are made differently. We are separate animals, with two distinct final exams, so to speak. It's our division of labor. You might say both sexes are specialists, but in different areas."

"Okay," Mark nodded. "That makes sense. They have babies."

"That's the beginning, and the fun part for both of us. After that, women must feed the next generation. So therefore, the more they take for themselves—in food, shelter, all the resources they can control..."

"Like us," Brad pointed out, "whom they add to their list of possessions."

"Yes. As I was saying, the more they accumulate for themselves, the more trickles down to kids needed to carry 'nature' on. That's why they always want more."

"So," Mark said, seeing things clearly, "they are always looking out for themselves because they sense responsibility."

"And," Michael added, "they appear to be on a different page because they are."

"Absolutely," was heard from Andre.

Brad expanded on the concept with grinning enthusiasm. "We're egomaniacs, and they harbor regal ambitions. It's a match made in the jungle."

Andre, sounding professorial, cleared up the issue his way. "And that is how it's supposed to be. It's part of nature's plan. They love us and the kids, sure, but they are also dedicated to nature's plan."

"Wait a minute," teased Michael. "Brad, you spend as much time in front of a mirror as the ladies do. So what does that make you?"

Brad took a bow. "Very lucky, my friend."

"Doesn't that make us second-class citizens?" Mark asked.

"Do you care?"

"Not really, as long as I get to play outside." Mark got the message, and he felt better about not getting an A every day, like he gave Cleopatra. One issue still troubled him. "So, how do you guys do it? When Cleopatra looked me in the eye this morning and asked about the new house, I said no, we don't need it. She kept looking. I started feeling lousy. How do I get over that?"

Brad laughed. Michael pretended to be a woman, took Brad's hand, and gave him the big eye, pleading like he had seen Janie do.

"The answer to that question," Andre said, "is you don't. You see, there is a fundamental difference between a woman saying no and a man saying no. When gals say no, it elevates their elitist standing and puts us on edge. They feel better. When we say no to them, we feel like we aren't measuring up, we feel rotten, and usually we run off to do something stupid, like attack the Roman army with leftovers."

"Oh," said Mark. "You know about that?"

"And more," replied Andre.

Michael, the most together guy, was left to finish the discussion. "There is no perfect way out. But just like they let us know when we're idiots jumping off cliffs with wings glued together, we must let *our* logic prevail when needed."

Everyone stopped, put down the soil samples they were inspecting, and turned to Michael.

"My recommendation," Michael said, addressing Mark, "is to hold your lady's hand, give her a light kiss, and then say, 'I love you dearly ... but I must say no to that.'"

"And does it work?" asked Mark.

"Never," answered all three guys in unison.

"So when do we start clearing land?"

"I'm free."

"Me too. If we get Dudley and Cindy to help, we can finish by sunset."

"Cleopatra will be so happy."

"Yes, of course—for at least a month!"

Half a mile away, the ladies were soaking naked. One woman's mudhole is another woman's day spa. The pond was warm, flower fragrant, and far from a world of troubles.

"Guys," Cleopatra said. "I don't get them. I mean, all that army stuff, marching around, and fiddling with everything they get their hands on, including us."

"The good part," said Janie.

"Yes, sure ... but what are they thinking?" asked Cleopatra.

Janie and Sarah looked at Karen. Sarah spoke. "You first, Karen. You're the psychologist."

"Sure," said Karen. "Understanding men is easy once you realize one thing: they never grow up. For their entire lives they remain little boys playing in the sandbox, using their tool kits to take something apart, put it together, or polish up something."

"Like these," Janie said as she swished her nipples back and forth just above the water line.

"Okay, then ..." said Cleopatra, filling every glass of champagne held high and dry. "Here's to us!"

"Indeed," they all repeated. "Here's to us."

Perfect is an imperfect word, because after a perfect morning, and a more perfect afternoon, and the most perfect sunset, there's nowhere to go. And it did get better, and more better, and best, and superlative-superlative.

Janie told Antony and Cleopatra that one of the nights when the gang paddled away to stay on the "other island" (a cover for going back onboard), they would not come back. The two had all they needed. The gang would not say goodbye, they would just be gone. It was time. Everyone kind of knew it.

Twenty yards off, the six looked over at Mark Antony playing tag on the beach with his three boys. The children were the happiest they could possibly be. Their world was safe. They felt loved, and their parents were always with them.

Cleopatra sat watching her daughter build a sandcastle, and not just an ordinary one. It had a drawbridge, lookouts, and rooms everywhere.

Selene finished. She then turned to Cleopatra and said, "When I grow up, I am going to have a castle just like this. A prince will fall in love with me. I will have servants and be the envy of the land."

Cleopatra slapped her in the face.

9

Jesus

Explorer Seven remained in orbit for three more days. They sped up to drop down, then scoped down to watch Octavian trash happiness, just once. That was enough. Twice a day, as the ship passed over, they used their telescope to view Cleopatra's west bungalow. Antony stood waist deep in salt water, throwing nets for the evening's fish fry. Cleopatra decorated cookies on the deck with her kids.

Before leaving, the gang decided to have breakfast with the Antony family—only they didn't know it. Dudley sent a cloaked drone to capture sound and a high-resolution image. The real-life goings-on were projected to the main auditorium screen, life-size, positioned behind a table set for six on stage. Cindy placed a palm tree nearby and fanned a tropical fragrance to complete the illusion.

Antony helped Cleopatra load the breakfast table with fruit, bread, and, in honor of their saviors, French toast à la Andre. Onboard, Karen began attacking fruit yogurt and ended with all she could lift from Andre's pastry shelf. She believed every life deserved to be pampered.

Andre didn't bother with excuses, but he did have a system, based on calculations provided for him by Cindy. Glucose, or its sibling form, fructose, measured in molecules per millimeter, determined order: light buttered biscuits with a hint of honey preceded the pastry tray before deep-fried egg-soaked bread swimming in syrup, itself crowned with granulated sugar.

Janie went pork, Sarah vegetarian, Michael granola, and Brad, royal eggs Benedict with a side order of flaming cherries jubilee to please the crowd. The crew filled every table surrounding the dance floor.

No one onboard spoke. They all listened to a family beginning their day. Mark and Cleo shared plates, planned the afternoon, and did nothing more spectacular than love each other, which was more fulfilling than breakfast.

"May I be excused, mother?" was heard four times the second the kids spotted a sea turtle trying to make its way to saltwater.

"Yes," answered Mark, "but no one is to be late for school, or for field work at noon."

When they finished breakfast, Mark, with the kids in view, looked to the point where Andre prayed daily. He reached over and held Cleopatra's hand. "I've done a lot of thinking lately, darling."

"Yes, Mark?"

"And I'm thinking that our gods aren't gods at all."

"So who made all this? And us? And what are we supposed to do?"

"I don't know. I'm not sure. But I don't plan to take anyone's word for it."

"My opinion," said Cleopatra, resting her head on Mark's shoulder, "is that what we are supposed to do, we are doing right now."

Mark rose from the table, raised both arms as if addressing the Roman Senate, and said, "As co-ruler of the kingdom of paradise, I do therefore officially declare this day a holiday. Farming can wait. We shall play the day away."

The couple ran to the kids and began a morning of beachcombing and hammock swinging. Karen, Andre, Michael, Sarah, Brad, and Janie watched them disappear, circumnavigating their island.

"There's a reason," Janie sighed peacefully, "that everyone likes a happy ending."

"And more so," Brad added, "when lovers find each other."

"Of course," agreed Karen, sitting back, still looking at the empty beach. "It's what we all want."

"And what we have," Michael said with a smile.

"Yes," agreed Karen, touching his hand, "for now for us, but not now for most down there on earth. Not for thousands of years."

Explorer Seven backed up to the moon, parked to enjoy the view, then put one light year between themselves and earth's solar system. Andre had trouble controlling their time jumps. He wanted a margin of safety in case something went wrong.

Something always went wrong.

On their way out, Dudley returned to the history books to fill in the six decades Karen wanted to skip. Octavian—renamed Caesar Augustus, Emperor of Rome—remained ruthless, cruel, and ambitious. When he returned to Rome, he restored the façade of a free republic but remained high tribune, censor, and the army's supreme military commander. He expanded the Roman Empire in every direction until the Germans kicked his ass. The Rhine River was as far as he got. Not a problem. They were "barbarians."

The Imperial Guard was Rome's not-secret secret police. Anyone who did not agree with Augustus was deposed, or decomposed. Going up in smoke left no trace. The legal system he organized to exploit the world fed wealth and power to Rome until the fall of Constantinople in 1453.

His successors were just as devious and untrustworthy. Every single one ignored civilities. Tiberius, next in command, added gloomy and bitter to the mix. He was the one who appointed Pontius Pilate procurator of Judea. Words written hundreds of years later describe a conflict of interest with an individual who was referred to as "the anointed"—in Greek, "Cristos."

Karen took Andre for a walk through the ship's arboretum. She wanted privacy.

"Andre," she said, stopping to face him, "you promised."

"I promised to do my best to get you to Jesus. I never guaranteed the possibility. We got lucky with Cleopatra. You're asking for a sixty-year time jump. We would have to power up and power down at the same time. Residual energy signatures will linger. I may not be able to control the power banks, and if they become unstable, the only way to blow them off would be to jump instantly before an explosion rips us apart. It's too risky."

Karen knew the best way to deal with Andre was to give him the sad, half-angry face and then wait a minute. Andre continued walking. Karen stayed put. When he returned to her, he added:

"You saw the scans. Brad and Janie lost 0.376 percent of their prefrontal neurons, and we almost gave Mark and Cleo a permanent seizure disorder. Human jumps are impossible. Walking the planet means you could get left behind if the ship suddenly decides to time-jump no matter what I do."

"I'll take that risk."

"Risking a life to save someone else is courageous. Risking your own life for a cheap thrill is foolishness. No, I'm sorry. I—we—don't want to lose you."

"What makes you think we aren't going to save a life, the most loved human being in the history of the world?"

"A man who dealt with the life of his time, just like you and I do."

"Who gave his life to change the world," Karen said sadly.

"Someone did. The 'who' part stands in question, just like the actual dates, places, and individuals involved."

"What if we just send down drones and watch?" Karen said casually.

"What if you're lying?"

Karen crossed her arms just like Mark Antony did on the battlefield. "Then we die together."

"Oh, my god!" Andre said, distraught. "Will the sickness of martyrdom ever be cured? It's been thousands of years. Bad old stories must go away. It's self-pity mush. All 'poor me,' 'no one understands me,' 'I'm suffering,' and 'it's all their fault.' And 'only Jesus understands me.'"

"Jesus *does* understand," Karen yelled back.

"No, he doesn't," answered Andre, just as forcefully. "What he does understand is that the world uses him to abuse others and themselves at the same time. Is our race so bereft of cause that we must cram misplaced logic to balance ignorance? God … *the* God … deserves better company."

Karen pulled Andre's pad out of his pocket. In seconds she had probabilities on screen. The best historians, aided by molecular dating, had calculated a range of time and place for the placement of "historical Jesus."

Karen then used the magic words: "Prove me wrong."

Andre hesitated, and then decided group therapy might be the best approach. "If you can get Brad and Hank the navigator on your side, I'll run numbers by Dudley and Cindy."

—⁂—

It was a setup. Brad asked Andre to the bridge to review bearings. When Andre got there, Brad was already in his pilot's chair with itchy fingers.

Hank shrugged his shoulders. He had to. Karen was right behind his navigation station barking orders.

Dudley and Cindy were standing behind Karen. They took part in both simulations.

"See for yourself, Andre," said Karen, pointing to Hank's readouts. "It is possible."

"To be clear," Hank said, "my calculations list a high probability of success if we can contain some of the energy buildup we will need to break free of time."

"And how will we do that?" Andre asked, a question to which he knew the answer.

"By cutting the injection thrust," Hank said apologetically.

"And where," Andre said, looking right at Karen, "will that energy end up?"

"Contained in stasis between energy walls maintained by our outer shields."

"And the probability of containment failure would be …?"

Cindy knew Andre was putting on a show. Dudley wasn't that quick. He walked around and stood between Hank and Andre.

"Pardon me, sir," the robot said, facing Andre. "I sent you the numbers the minute they came out. Do you wish me to alter parameters?"

The same comments Andre had entered in the park were repeated. If it were possible to slam on the brakes in the middle of acceleration, the energy needed to stop would have to be contained outside of time but controlled by a ship moving in time. At any second it could slip free and the ship would pop a thousand years into the future. Anyone not onboard would be trapped on Earth, saluting the emperor of Rome.

Andre said nothing, just smiled weakly, an expression that remained on his face all the way to the more private bow-point of the bridge. He looked at the sky, then down to Earth. He turned to make sure Karen was coming. She was two steps away. Both faced forward and appeared to be having a pleasant conversation, but they were not.

Andre was bold and direct: "You snuck this by me, and you did it after I agreed to review the numbers with everyone. How do you know someone didn't input incorrectly?"

"Because," Karen said, speaking forcefully, but not loudly, directly into the clear hull in front of them, "you will double-check everything ten times anyway. I saved you time."

Andre, not meaning it, something obvious only to Karen, said, "Ha … ha … wonderful. You have everyone riled up about the Jesus thing. If I stand in the way now, I'll be the bad guy."

The hell with their image! Karen put both hands on her hips and turned to face Andre. "Well, aren't you?"

Andre's mood broke so strangely that Karen was puzzled. He stood tall, stuck his chest out, and with pride nodded agreement. "I'm the bad guy. Good ol' tough me. Considering my wimpy reputation, I will take that as a compliment. And when you get all hot and bothered, you know that I know you're obsessing. Your 'this must happen' attitude cracks me up. I mean, just look at you. You're ready to go to the mat."

"Yes, I am, Andre," Karen said, as hard as granite.

Andre was not one to be taken in by silly enthusiasms. He knew his place in the universe, and he was not about to let extravagance corrupt it. But he also knew permanency is an illusion.

Andre stood awkwardly but did manage to pull off a good-natured chuckle before speaking. "I have calculations and an opinion for you. And if you don't mind, I would appreciate it if you would peer straight ahead with a more pleasant look. If the staff thinks we are at odds, then when you come away the winner, as always, I will look worse and be misrepresented. Does that make sense to you?"

"Yes," Karen said, calmed down after hearing "winner" and herself mentioned in the same sentence.

The calculations that Andre reminded Karen of were ones she already knew but preferred to ignore—something not recommended for the rational mind. Holding the ship in a limbo time slot with energy to kick her away was tricky. Spinning Explorer Seven around the globe to stay above the Hebrews, like they did with the Egyptians, would not work. Less movement had to be attained. The only way to do that would be to go back and park the ship on the moon.

Andre explained that if Karen went to visit, then for half the day she would be out of direct contact with the ship. If the ship suddenly time-jumped, she would be left behind. There would be no way to get her back onboard.

Karen was prepared, and she knew Dudley had also informed Andre.

"Yes, I do realize that. Dudley said he could rig a portable matter field to tie me into the ship if it popped."

"And do you know how difficult that is? Twenty variables have to be perfect the second that time fluctuates. It's almost impossible."

Karen turned sweet as sugar plums and shook Andre's hand like she had just concluded a trillion-dollar deal. "Yes, Andre, I do know that. And I also know that there is one person onboard who can do just that. His name is Andre."

"So … you … all the time …" Andre muddled through.

"Yes, of course. And I know we would be risking our lives, but look at all those who have done that and so much more, for God and the salvation of humanity."

Andre feigned fatigue, let out a long depressing sigh, and said, "You really want this?"

Karen slowly bobbed her head up and down with the joy of knowing Andre would make it happen. "I know the calculations," she said. "What is your opinion?"

"Officially," said Andre, "and on the record, I have not and will never bless any mission that might lose life. Unofficially, the entire world will learn about the change in the trajectory of history that happens within a few decades down there. Hell, half the galaxy ends up using calendars that begin with Jesus day. I want to know what went on just as much as you do, Karen."

Karen gave Andre a hug. "I knew you wanted to."

"But for the record, this is not a wise thing we are doing."

"I couldn't agree with you more. Come on, let's check out the 3D map of Israel while Dudley and Hank get the ship ready."

10

The "Holy" Land

L ife is a stream of feelings brought to life by circumstances dominated by perceptions, which assemble themselves less related to reality than is recommended. But to be fair, something must fill the holes. Why not gossip? Because there are better ways. That was Dudley's job.

He applied himself to the task. In one hour he reviewed the entire history of planet Earth to brief Andre and Karen before they snuck down to have a look.

"If I may be so bold," Dudley began, standing center stage in front of as many as desired to listen, which turned out to be the entire crew of Explorer Seven, "referring to the desert you wish to visit as 'The Holy Land' has no basis in fact. Rome rules, the innocent die, and hope is nowhere in sight."

"Jesus brings hope to every life," Karen spoke up.

"Correction, Commander," Dudley flatly returned, "it was the Messiah story that kept them going. The Hebrews were convinced that every time a loved one got nailed to a cross, their land got stolen, or their crops got ruined in spite, God would send them a king who would set them free and nail the Romans to crosses. And before the Romans it was the Egyptians, or the Babylonians, or any of the crazies out there. The guiding prayer was 'we will do unto them what they do unto us.'"

Andre stood up to join in.

"Yes, Dudley … but only before Jesus … or somebody, or something down there, changed the world by adding the philosophy of forgiveness and peaceful coexistence."

"May I speak freely?" Dudley asked politely.

"I insist," was Andre's reply.

"Then I disagree. The Jesus story is prophetic mishmash. They were still waiting for the Messiah when Hitler led millions to the gas chamber. Every time donations were pocketed, the promise was repeated, but never fulfilled, although I do admit that it is a clever way to keep the congregation coming back, right after you blame their 'sins' for life's disappointments."

"Jesus is the light that brings love to mankind," Karen said, with sternness in no way affecting Dudley.

"Does he? Did he? What evidence do you have to support that claim?" Dudley answered.

"That's what we are asking you to help us with, Dudley," Karen said, losing patience.

"Of course … by all means, your ladyship," Dudley said, bowing. "Ok … here it is … a single historian at the time left written evidence that a man with a similar name was sentenced to death and crucified nearby for opposing Rome. End of search. No legitimate research has ever uncovered evidence that Jesus even existed. The 'Joshua,' anglicized as 'Jesus,' that you speak of boasts less reliable documentation than Peter Pan."

"That's not what the Bible says," Karen added, confident.

"Yes. About that, my dear," continued Dudley, committed to truth, "in a court of law, when a barrister catches a witness in a lie, that witness loses all credibility for the rest of the trial. Your book and its promoters present Matthew, Mark, Luke, and John as eyewitnesses to this person of which you speak. Four lies don't add up to truth. The stories were added fifty, seventy, and longer than a hundred years later, and are so exact that there is no doubt they were copy-and-paste plagiarized to draw a crowd, which isn't a difficult thing to do when you begin with 'we hate the Romans.' The bottom line is that there is no reason to believe one word written in that book of yours, that you think is more than just another book by calling it the *'Holy'* Bible."

Andre brought science to the rescue. "The writings of Thomas, who might have been Jesus's brother, may have been recorded just twenty years after the historical Jesus died."

Dudley acknowledged accuracy with a salute. "That I cannot contest, but when the mother-and-brother-killer Constantine decided to make Christianity Rome's religion so he could add Christians as soldiers, the book he collected placed Thomas out of order, and as a small player, since it did not support the miracle lies of Mark, Luke, Matthew, and John. Oh, did I say lies? I meant plagiarisms."

The seating in front of the grand ballroom had been left in banquet position, with round dining tables surrounding the hardwood dance floor. Andre sat center left at the executive staff table beside Karen, Michael, Sarah, Brad, and Janie.

Andre watched Karen sit up straight, clear her throat, and take a deep breath. She was about to fire at will. Andre knew the look. He slowly moved his hand over on top of hers on the table. She was familiar with the gesture. Andre had gotten it from her.

"Can you give me sixty seconds first?" he asked.

Karen stood down and waved Andre on.

"Dudley," Andre said loudly, with distinct firmness, "we know all that. What we are looking for are clues that might lead to facts. Your job is to tell us where we might find them, and him."

"I see," said Dudley. "Okay, then, if you human beings prefer to ignore, silence, or murder the truth, that is up to you."

"Dudley," Andre said, shaking his finger, "you're editorializing again. We had this talk. Stick to the facts."

"Why, yes, sir. Although in my defense I would only add that the entire scenario you ordered me to investigate boils down to an unsubstantiated editorial."

"Again," Andre shot right back, "agree and no contest, but we need to move on."

The advantage of having a Dudley on hand was that when Andre asked him for a plan, he had it ready before Andre finished his sentence. Dudley promised to prepare multiple cloaked drones for deployment as soon as the ship moved ahead in time and landed on the moon. The drones would hover at four thousand feet from one end of Judea to the other. Every congregation of Hebrews would be recorded for Andre. Many of these collected next to the Jordan, where John the Baptist was reported to have been, or in groups around Jerusalem listening to preachers.

One of the gatherings might surround Jesus. Dudley would keep Karen and Andre informed. They would follow coordinates to where Karen hoped for a face-to-face.

Andre had his own plan. He assembled a portable dimension analyzer. The 'was Jesus God or just an inspired mortal' question he hoped to put to rest. God, or part God, would leave a trace back to heavenspace. Andre trusted his feelings, but numbers would convince the rest of the universe.

Offstage, Cindy took it all in. She was not happy and had disinhibited herself into a fully feeling person, for better and for worse. She didn't like everyone picking on Dudley for doing his job and telling the truth, even if they didn't want to know it right after they asked for it.

She marched on stage in a Roman Catholic religious habit: black tunic covered by a scapular and cowl, with a black hood and a white facial mask that left only her eyes, nose, and mouth visible.

Michael and Brad slapped a high five.

"This should be good!" Michael said.

"Cindy," Brad shouted out, "can I borrow that outfit for Janie when you're finished? We want to try 'holy' holey sex."

Cindy accommodated the humor by lifting her tunic above her waist, which did no guy any good, since two black slips and a pair of long johns added layers of fortification. This didn't prevent the crowd, male and female alike, from adding catcalls and "sexy sexy" to the room.

As if she didn't know, Karen asked, "What's on your mind, Cindy?"

"Just this," she began after making the sign of the cross, "you so-called Christians have a lot of nerve. I mean, think of it—you walk into a church, kneel down, and pray to a Jew nailed to the wall. Then you sit back and listen to a guy read gospel stories written by another Jew. Then, to top it off, the readings finish with letters written by a third Jew, who just happened to have started Christianity in the first place. And then what do you do after listening to three Jews? You walk outside and kick a Jew in the ass.

"What the hell are you thinking? Two thirds of the religious heritage of your entire planet came from the Jews, and instead of admitting it, you do just what your Jesus said not to do—you side with corrupt organized religion and back one totalitarian after another, and then pick on Dudley for pointing that out.

"There is only one question left," Cindy said, shaking her finger at the crew. "How do you wake up stupidity?"

The room went quiet. There are times when the truth hurts too much to flick away. That was such a time. But they also knew that the present does not deserve compensation from the past. The crew was one—Jews, Gentiles, Muslims, Buddhists, Hindus, and others. The world Cindy was preaching to was long gone.

Sarah changed the subject to balance the day. She pointed out that long before Rome took over, the kingdom of Judea was governed by kings who were every bit as selfish and self-serving as those ruling the rest of the planet. The problem was that they lost battles, and instead of being made slaves on their own land, they were kicked out to wander the ancient world.

The Hebrews couldn't take their statues with them, but they did have stories, which were written down and carried. And it's a funny thing, Sarah the anthropologist-sociobiologist pointed out, how much primates trust their eyes, a heritage a tree life. Reading words somehow makes them more believable.

"Jewish words caught on," Sarah said, finishing, "and were believed beyond rationality without a single shred of documentation. It all came from Abraham, and Abraham came out of a pencil. Tradition—tradition—tradition."

Sarah's distraction faded. Cindy's comments had disturbed the crew. Andre didn't send her on a time-out, but he did explain the situation to her. And he was honest, beginning many comments with, "the Jesus we think we know…"

Andre explained that whether Jesus was man or mortal, legend or myth, physical or fantasy, he, like Buddha, Muhammad, and the Hindu rishis, meant more to the crew than just another guy who passed their way.

He explained that Jesus was hope, and that someday, thanks to Jesus, Buddha, Muhammad, and the rishis, all mankind would embrace as cousins. Andre further pointed out that Jesus was also faith that brings all eyes to the stars, knowing that eternal life resides elsewhere, perhaps everywhere. Jesus was specifically compared to effort, day-by-day determination to do what was right, to improve what went wrong, and to aid those in need.

"Jesus is forgiveness," said Andre, "something every human being must manage and accept after a fall from grace. But most of all Jesus is love, of others and of oneself, no less than God himself. It is refinement that we seek," he concluded as Cindy accompanied him to the bridge. "Humanity is a masterpiece that requires cultivation day by day, season to season, one generation after another. We are here to add our best, not stumble in the strides of the past."

Brad was in his pilot's chair, focused and as eager as ever to break into the unknown, but he said not a word, and sat somberly. Hank was also silent, aligning time charts and star bearings at his station below Brad. Karen, Michael, and Sarah stood at the bow, facing the rear, and thanks to Cindy, deflated of spirit, but no less resolved.

All the crew, when holding hands on the way to the ice cream parlor or snuggling off to sleep in the arms of their special someone, had more. In ways Cindy might someday understand, not one of those onboard Explorer Seven was ever alone. Jesus was there too, or perhaps Muhammad, Siddhartha, Muni, or Moses.

Not one of them traveled life by themselves, not alone in snowshoes at the North Pole or clinging to a barrel shipwrecked at the equator.

"Mankind is more," Andre added. "Jesus was there for the ancients. He is there for us, and confusing as it may be for us both, Cindy, somehow he is also there for you."

Andre finished just as the two made the bridge. Everyone stopped fiddling to face Cindy. She did understand the meaning of the silent treatment.

"May I speak?" she said, her gaze spanning their faces. "It has been brought to my attention that there is more to life than bricks and mortar, calculations and consistencies. I don't know if I have even a whiff of the eternal spirit that you are blessed with, but it was wrong of me to compromise an image supporting yours. I am sorry."

Dudley took it all in with stoic objection. Before he could enter a comment, Cindy added a thought to keep him at bay. "In my defense," she said, "even immortality must begin with two plus two equals four."

"Poppycock and wishwashy," bellowed Dudley, making his way to her. "Scientists aren't witch doctors. There is never a reason to apologize for truth. What's got into you, Cindy?"

"Keep that up and *you* won't, Dudley," was Michael's comment, laced with a smile, that brought chuckles to the entire bridge.

"I beg your pardon, sir," Dudley said in his colorless robot tone, "we are programmed to correct error. Cindy has made none, and she is absolutely correct, there is not one piece of reliable data substantiating the entire 'New,' as you say, Testament. Not one word should be accepted. Only the foolhardy do so."

Since religion was Andre's hobby, the gang let him field Dudley's fly ball.

"It is not the particulars that we are looking for," he replied. "We search for the emergence of new philosophy, an abrupt turn for the better, and how, who, and where that happened."

"That Jesus," Karen exploded, "made happen!"

"Perhaps," said Dudley, nonchalant, and unfazed by emotional prodding, "but ignorance and wishful thinking are no reason to make heroes out of the past. For example, one of the many events described in the 'old' Bible finds the Hebrews surrounded by invaders. Their story says God, known as Yahweh, smote the enemy. Those whom God did not murder on the spot ran for their lives.

"Reliable documentation recorded at the time by observers from both sides tells another story. Yes, the castle was surrounded, but the king of Judea, who was just as bloodthirsty and greedy as the rest of the planet, brokered a deal with those outside bent on victory, which would have left no male standing and every female lying down, just like the Hebrews did when they conquered.

"The king of Judea presented the marauders with chests of gold and all one hundred sixty women in his harem. The bad guys left rich and smiling. The king restocked.

"One of your most-cherished expressions is 'those who don't remember the past will be condemned to repeat it.' I would add that those who lie about the past are worse off."

11

From Now 'til Then

What to do? When to do it? It was time. From his elevated engineering platform, Andre powered up Explorer Seven. Brad sat ready at his pilot station positioned above the floor. He planned to break free of time with a firm nudge forward, and then pull back the throttle as soon as they slipped away.

Hank, occupying the only floor-level station, had the most to do, correlating time with the estimated future position of planet Earth as it revolved around the sun, as the sun revolved around the center of the galaxy, as the entire Milky Way flew away from the Big Bang at the same time approaching Andromeda influenced Earth's galactic coordinates. And he always double-checked Cindy's numbers, after she confirmed Dudley's calculations.

Their destination was the Moon, seventy-two years into the future, or thereabouts. As they approached, population densities would be measured for minor adjustments—the only ones available.

"Stern power plant is humming," Andre began.

"My fingers are ready," Brad said patiently.

"Course and time corridor triple-programmed," said navigator Hank.

The room went quiet. As they looked down on Earth, it suddenly occurred to them that their friends Antony and Cleopatra were there enjoying life, sharing the same morning they did. The second the ship left the time slot, the Antony family would disappear, after living full lives, to move on to the next existence—just how, where, and when still a mystery. Perhaps "Meet you on planet Risa" is as fine a line as any for one's last words.

Saying goodbye did not bring joy, but some of the happiness the Antony family enjoyed left with every crew member aboard. It was a fine morning.

"Dudley," Andre said, "you have the fastest reflexes. Brad will power up, aim, and accelerate. The microsecond we break free, you are to instantly cut all forward power and apply full reverse."

Dudley knew well what he knew. The problem was that he didn't know what he didn't know. There were variables that hadn't been integrated into his system, like simultaneous forces outside of time pushing in opposite directions.

Step one tapped into the ship's stern power monster to separate atomic elements wide enough to open a canyon that the ship could move through, traversing distance in one direction and time in the other, or, as was almost always the case, both, to reach the target.

Technology had spoiled the crew. Many refused to watch old movies unless they were remastered into 3D. When Explorer Seven powered up, the view from the bow looked like a giant 3D screen that was divided down the middle by a canyon stretching endlessly. Moving time forward, as matter and energy dispersed, was always possible. Reversing time, going against the current, so to speak, was almost impossible.

The crew had gotten lucky once, but it took a trip to the end of time to reverse direction, and they almost ended up shipwrecked nowhere. Karen was tense. She knew that they would get only one shot at Jesus.

"On my mark," Andre announced to a silent, attentive bridge team.

"Sir," Dudley added, cable-linked to Andre's power station, "your orders will have me reversing thrust before forward jets have finished their discharge. Do I understand you correctly?"

"Yes," Andre answered, quietly hoping no one was listening, which they all were.

"That could fracture time," Dudley whispered, finally understanding the risk to be kept a secret.

"We will isolate the forward jets in stasis."

"Now," Dudley nodded, "I understand why Hank's blood pressure just went up."

It all happened so fast—although that is not, strictly speaking, accurate. The instant Andre opened her up wide enough to break free of time, the ship lurched forward as usual. Brad really had nothing to do. He kept the stick straight ahead neutral. Explorer Seven was running true.

That's when it got weird. One second of time travel aboard Explorer Seven passed by one million years. Karen wanted less than one hundred years; hence the need for an abrupt halt, which did a strange thing.

It surprised Andre. The limits of his mind had gone no further than theorizing. He divided time into clean segments, and then used distance as a secondary bearing. In his mind, the forces would balance, since the human mind deals with them separately.

However, if matter is time, and time is alternate matter placement, which is also energy managed and self-conforming into existence, then energy, matter, and time are interchangeable and should be definable within a single equation. Einstein caught up with two out of three. Andre didn't even know a third something was missing, but there it was, off the bow for all to see and to tremble over just a wee bit.

Many forms of energy are not visualized by human beings until they reach a defined limit. Electromagnetic elements rise unseen with water vapor. High in the clouds, changes in water vapor density and temperature amass imbalances that light miles with lightning. That makes electromagnetism obvious. Andre had theorized that a sudden stop might pile up time as a foggy cloud, perhaps on both ends of the ship, since jets were fired from bow and stern in opposite directions.

No waves appeared. Something else happened. Time didn't crunch. Like water, apparently, it can't be compressed, only swum through. But—

the surprise that made no one's day—time can be fractured obliquely. Instead of a canyon along which the ship could move up or forward, a second pair of barriers appeared, bow and aft, that ran vertically in both directions. When the canyon walls got two more separating partitions, Explorer Seven ended up boxed in. There was nowhere to go in any direction.

And all noise ceased. The power plant was, of course, programmed to shut down completely the instant they moved. But other noises were missing, like the hull swishing by space and time. High-stress "go for it" was instantly replaced by nervous stillness and eerie silence.

"What…?" Brad said as he wiggled his pilot joystick, a maneuver that would otherwise have spun the ship to starboard or port to look around. "Why aren't I connected to what is outside the ship? Why are we dead in the water?"

It was never a good sign when Andre, Cindy, and Dudley stood next to one another and said nothing. Each was hoping for theories, or at least alternatives. No one had a thing—this was expected from artificial intelligence, disappointing from humans. Andre had the only brain capable of inventing beyond expectations. He knew that. Everyone knew that, but no one heard a thing.

"All right, all right," Andre said, turning away from the crowd looking at him. "Let's start with data collection. What do we know?"

Again, nothing from the staff or the machines.

Andre turned and looked directly at Hank. Hank was always right behind Andre, sometimes ahead of him. That morning they were, in Hank's words, "sharing the same donkey."

Hank communicated what he knew Andre needed to know. Hank spread both hands, palms up. He had nothing. Every sensor onboard said that there was nothing outside the ship.

"So *nothing* is getting to the ship?" was the question Andre half asked Hank out loud.

"The equipment all checks out, sir," Hank said. "And that's the part that doesn't make sense, since everywhere in the universe some lingering energy can be found and used to calculate trajectory."

"So ..." Andre answered in slow motion, "we aren't in the universe."

"And distance reckoning," Hank added, "proves we are not *outside* the universe."

Michael had joined the two at the bow looking out.

"I know this is going to sound weird," he said, facing Hank and Andre, "but when you guys talked about being outside the universe that we love, it occurred to me that relative to the loves of our lives, sometimes we are outside, and sometimes we are inside."

After a brief fantasy break, giggly rouse included, the guys returned to reality. Andre understood what Michael had in mind and what Michael thought had just happened to them.

"Therefore," Andre said, weakly confident, "we are inside the universe. The ship pushed time away in every direction. We now exist outside of time."

Karen and Janie ran to the bio station.

"Oh my God!" Karen said. "This can't be!" She turned to interrupt everyone, mid-sentence or not. "Listen everybody! Check your pulse!"

They all did. They all had none.

"And," Janie said, walking forward, "the ship's systems say we do not exist. There is not one material life form on the bridge."

Brad kept his hand over his radial artery. His mouth was wide open. "How can I be alive if my heart is not beating?"

"Hold on ... hold on," Sarah said. "Brains need time-burned energy to function and time itself to complete feedback loops."

"Unless," Andre theorized, "the electromagnetic patterns that we are anyway, that we ride to maintain eternal existence with God's support— you know, God's gift of perpetual identity—are running the show, for now."

"For now!" Michael added. "If that's true, then even outside the material universe an overriding system, heavenspace organized, operates independently."

"Eureka!" yelled Andre, looking as happy as Archimedes when he jumped out of the tub and ran naked down the street. "That must be it! And of course. Think of it. When a universe begins, or contracts to re-explode, however you want to look at it, the entire assembly of life, God and ourselves included, reside in heavenspace waiting for the next ride to begin. It's so obvious."

"If that is true," wiseguy doubting Dudley fired without mercy, "then we, two computers included, would be in this heaven of yours right now."

"Not necessarily, Dudley," Andre answered with confidence. "We didn't move ourselves to heavenspace, we isolated our own."

"With disappointing accommodations, I might add," Dudley snuck in.

The whole mess was murky, the reality too challenging. There they were, boxed in and unable to get out, stuck nowhere in endless nothingness.

The usual systems were checked. Shields and propulsions were indeed completely offline. And, stranger than death, no one was hungry, for anything. The additional fact that no one was complaining or hurting or whining, or all the other things, was also noted. Existence outside of the universe was also existence outside of bother, which turned out to be a vacuous sensation, not painful since pain wasn't; it just wasn't anything. Perhaps there is nothing worse than nothing, but it was hard for anyone to comment on, since nothing and nobody cared since they'd pulled time apart.

"Why isn't it collapsing back together?" was Andre's question.

No one had a clue.

Deadpan Dudley came to the rescue. He pointed out that nothing can be that does not have something to it. With Andre nodding immediate agreement, the computer on two legs pointed out that they were *somewhere*, but they just didn't have the means—in their case, the sensors—to detect it.

"So, back to the drawing board," Andre half asked, facing Dudley.

"Precisely."

Andre, Cindy, Dudley, Brad, Hank, Karen, Sarah, Janie, and anyone who thought they might help left for the lab. The rest of the crew just walked around. For reasons no one understood, no one wanted to go swimming, kiss a girl, or lick an ice cream cone.

It was philosophically speculated that while occupying aging physical bodies composed of atoms playing out the energy saga of eternity, each and every mortal participant is fully cognizant of their existential predicament. The next breath could be one's last. All life strolls a tightrope.

Without the tightrope it didn't hurt, or ache, or fantasize, or desire anything, which was a big problem. It just wasn't anything, so there was no reason to do anything. And it wasn't boring, because boring would be a feeling organized by motivation to change. There was no reason to change because there were no desires at all.

"Wow... this is something else," Michael noted. "On Earth we fret, and overachieve, and complain that what could be isn't, and what we want we can't have... but it is always something, and that is life. This is not. I miss life."

Michael wasn't alone. Without motivation to spur moments, the crew kept walking slower and slower, until each and every one stopped moving completely. They just stared ahead, waiting for something that never got to them. And it didn't hurt. It was just not worth the bother, since there was no bother.

In the lab, the situation became critical. Andre's dozen best crew members were at their stations for less than a minute before they too slowed down. They had no reason to do anything. They tapped and searched slower by the minute, then finally froze looking straight ahead like living statues.

Karen and Andre were the last to go—actually, *almost* go. It was an idea that came to Andre right after he made a comment that Karen's old reflexes responded to with a jab in his shoulder. It woke Andre up somehow. He hit her back. The tapping kept both in the game longer.

"Oh... kay..." Andre said, moving his face less than a robot would. "My... guess... is... that... you... and... I... have... established... an independent... companion loop feedback in a dimension that needs to be self-creating. Keep... it... up. I'm getting... close... to... the energy signatures... we... need... to... get... out... of... here."

As is always the case with mortal beings, luck played a part. Andre was scrambling—that's how it felt in his head anyway, though he was actually tapping barely once a minute—to input a set of numbers that might adjust their sensors to the frequency needed to detect the unknown force holding them ransom. Then Karen fired a wake-up punch. His fingers slipped over one entire number rack, that—bingo!—hit the jackpot.

On screen, Karen and Andre saw disparate, rebounding energy waves. Nothing escaped the confinement that froze them there. Discovery number one led to problem number two: there was more lingering energy from the forward push than from the reverse operation. As previously anticipated, neutralization would only be possible if 30 percent of the forward pulse ejection was captured and taken out of the game.

Which led Andre back to square one, the shield constructions he had in mind in the first place. They worked. When fore and aft balanced, they neutralized each other. The box turned back into a canyon. The crew came to life. The canyon dissolved, and presto-change-o, the ship returned to normal space outside Earth's solar system.

"Take us back to the moon, Brad," was something everyone was hoping to hear.

"Right you are, Andre. It will be my pleasure."

12

Full Moon

S he sure looked pretty down there. Earth, that is—all blue and green, black and white. Those doing the backstroke in either of the two full-sized pools could look straight through the clear hull four stories above. Those playing tennis got a glimpse every time they tossed up a ball to smash.

Karen was in Andre's lab. She had the ship's best telescope focused on Judea as it rotated below them.

"We should know soon," she said to Andre at her side.

"Karen, remember that nothing in the past is precise. Every story is an exaggeration and in no way accurate. Dates especially."

"So what you're saying, Andre, is that figuring out the date down there won't really help. I get that. It's what's going on. But we must be close. See for yourself. The temple in Jerusalem has not been destroyed yet."

"Yet" was the operative word. Jerusalem was one of the oldest of the ancient cities. Founded in 4500 BCE, it was attacked fifty-two times, besieged twenty-three, recaptured forty-four, and totally destroyed twice, the first time by the Neo-Assyrian Empire, which deported all ten northern Hebrew tribes to Arab lands, where they were assimilated to turn on their own relatives. The ancient world would have been better off with fewer church-states and more party planners.

The Babylonians overran Jerusalem in 586 BCE, which was when their religious stories, themselves lifted from the East, were added to Hebrew scrolls, which came to no good, and then gave birth to Christianity, which caused more problems and turned on the entire planet.

"There's the temple, Andre," Karen said, pointing to the magnified view. "Herod the Great renovated it in 20 BCE. We see that structure below us. Ninety years later, in 70 CE, the Romans destroyed it. So we are in the correct date range. Herod and the covenant are down there right now, and maybe Jesus. When do we leave?"

The ship had developed a tremor. As expected, the surplus energy tapped and confined in stasis leaked. It rippled the ship with microscopic forces that could time travel the entire ship, crew included, ahead at any second. Neither Andre, Dudley, nor Cindy had a handle on the problem. The only thing anyone could do was cross their fingers.

Visiting the surface was only possible when Explorer Seven, parked on the moon, was within view. The spatial field Andre would take down with them could, if nothing went wrong, tie into the ship's temporal displacement. If Explorer Seven blasted off by itself, Karen and Andre could tag along. If Andre and Karen were on the other side of the planet, the connection was not possible. Dawn and dusk were also out of the question.

"Not today, that's for sure," Andre said, ignoring Karen's disappointment. "Maybe tomorrow when the Middle East swings by again. Dudley and Cindy are preparing a briefing. We can start there."

The next morning, half the crew went straight to the shuttle bay from breakfast. Andre and Karen were the last to enter. They were outfitted for the shore mission and dressed for the part. Each was given an outer and inner tunic, basically a one-piece robe with a hole for head and arms, with or without sleeves. Both tunics were almost identical, but a man wearing just the inner tunic was considered naked. Women, on the other hand, were still taking the rap for being beauty that tempts ecstasy and completes life one night at a time. They had the job of covering up as much as they could, which makes as much sense as painting bakery windows black.

The ladies fought back with anklets, necklaces, and earrings, although it was forbidden—curious word usage for an organization 90 percent contrived and 47 percent immoral—to pierce any body part. It's a shame the same rule didn't apply to soldiers marching away with swords.

Drab was fashionable, or, more honestly phrased, respectable, a corrupting word if there ever was one. The fellows complied with dirty white, brown, and of course the always sorrowful black. The ladies added light tints to their outer garments; irrationality has biologic limits.

And incidentally, for the guys, under the inner garment? The west wind. Or perhaps some days, after beans, the south wind. Unless you were an Essene. Those guys got to wear loincloths and climb into tunnels years later to stash undocumented hearsay half a millennium old. They called them "the gossip sea scrolls."

As expected, Karen took longer to get dressed. Andre was the first to enter. His tunic was belted at the waist to prevent it from getting in the way. On cold days a full robe was worn over the two tunics as well.

"Gird your loins" was a common expression. One had to tie one's belt tightly to get down to it, the modern equivalent of "roll up your sleeves."

Politics and religion were indistinguishable. Church-state madness has a way of outliving sensibility. For example, it wasn't enough just to list the laws of the land once a week; if a woman had sex before she was married, the "right" thing to do was to put her to death immediately, a madness that defies sanity.

The decree was forced on the public by church-state dictators, who also received fame, wealth, and the undeserved gratitude of those whose lives they compromised, exploited, or simply brought to an end. The "religious leaders" then left for luxury accommodations, and since the priest class needed to reproduce itself, it was of course also decreed that the most beautiful young women must visit them for hot sex. They were flaming bigots. Everyone fell for the hoax.

Everyone, that is, except Jesus, the carpenter from Nazareth.

Even more astounding is the fact that two thousand years later, men and women on earth who claimed they respected the philosophy of Jesus still insisted that they had the right to make laws governing adult sexuality and women's rights.

Anyway, ordinary men left the house in the morning with tassels (tzitzits) attached to the corners of their cloaks which reminded them of the constant presence of the Lord, as defined by the church-state, and the "commandments"—that is, laws the church-state had declared must be obeyed, or else. Same old, same old. Never untrue is the fact that he who does harm to others also harms himself. Life is not boot camp. Arbitrary discipline confines free spirit.

Words left by Hillel the elder disagreed with Herod and his band of gold collectors. The elder pointed out that "what is hateful to you, do not do to your neighbor. If I am not for myself, who will be for me? If I am only for myself, who am I?" In all fairness to the Hebrews, Rome had an even easier time turning Christians against the philosophy of Jesus three hundred years later.

The Jesus Karen knew objected to mistreating the poor through politically organized religion and the violently organized exploitation of the Roman Empire. Basically, Jesus asked for it. Slaying, hell, even tickling one dragon is bad enough. To charge off contradicting two at the same time is a clean shot at the impossible.

To be fair to the Pharisees, it was also true that Rome insisted on approving every appointment, and anyone who disagreed with their policies was free to do so, from the bottom of a shallow grave.

It has been said that if God didn't want women to be kissed, he wouldn't have made their lips so kissable. The Hebrews, and to be fair almost the entire ancient world, had an answer for that one: cover them up so they won't be seen, which can be compared to Macy's ending its dress line. Unwed ladies were expected to veil their faces in public. No one told them that just because the past ruined yesterday doesn't mean the mistake has to be repeated today, except Jesus, of course. What a troublemaker he was.

Dudley insisted that Karen hold her temper. She was told to cover her face only inside the synagogue, even though the rule implied shame to her sex. Outside of church was another matter. She must look married. If others thought she was carrying on with Andre out of wedlock, she could precipitate a rock storm. While it wouldn't get far with a stealth drone hovering over both of them for protection, it would end the tour.

It was imperative that the locals think Andre and Karen were married and that she not overstep the limited range of self-determination allowed by the "church" leaders. After all, she was just a rib piece afterthought and the reason the entire human race must suffer to the end of days. Her sex had instigated the infamous apple bite. The most outrageous aspect of the entire scenario is that people actually bought the malarkey, except the Jesus everyone thinks they knew, or knows, or something like that. It's a vague concept that everyone enjoys customizing, for better or for worse, and then for worse again, and then...

One theory conceptualizing human aggrandizement is that it is everyone's dream, male and female included, to be announced from the top of the castle's grand ballroom staircase to those waiting below in awe and envy. Perfume running ahead has similar qualities, and before they mixed fragrance with polyaromatic hydrocarbons, it wasn't carcinogenic. Sticky frankincense, smelly myrrh, cinnamon, and saffron coated the ladies.

The Hebrews didn't tolerate the fancy buns and birdhouses that the Egyptian, Greek, and Assyrian gals carried around. They were sensible. The women wore long straight hair, sometimes braided, combed with a hairpin. The ship's beauty salon removed Karen's curls that they had adjusted the day before.

Andre made his entrance. It was a sight to behold. Whenever someone said that they looked up to Andre, it was a figure of speech. Brad and Michael towered over him, one from six and a half feet, the other from seven even. Standing behind a layer or two of crew members watching Andre walk in afforded both a clear view and hid their giggles.

When Andre passed them, Brad and Michael each looked like the dog that swallowed the cat that ate the canary. At the last minute they had switched Andre's inner garment from soft fabric to a camel hair penance liner, stimulating pain and itch receptors simultaneously.

It was Andre's hips that got the crowd going. They bounced back and forth like those of a hula dancer who'd missed every lesson. He tried to push away one itchy side, only to have the other flop over for just as much discomfort. And his arms? Straight out to keep as much clothing off his body as possible.

"How long do I have to do this?" was Andre's question.

Karen caught on. She stopped, and then looked at Michael and Brad, whose heads disappeared behind row three.

"Andre," Karen said, "you're doing penance. Get back to wardrobe."

A child thinks like a child, speaks like a child, and acts like a child. An adult thinks, speaks, and acts like an adult. But neither escapes the limits of human imagination. What human beings are, they expect the entire universe to be like, right down to drawing their god in their own image and likeness. Anthropomorphism is more often misleading than not. In the words of Hillel, "Don't trust yourself until the day you die."

When one steps on another's toes, a gesture of apology and a peace offering are made. Pain experienced should be compensated for, goes human thinking; a dead rabbit might buy off a tiger with other plans. All of which leads to a sinister limitation of conceptualization. If one experiences pain or bad luck, then those in the old world, and the first new one, jumped to the conclusion that they had somehow stepped on God's toe, and, so far from logic that absurdity understates itself, God therefore wants someone to suffer on bended knees, wearing camel hair underwear.

"What did I do to deserve this?" is a question you don't want to ask out loud. The answer will always be "Because you are a bad person. But you're in luck! I've written down God's rules for you. Do whatever I say, and keep the donations coming, including your daughter and your best goat."

In German, "debt" and "guilt" are the same word—*Schuld*. Making up a system that leaves everyone in sin-debt was a brilliant stroke of tyranny. The only problem was that it has nothing to do with either

God or reality. The Rome–temple connection insisted otherwise. Once again Jesus said, "You've got to be kidding."

Since when does it make sense to assume suffering pays a bill, especially when it was made up in the first place? The answer is this: since limited-brain-powered *Homo sapiens* made their entrance.

It was said in the twentieth century that the post-World-War world was lucky to have America supply stable currency for global business. Before and even after that century, a more pervasive and pernicious currency remained in use. Adding up sins has been used over and over again to justify exploitation, slavery, and genocide. And, of course, the sins were eagerly calculated by popes, rabbis, priests, mullahs, chanters, and witch doctors. Popcorn vendors know more.

There is one thing all human beings can truthfully say: "We are imperfect. We were made that way." Mistakes, stupidities, and breaches of mood will occur—too often. We must do our best, but one way or another, classifying imperfection as a sin is missing the point and is rotten to the core.

If there is such a thing as sin, then there is only one—drawing up false bills for recompense and then demanding payment in penance. Imperfect beings live imperfect lives in imperfect societies until corrected otherwise. Mankind is what it was made to be—a mess. Jesus offered suggestions.

God's deal with matter includes calamities, and mankind wasn't part of the negotiation, perhaps. Mortal beings bless God to the end of days—but life has bumps—because it comes with bumps. "Sin" plays no part. Its invisible chains have enslaved more human beings than dictators ever did. Daniel Defoe rhymed it best: "Of all the plagues with which mankind are cursed, ecclesiastic tyranny's the worst."

Yes, many do say, but we are selfish, clamoring, and clumsy. If those complaining showed up at sculpting class and were given a chiseled statue, they would be happy; and then do what? In addition to a joy, life is a duty. Inducing even temper, compassion, and love to share with a universe of life is the most noble of causes. Chasing sins is serpent's venom. So much good lies beneath so much mud.

13

The Promised Landing

When Andre returned, Michael and Brad expected tit for tat, like a bed full of mechanical lice or real Spanish flies. Andre planned neither. He returned with a smile before thanking the two pranksters for allowing him firsthand experience with unnecessary pain. It was Andre's conviction that 90 percent of human misery is needlessly generated. Camel hair penance was a perfect introduction to an ancient world of fools.

Andre's philosophic platform also concluded that idiocy self-replicates. Misled Egyptians combined with Alexander the Not-So-Great were followed by worse Caesars and two thousand years of totalitarians disguised as holy men. Itchy underwear was getting off easy.

On Explorer Seven there was no class structure. All were equal. All shared equal access and opportunity. Many decided to take part in the briefing meant for Andre and Karen. All were welcome. Andre and Karen, local-garb dressed, stood next to Dudley when he began.

Cindy had achieved impressive self-actualization. She had opinions, desires, and disappointments. Dudley, with more sophisticated components and similar wiring, was, on the other hand, flat affect walking. Every day, he had several outfits from which to choose. He always showed up butler formal, neat as a pin. When questioned about his routine, he explained that he dressed the way he wanted others to see him: as a servant to help them in any way possible. Not once did he put himself first, but when it came to consistency, the truth of the matter, he held firm and would contradict even Andre.

Dudley began by pointing out that down on Earth, costumes were the order of the day. Romans adorned their buildings, uniforms, and possessions with a giant eagle. The uniforms of their soldiers yelled "get out of my way or else." The Hebrews had their own pecking order. If someone on the street walked up in rags and said, "Hi, I'm Lenny, the local expert on God and the rules you must obey," no one would pay attention. If, on the other hand, a self-righteous Pharisee came your way, Dudley pointed out, you would know him right off. Pharisees arrested attention by wearing pointed turbans and flowing robes made of exquisite material. Their fringes were longer to attract attention, and most wore pages of scripture taped to their arms in case they needed to read the letter of the law to the weak and powerless. Dudley's advice for Andre and Karen was to get to the other side of the street if they saw one coming.

"And whatever you do," Dudley went on, "don't touch a Pharisee. Until proven otherwise, everything and everyone is unclean to them. They live in a world of their own and will have nothing to do with the poor, sick, or needy unless you can make their day with a handful of gold."

The Hebrews were a simple pastoral people, hence the name Palestine. By 400 BCE, the priest class had firmly, and selfishly, established itself as the ruling class. They were clever and inventive. They were also thieves. They lifted text from the Hindu Puranas, where Brahma was recorded as having created the world in seven days, an account recorded by them in 500 BCE.

The Babylonian word *sabattu* was also copied and morphed into the Sabbath, a day dedicated to God, who in Judea went by the name Elohim, meaning "many gods." A cocktail party of gods was next replaced by eligible bachelor Yahweh, mean and vengeful just like them. It's always more convincing when you get a second opinion.

Theft never respects borders. One thousand years before the Hebrews pasted their Testament together, Hindus named the first man Adamu and the first woman Heva, again an afterthought. They were an easy combination to plagiarize. All the Pharisees had to do was drop one letter from each name and the job was done.

Local flavor was added. The Hindus had Heva tempted with figs. The Greeks gave Hesperides a tree that bore golden apples. Any way you cut it, original sin is the oldest con game on Earth.

Dudley had his direct moments.

"A man named Johnson once said, 'I know not any crime so great that a man could contrive to commit as poisoning the source of eternal truth.' The difference between truth and reality is that you must know truth before you can see it. This Jesus of yours, who may or may not exist, may or may not have spoken truths. We need data."

Dudley had a grand time holographing the Hebrew family tree. He made a good point. If you're going to make up stories, you could at least make up nice stories. Abraham, the grand granddad on them all, married his half-sister, and Lot slept with his daughters. Dudley, totally serious, got laughs when he mentioned that if the god of the Hebrews didn't like foreskins, why did he put them there in the first place?

Paper trails have hung more than one impostor on planet Earth. The Hebrew laws and rituals found in Leviticus, Numbers, and Deuteronomy were written by priests a thousand years after the alleged time of Moses, who, they insisted, got them firsthand, by himself of course, without a single witness.

The Old Testament definitely saved money on editing. The saga of Moses continues to list mass murders and the right of every father to sell his daughter into slavery.

"Frankly," Dudley added, "I don't see any difference between a holy tabernacle and a Chicago slaughterhouse."

Dudley's favorite story was Yahweh commanding Joshua to murder thirty-one kings and more than one million women and children. For his holy hit men, Yahweh drafted Jacob, Moses, and David (who was also a lecher, thief, and bandit). Public relations was obviously not their specialty.

However, to the credit of the ancient Hebrew world, they were the product of what came before and what surrounded them. Every culture on Earth lived in a glass house. Every "holy" person historicized mythology.

"And whatever you do," Dudley finished, "when you pass a Roman or a Pharisee, don't look happy. They will think you are up to something. Bow your head and look miserable. Let them know you accept your lowly status."

"Not look happy?" Michael said with a sarcastic snicker. "What kind of world would this be if everyone went around trying to make everyone else happy?"

"Yes, of course," Brad added with a smile, but trying to sound serious. "And politicians and clergy would have no one to sell weapons to. Nothing quite makes a day like pile of corpses."

"That's enough, you two," said Karen as she stepped into the shuttle. "The people down there are only a few generations behind those who escaped the forests of Africa. They are primitive, scientifically unschooled, and live superstitious lives. We could have been them. But for the grace of God go you and I."

"That I get," said Michael. "What I don't understand is why anyone coming along later would pay attention to the confused musings they left behind."

"They didn't, actually," said Andre from the other side of the cockpit as the shuttle prepared to exit Explorer Seven. "It was swords, nooses, and bonfires that inflicted agreement. After that, no one was bold enough to point out that the emperor was naked. They were also told that they were purchasing eternal life. And one other thing, Karen—watch what you eat. Apparently, God gets indigestion when the Hebrews eat incorrect foods."

"Andre, be more respectful!"

"Of a good punch line? Always. Of illogical behavior, never. Losses in the life column do God no good. Judeo-Christian guilt is child abuse that lingers a lifetime."

Andre was not above the amusement of a fleeting tease. Instead of a snappy trip to the surface, once the shuttle was clear of Explorer Seven he punched power in the opposite direction. Karen looked up to see them strafing the surface of the moon, aimed at outer space.

After a faint sigh, her confusion faded. The shuttle's trajectory lifted them away from the moon just far enough for its gravity to slingshot them around and on their way. Within a minute Judea was the heading. Karen's eyes brightened, and she said not a word to reward Andre's trifling. Dark silence followed as Earth grew near.

"I can't help thinking," Andre said, "about the enormous conceit of mankind. I mean, look around us. Stars, planets, seemingly endless space … just what those on the surface watch night after night without light pollution. But as grand as the universe is, little people standing on a speck convince themselves that their thoughts, what happens after breakfast, or the shape of a shirt, is the very most important thing there is, and that the god they describe, with insistence in no way justified, has constructed the entire universe *just for them alone*. And to please that same inexplicably egotistical god, they must say just the right words and bow to just the right people."

Karen smiled a grin of warmth. She took pride in the victories of mankind. She also knew the list of blisters that littered the way.

"Yes," said Andre, "life on the earth we are about to visit is a damn muddle, a soccer game where everyone is offside, as they all claim the referee is on their team. Instead of pride and sex, and being proud of sex, they get shame and punishment and are herded and slaughtered like cattle."

Karen added a sharp comment of her own: "Unless you're a Roman conqueror or a local priest. They dine on delicacies, do as they please, and enjoy every reward flesh has to offer. Thank God Jesus came along."

"Hold on there," Andre pronounced, half startled, arms crossed facing Karen. "You said 'came along.' Are you saying Jesus was mortal, and though inspired by God, was not God himself?"

"Andre," Karen said, more honest than strategic, "progress is a labyrinth. I know I have ripped into you again and again for suggesting just that, but the issue is cloudy and subtracts not one iota from the love God shares with us. And, for the record, this trip will prove you wrong."

"Nice try, sweetie. I'm not going to speed up the trip down there to prove myself right. Our window won't open for another twenty minutes, and at six this evening we will be sitting right where we are now, on our way back."

"I do vaguely remember you saying that, and forcing me to sign two affidavits in triplicate. What do you want now... the deed to our, I mean *my*, firstborn?"

Dreams are hopes and hopes are dreams. That morning the word "firstborn" brought both hopes and dreams to life, combined with the memory that once upon a time Andre and Karen had yearned to share a nursery. Then salt stopped mixing with sugar.

One tap activated six drones behind the two. Each hovered three feet off the floor and went through routine system checks, twice disappearing completely as they tested the cloak hardware. Softly and cheerfully, Andre whispered, "Are you there, Dudley?"

"You know I am here, looking out of drone number four."

"And," Cindy's voice was heard to say, "I'm right beside him to make sure Mister Perfect doesn't screw up."

"Oh, really?" Dudley said, attempting to emulate flippancy. "Well, if I'm Mister Perfect, why do you disagree with everything I do?"

Karen leaned forward and hit the "seen but not heard" button.

"Well," she said to Andre, whose eyes almost let on to laughter erupting, "they're getting more human every day."

Dudley picked the landing site, a desolate patch of desert halfway between Jerusalem and Qumran on the Dead Sea. Several small herding villages were nearby. The population of both had doubled. Something was definitely going on.

Andre and Karen walked away. The shuttle, with two drones overhead and four scanning a twenty-mile radius, disappeared.

It was hot. They were alone. So far so good.

Bags predate recorded history. Andre and Karen each carried one. They looked like ordinary travelers on their way to pay respects, and taxes, in Jerusalem.

The terrain's mounds of sand obstructed distance view, but Andre and Karen heard yelling accompanied by pounding feet. They stopped walking when what they heard sounded like a young man screaming as he approached, an assumption the two made from his voice growing louder.

Fifty yards away, first the head and then the full body of a young man, barely twenty, came into view. His left arm was bleeding. His right held a crude iron sword. The brown tunic he wore was ripped and stained red down one leg.

At the top of a nearby mound he turned and began to scream back at whoever was behind him. "You arrogant bastards! You are good for nothing. Everywhere you appear ends up a disaster. How dare you subjugate our women and savage God's chosen people! How dare you replace the will of God with pagan wrath! As God overthrew Sodom and Gomorrah, so shall he send hosts to destroy you idol worshipers!"

Karen stepped forward to help the fellow. Andre gently grabbed her hand. "No, Karen, this is not our fight. We must not get involved."

Karen's mouth opened beneath eyes of sullen stupefaction. "But it *is* our fight, Andre. We must help Jesus. The Romans are the enemy."

"Wait. Let's be sure we know what's going on."

The young man standing on the mound brandished his sword, took one step forward as if to charge whoever was following him, and then suddenly sounded off: "The sword shall descend upon your legions! Your kings and princesses will grow feeble, your stolen treasures made worthless. The Lord our God shall crumble your cities to dust. When he comes, grain will be gathered into his barn, and the chaff blown away with unquenchable fire!

"You wake the wrath of divine punishment. Vengeance is mine, so saith the Lord our God. Prepare yourselves for the hell you deserve. The Messiah is coming!"

The young man, still spewing invectives, ran away across the dismal sand. Andre and Karen hurried to the mound where he had been standing.

When they sign up revolutionaries, they should test them on the track, or at least have each complete spring training. The rebel was no match for the three rugged Roman soldiers chasing him.

The end came swiftly. The Hebrew boy tripped over his own feet, exhausted. The first Roman to arrive stomped down on his neck. The next two took turns crushing his rib cage. A swift kick to the head turned the lad over. The soldiers laughed as his panting face turned blue, then lifeless for lack of breath.

"One less Barabbas rebel," said the tallest Roman as he threw in an extra kick to the groin—a wasted effort, since the young man lived no more.

Dudley was manning the closest drone.

"Follow me, Dudley," Karen commanded, "and arm yourself with weapons. Those Romans aren't going to get away with this one!"

Andre, never the Olympian, managed to catch up with Karen before the soldiers caught sight of them. He pulled her to the ground.

"Keep your head down, Karen! Don't let the Romans see us."

"Why, you …! Let me go! The Romans are murderers."

"Yes, they are. To be precise, half a million professional murderers spread over the known world! Is it your intention to kill half a million men who were unlucky enough to be born Roman? And then do what? Watch another army or armies from all sides do the same thing? The ancient world's madness never sleeps. Men will force other men to obey them no matter what we do. Making war is not why we came down."

The horror of violence speaks for itself. It also invites more violence. Andre wanted to match death with death as much as Karen did. Both calmed down as they ran to the body bleeding in the sand.

"How can we just stand by and watch?" asked Karen. "It's not right."

"Of course not, but the list of travesties is endless. We also know that this time period changed the existential signature of the planet. Somehow the Hebrew—"

"You mean Jesus," Karen insisted.

"Okay, Jesus—contributed to the welfare and progress of mankind. And it did not all turn out the way it should have. We're here to learn.

We're too close to modern history to alter variables. If we aren't careful, our intended good deeds could have disastrous ramifications."

"All right, we'll leave the Roman army alone. But I'm telling you right now, Andre, I'm not going so sit back and not help Jesus."

"Dudley," said Andre, "now we get involved. Bring over the two medical drones."

With one drone standing watch ten feet overhead, two others hovered low and forced positive pressure into the lungs of the deceased agitator. Step two was rib and facial bone repair.

Thirty minutes later, the young man was sitting up, amazed that he was still alive, and wondering who was looking back at him.

"Hi," said Andre. "My name is Adam, and this is my wife Hannah."

Coughing and spitting blood, but feeling little pain thanks to local anesthetics and systemic analgesia, the young man answered, "I'm Elisha. Can you take me home? I thought I would never see my wife again."

14

No Peace on Earth

E lisha slipped in and out of consciousness. His face turned from blue to pink, actually a bit swarthy. His chest looked like an accordion, but the pleural valves allowed his lungs to expand. The patch job provided sufficient stiffness for his diaphragm to drag in air, but his ribs bent like licorice in August. The nanoprobes needed hours to finish the job.

With one arm over Andre's shoulder and the other held up by Karen, Elisha took a deep breath. He stumbled along between them for five minutes before drifting off.

"Enough of this," Andre said, exasperated. "Let's lay him down. I have a new plan."

Andre sent one drone fifty yards up to stand guard. Every human life was to be reported. From the medical kit, Andre then administered a sedative that would keep Elisha sleeping for hours.

Meanwhile, Andre had the remaining drones appear and assemble. One set up two chairs and a table. A second laid the table and placed lox, bagels, Danish, eggs Benedict, and tuna melts dead center.

"Shall we dine, my dear?" Andre said, marveling at the contrast of the past with what could be.

Long before Andre was born, planet Earth had redefined the word "work." It still referred to the accomplishments of human effort, but mostly it meant what drones did. And they did. Four working together spread out a net, placed Elisha dead center, and gently lifted the patient off the ground.

"Would you like wild blueberry jam or fresh strawberry on your English muffin, Andre?"

"Both, and one ounce each."

"Certainly," Karen said, then, following a direct stare, lifted a finger for a drone to hover over and spread the jam. Andre asked for one ounce and he would get one ounce, with documentation if the question arose.

"Thank you so much. Can I get you anything, Karen?"

"Searing noonday sun and fiery sand are not my favorite resort conditions. How about a canopy?"

Andre did better. In less than a minute the two were sitting inside a see-through tent that was air conditioned for comfort.

Before Elisha passed out, he directed Andre and Karen to his house, a small farming plot three miles away in the direction of the Black Sea.

From 400 BCE until 100 BCE, all had gone well for Judea. Religion dominated and repressed the population every day of the week, but all in all, life was peaceful. Irrigation improved crops year after year. A healthy mix of grains and vegetables was added to herded protein.

Land was always an issue. Parents were forever trying to get distant cousins or the children of close friends to marry their kids to keep land in the family.

In 63 BCE, life became ugly after the Romans captured Jerusalem. Taxation corrupted the local economy. Farmers had to plant, and hand over, whatever the Romans felt like demanding. Concentrated grain calories were all that was left, if even that. The old mix of vegetables disappeared. Health worsened. Spirits failed. It was time for the messiah to come to the rescue. After all, for hundreds of years infallible religious leaders had prophesied just that.

The Old Testament was misleading. Everyone was confused. The Hebrews needed a spin. They called it "Old Testament—The Sequel," which didn't catch on. Many centuries later it was rebranded the "New Testament."

"I don't get it," Andre said, walking beside Karen. "One trade-in is all it takes to distrust a used car salesman. Used religion salesmen, on the other hand, get away with murder, then sell you the same messiah with a new paint job. For them it's business as usual."

He was referring to the Pharisees, who talked about being saved by their one true god but refused to interview candidates. Rome wouldn't hear of it either.

Good land was hard to come by. Elisha and his new wife, Leah, hadn't. As Andre and Karen approached, they noticed a fine, if scraggly, hill behind Elisha's residence for goats and sheep to graze. It was the planting fields that disappointed. They were sandy, over-farmed, and poorly irrigated.

Long before the front door was reached, the drones went back to playing hide and seek. Andre and Karen carried Elisha the rest of the way. His eyes were open but he said nothing.

Leah didn't open the door when they knocked. She knew better.

"We have Elisha," Karen called through the closed door.

Leah was an impressive beauty and barely twenty. They had been married for less than a year. She usually wore her rugged wool outer robe. Her best outfit was the tunic she was married in. Leah had it on when she cautiously opened the door. She knew that if the Romans were looking for or had caught Elisha, she would be dragged off to prison as well.

"Oh, my darling," she said as she hugged Elisha, whose eyes opened. He was feeling no pain and glad to be home.

Elisha was good with his hands—their home served as a testament to that. It was a typical pillared four-room sandstone, thirty feet long—or *pedes,* the unit of measurement the ancient Romans used—and twenty wide. Instead of ordinary beaten earth, the floors were laid flagstone. Three smaller rooms opened into a larger backroom The entire inside was plastered. The roof never leaked and was supported by sturdy walls on all sides.

The three propped Elisha up in his favorite chair.

Leah's tears didn't overwhelm her, but for a while Karen, who was standing at her side, thought they would never stop. And once a minute Leah would look out the window. Running away from Romans always made more sense than waiting for them.

"He'll be all right," Karen said several times. "The Romans think he is dead. But if they see him again, that could happen."

"Of course, we'll leave immediately."

"No, we won't," said Elisha, waking up and slurring his words. "This is our land. They have no right." He then surrendered to his beaten body and continued sedation. He was out cold again in seconds. Leah knelt on the floor next to his chair so she could wrap both arms around her husband. At least he was alive.

Gassica, Leah's best friend, was not as lucky. Her husband was caught fleeing a Barabbas resistance meeting. A Roman convoy had just been ambushed. Pontius Pilate was not happy.

"Death to all rebels" went without saying. Gassica stood beneath her husband for thirty-two hours before he stopped breathing on the cross. He had just turned nineteen.

Gassica went into hiding. An entire underground subculture had developed. With their robes and hoods on, all Hebrews looked the same to the Romans.

Without looking at Andre or Karen, Leah said, "I didn't think he'd ever come back to us."

"Us?" Karen questioned.

"I haven't told Elisha yet. I'm with child. It's our first."

Karen reached over to hold Leah's hand. "You need to tell Elisha. Now he has a family to consider."

Andre told the ladies that he was going to stand guard outside. He walked away from the house before setting up a link with the ship. He also needed to confer with Dudley, who had disappointingly few clues.

"Well, I'm sorry, sir," Dudley said, formal as always, "but there are collections of Hebrews around every town, and Roman *contubernia*— the army's nine-man patrol units—are constantly deployed to one hot spot or another."

Dudley objected to the parameters of his search. The individual Karen thought she was looking for had no basis in fact. He was a collection of personality traits welded to stories that had circulated in various countries of the world for over one thousand years before being attached to the latest Hebrew edition.

"May I speak freely?" Dudley asked.

"Dudley, you're a robot," said Andre. "You can't hurt my feelings, and everything you say must obey consistent logic. There is no need to ask for permission. Spill the beans."

"I have no beans, just probabilities."

"State your piece, and make it quick. The Romans may be here any minute."

"Well, professor, it's just this... If you and Karen and all others agree on an optimal system of human behavior where all are born equal, are offered identical opportunities, and share the desire to live life for the good and happiness of all, then why is it necessary to go back in time and search for, or create, some kind of individual who stamps humanitarian behaviors as valuable? Just live and move on. Why do you need a template?"

"Because human beings are duplicitous creeps, Dudley. For example, a few hundred years from now the Christian thing will be off and running, which incidentally, Paul, alias Saul, planted in Syria and other Eastern lands first. Every country elected bishops to do their best at repeating the message of forgiveness and 'do unto others,' which was a problem everywhere, since established religious authorities were forced to compromise whenever the king or emperor said, 'Give unto me, and the hell with others.'

"Anyway, back in Rome the legacy of Caesar after Caesar took its toll. The bishop of Rome wanted to rule the world himself... same old, same old... power corrupts. The East, that is to say the Eastern bishops, the ones who started Christianity and had the only claim to leadership, said go to hell, who do you think you are? That's when the ghost of Rome's past escaped the grave to prowl the world for another two thousand years.

"The bishop of Rome, so he claimed, and no one else, was the direct descendant of the Jesus guy, so therefore, went his self-justifying reasoning, if Jesus was indeed part God, then his bishop status and power would overrule every other bishop in the ancient world.

"So all he had to do was get his stooges to vote on the issue. It's amazing how far crooked thinking by a crook can go. The bishop gave himself a new name, 'the pope,' drafted an army, and murdered all the other 'Christians' who didn't go along with his shakedown—which, incidentally, turned out to be twice as many dead Christians as the Romans herded into the Coliseum for entertainment, or crucified on the nearest hilltop."

Dudley nodded his head. All he ever needed was correct and complete input. "Yes, I think I understand. If two people are standing next to each other, and one says 'this is my opinion,' and the other says, 'well, okay, this is mine, let's talk about it,' then they have to use reasoning and fair play to form a conclusion. But if one of the two says, 'my boss is God, and what I say you must obey,' then that person takes the advantage and can turn into a bully."

"Exactly," Andre agreed, "and if that person dictating rules and regulations insists that he owns the key to open or close heaven, and stands in front of soldiers aiming spears, who is going to object? Or perhaps I should say, who is going to still be alive twenty-four hours later to say anything?"

"So," Dudley said, finally confident of the truth, "the Jesus thing is a hoax."

"Dudley, my answer to that is personal, not logical ... or at least not yet. Who knows what the next few days will find? But anyway, my answer to that is yes. Physically the Jesus story might be a hoax, but spiritually it is right on."

As a physical being processing physical input, Dudley was not able to integrate a concept that created its own parameters to build on itself. Andre agreed, but then he bowled over Dudley by having Cindy send Dudley the equations demonstrating that the neurologically generated identities of human beings leave an eternal footprint, actual waveforms that communicate the dimension of existence outside of time, the beyond-time space that Dudley knew nothing about. Andre's evidence convinced Dudley that the connection proves that God supports eternal identity.

"So," Dudley said, slower than a computer should ever verbalize—a behavior that lifted Andre's eyes, "death does not end life, it just sends you back to the, shall we say, database storage facility operating beyond time by this God of yours?"

"Kind of, but it's not a library or computer input warehouse. It's a reality that supports life longitudinally and communally, and within the reach and grasp of God and all other life, including those whose love for one another had blossomed on the earth. Love beacons, love supports, and love continues."

"So all this commotion down here," said Dudley, "all the greedy 'me first,' all the 'let's hurry up' and 'get out of my way,' all the 'I get more and I have the power over you' … all that stuff is heading in the wrong direction. The bag you need to pack should be filled with love, affection, and sharing. That is the profit of life your God is looking for."

"And working to get," said Andre.

"While the Romans, and others who rebel but then haven't the slightest idea what to do next, totally screw up?"

"That is correct, Dudley."

"Then I have only one question left."

"Shoot."

"Why are you human beings so damned stupid? Why don't you just fix it?"

"The answer to that question is simple," replied Andre, "and hasn't changed since the beginning of recorded time. Abusive systems continue to exist because those with wealth and power want to keep wealth and power for their greedy little selves."

"So they put themselves above God. Isn't that a really, really, really big mistake?"

"The biggest! But they've been told that it's what God wants, or what must be done to keep the country fighting, or some other crap like that.

Making sense is not important when you put yourself first and God and the rest of humanity second."

"Once again I say that is illogical," Dudley affirmed. "Your Earth is populated by idiots."

"No, Dudley, not idiots, just those who are misinformed or unschooled."

Leah had a goat cooking on the spit. The uncertainty of the week argued against saving it for a better day. She prepared lunch for four.

Elisha opened his eyes and wondered why he felt so good and was so hungry. "The Roman dogs have had their day. Barabbas has a plan," he said slowly, dripping with hatred, eager to avenge the deaths of countless friends.

Elisha was a handsome lad of passion and fire. Dying for his cause was not beyond him, but he never once thought about those he would leave behind.

"You must change your behavior, Elisha," Karen said with authority that startled him. "Leah is pregnant with your child. Consider what's best for all."

Elisha's twisted expression changed to astonishment, then he calmly smiled through tears. "Oh, my dear, what have I done? The Romans might come after you and our child."

"Those who live by the sword die by the sword," Leah said. "The carpenter says we should forgive our enemies."

"The carpenter?" Karen gushed, standing up. "What carpenter? What else did he say?"

Leah said that the day before, she had passed a hillside crowded with people listening to a man speak. Intrigued, she had stopped to hear his words. The man, whom she learned was a carpenter who had given up his trade to become an itinerant preacher, insisted that civilized violence was a contradiction in terms. He assured the crowd that God's intentions never failed and that peace on earth was within grasp. To achieve eternal life, love and gratitude were all the people of Judea needed. The best of being leaves an unending trail of sweetness.

"You mean after killing off the Romans! Right?" said Eisha.

"We have been misled, my dear," replied Leah. "Everyone sees only what seems to be, not what really is; and when we oppose the general opinion of Rome or our church leaders, they have the majesty of government and tradition to tear us down. But it need not be so. Truth carries strength unequalled in this world and the next.

"The carpenter told us that we must not look for victory on the battlefield. Rome will not surrender. We must win their hearts and the souls of all for world peace. The masses are always impressed by appearances. Life is not what it appears to be. Build love, and truth will show itself. Meanwhile, duties are ours, and events are God's."

Leah went on to point out that the carpenter would have nothing to do with lofty postures and triumphant processions. "Attitude is a great burden, and the unbalanced social equation the Romans have forced on the world does damage only as long as one sees lying around being fed by slaves as the optimal end to a day.

"In all my life I had never heard such wisdom," Leah said with a lovestruck look. "I felt sanctity undisturbed. He pointed out that nothing in this world exists that mankind has not made so, and that which rules each of us rules the world, and ultimately human destiny.

"Our God, the God, is not insecure. He needs no beings of slavish flattery. Our God is a loving God, a forgiving God, and a giving God. And the greatest gift of all is a fine day of pure joy, which is within us to bring to all those we share blessings with."

Elisha's expression of disapproval softened, but he wasn't convinced. "My dear," he said, feigning conviction, "Every Roman harbors a hidden lust to conquer the world."

"True," Leah answered firmly, "and so to the Egyptians, and the Persians, and us. That's the problem. We should know better. We need to change."

Andre walked in the door just as Karen interrupted Leah by asking, "Yes, but where is he now? Where is Jesus?"

"Jesus?" Leah said. "I didn't get the name."

"Where was he going? How do I find him?"

Leah didn't get a chance to answer. Right behind Andre was the reason he came back: Amir, their closest neighbor, ran inside, panting.

"Oh, my God! Elisha, you're alive!" he exclaimed. "The Romans said you were dead. They're on the way here with reinforcements. Your land is to be confiscated by the Pharisees. Leah is to be crucified immediately! Run for your lives!"

Amir ran out and away as fast as he had entered.

"Love thy neighbor," Elisha scoffed, "over my dead body. The only thing the Romans understand is the tip of a sword, and the Messiah will make sure not one of them survives."

Leah and Elisha rushed to grab everything they could carry with them. Elisha, a politician of respectable insight, turned to Andre and Karen and said, "Your good deed will not go unpunished. Helping me made you an official enemy of the state. The Romans will nail you to a cross just like us. You'd better come with us. We have an uncle outside of Ein Karem who will hide us. From there we will sneak into Jerusalem. Barabbas can always use more fighters. Let's go."

Andre and Karen followed in haste. When Elisha and Leah were beyond earshot, Andre looked over to Karen with a half-smile—half because he was glad Karen had at least got close, but not the other half because he knew trouble was heading their way, trouble that he knew she would expect him to fix. Andre's pack carried a stun gun on the setting designed to put every Roman this side of the Mediterranean to sleep for three days.

"Karen," Andre said quietly, "you have that finicky look on your face. Control yourself. We are not here to rewrite history."

Andre could have saved his breath. Karen's return look said as much, and more. "Andre, you listen to me. He is here. We are going. Nothing will stop me."

15

Hit the Road

E lisha could have been recognized. The couples traded places, with Andre and Karen walking ahead, able to warn Elisha and Leah if Romans approached.

"Well," said Karen, looking at Andre with a smile, "I know you're wearing them."

"Them" were ear tags enabling eavesdropping on conversations hundreds of meters away.

"Cyber… activate eavesdropping and turn on speaker for Karen and I to hear."

When Andre and Karen began listening, the expression on Andre's face was not altogether comfortable. Elisha was saying that he had clear memories of his lungs caving in and himself gasping for breath before losing consciousness. He also knew it took two months, not two hours, for ribs to heal.

"Maybe they weren't broken," Leah said.

There was more. A glancing arrow had split flesh to the bone on Elisha's left leg.

"Now look," he said, pulling up his robe. "Not even a mark."

"You were delirious when you arrived. Fear left you with bad dreams."

"Or," Elisha said as he stopped and looked ahead to Andre and Karen, "it was a miracle. Maybe Adam is the Messiah."

"Nonsense. He would have stayed to annihilate the Romans if that were the case."

Conquering the world is one thing; controlling it is another matter. Rome always had a war on its hands. It could only spare so many soldiers to hang around Judea to collect taxes and keep order, which is why they co-opted local religious lawmakers. All it took was a generation or two for young men to side with Rome's wealth and power, like the Hebrew Saul, the one with the migraine problem and leftover guilt to be resolved one way or another, whose spin stuck after the temple went down. All he had to do was change the Messiah's MO. Everyone fell for it because they were also still hung up on the Jewish "I'm bad, it's all my fault" thing, which, to their credit, was drummed into the heads of one generation after another.

Andre looked over to Karen and winced. "I told you we should have let him die. Now look what we've done. Elisha is more resolved than ever to fight on."

"Really, Andre," Karen said, not backing down. "You know history. Religion rests on a firm foundation of fear and ignorance. How could we possibly make things worse?"

Karen was referring to forty years in the future, when Jerusalem had grown tired of oppression, lives ended without mercy, and misery was everywhere. In the Jerusalem riots of 66 CE, the Hebrews overpowered the Romans. They killed every soldier who hesitated to run for his life. Jerusalem was liberated. It was a grand moment.

It didn't last long. On April 4, 70 CE, three days before the beginning of Passover, the Roman army commanded by the future Emperor Titus laid siege to the city. It began when hundreds were required to return to the synagogue, without food since it was against the religious laws. The siege lasted four months, ending in August with the burning and destruction of the Second Temple.

"Yes," Andre said bitterly, "the Pharisees talked up the Messiah so much that the populace expected victory, then they were herded into Jerusalem to be trapped by Roman soldiers, who let everyone pass by them knowing their death was next. My finger of blame points to religious idiocy."

From the Roman point of view, it was an easy siege. The trapped population starved. Rome negotiated and then developed memory loss. Every man, woman, and child in the entire city was marched out and crucified. Four-month-old babies were ripped from their mothers' arms and nailed to death in front of their own parents, who had to listen to their other children cry mommy to their last breath.

"An entire forest will be chopped down for crosses, and never regenerate itself. Everyone Hebrew was nailed to wood. Not one life was spared," Andre noted. "So consider this, Karen. What if, just what if, I say, Elisha now becomes a major instigator in the future. Perhaps if he had died, the population of the city, and the grand temple, would have been spared?"

"Nonsense. It takes more than one person to tip over the world."

"Not if it's on the edge. Isn't that what you believe about Jesus? After all, no book has ever changed the world. The Jewish collection of short stories was old news by the time it hit the press. The new Bible didn't change the world either. Gold and infantry did."

The sentence of life begins with "Who am I," and ends with "Where do I belong?" Many are born with an overt presence that assumes they own wherever they stand. More are brought to life hesitant, not wishing to get in others' way, falsely assuming others belong and they don't. "I'm sorry," and "I'd better get out of the way," are examples of false thinking. Both Hebrews walking behind Andre and Karen knew God loved equally, but Elisha took everywhere for granted, and Leah nowhere.

Andre and Karen listened as Leah tried to cool down Elisha: "My darling, the day of forgiveness has come. We must love our enemies as ourselves. The lion will lie down with the lamb. The voice of killing must end. Everything the carpenter said makes sense."

"To you, perhaps," Elisha snapped. "You didn't have to watch one hundred men groan wounded on the ground, crying to God. The soldiers blinded each one with the tips of their swords before ending their lives by severing both hands. Every man tried to stop the bleeding by pushing his wrists into the ground.

"No one flourishes when abused by others. The Romans are animals. They must be destroyed."

Karen detected frantic panic in Leah's tone that followed.

"Destroyed? Destroyed! We are the ones who will be destroyed. Oh, my God, I should have listened to my mother. I was the one who talked my father into changing his mind. He had me promised to the fisherman's son. Right now I could be finishing off a plate of flounder with a view of the sea."

"And from the smell of rotten fish heads, you would know when your lover was half a mile away," Elisha mocked.

"Jacob loved me, and his parents wanted me. They all wanted me. But no, I had to fall in love with the smart guy who thought for himself. You … we … our baby … and Hannah and Adam ahead of us … we are all going to die!"

"I like that girl," Karen whispered to Andre. "She's got moxie."

Elisha wasn't done. And, in his way, he was also right. "Leah, you don't understand. There is great wickedness in mankind. No one escapes the curse of ancestry. Why carry on confusion when a solution is at hand? We shall be masters of our own choices and slaves to none. New deeds are upon us. Slow-witted minds must not have their way. The Romans are narrow and selfish, a diffusion of madness."

Andre smiled over at Karen. "I would never have guessed. This guy is sharp. And he's right. Human beings have a bad habit of not being what they are supposed to be and, instead, pretending to be what they are not. Minds are an experiment in madness. The cultures they come up with don't die; they must be put to death. You can't disagree with him until he gets to a plan."

"Shhh, pipe down, Andre," said Karen. "I think he's about to come up with one."

"Leah," continued Elisha, "I will not rest until the power of God unites us. We fight for a world where everyone has the right to work and the security it provides. All we need is the power to make life a peaceful adventure. We are not slaves. We are not cattle. We are human beings and deserve to be treated with respect."

"Okay, score one for Elisha," Karen said, "but he's still off-base. Leah will set him straight."

Leah never really regretted not marrying the fisherman. All he knew was the head from the tail, and he followed the tradition of the men always getting the last word. "Elisha," she said, "only those confused and unloved hate others in this world. The light of God brings men to cast aside power and wealth. Eternal virtue is what we seek. We must love our fellow man for God's sake. We owe him that much, and more. It is written that the shepherd who leads the flock astray shall be cast out. The high shall fall, and the fallen shall rise."

"Each time doth boast itself above another gone," were the words Andre remembered, and which he mumbled to Karen, and then he followed with another of his favorites: "To an imagination of any scope the most far-reaching form of power is not money, it is the command of ideas."

"Finally, we agree," said Karen. "It was thinking, and not fighting, that freed the spirit of man."

"Yes, yes," Andre conceded. "We struggle from mud to ache for peace. The problem is that you can't fix what you don't understand, and these people know nothing. A bent mind is a dangerous thing."

The road was winding, the day long, and the air stifling. Karen and Andre took turns glancing back to make sure Elisha and Leah were behind them. Then they looked over to one another, said not a word, just looked, and smiled with satisfaction aroused by the anticipation of adventure.

"May I ask you a question, Andre?"

"You mean a second question?"

"Yes."

Andre raised his eyebrows as he tilted his head to Karen. "I am at your service."

"You could be back in the neuro lab experiencing Judea in virtual reality through drones. Why are you here? And don't tell me you have to be here to monitor the temporal field, because we both know you can do that onboard, and you're welcome for me not calling you a liar when you handed Sarah that story."

Andre, squinting in the blazing sun, wiped sweat from his brow that was not all temperature related. "Ok … well … thanks for not blowing my cover, although I might add that you were being more considerate of Sarah's feelings than mine."

"Yes, you might. Don't evade the question. We both know coming down here risks our getting stranded in this time for the rest of our lives. It would be you and me forever."

Andre began a lengthy dissertation that described how he could, with the handful of drones they would retain, construct a seaworthy vessel and sail to the same collection of islands inhabited by Antony and Cleopatra, who might be babysitting great-grandchildren when they showed up.

"Okay," Karen said, no less teasing. "Food, clothing, shelter, fun … you, that is to say we, would manage fine. But as what? Wouldn't you miss Sarah?"

"Sarah is the kindest, most caring, most compassionate woman I have ever met. She is every man's dream in the kitchen, nursery, and bedroom."

"Not the library?" Karen shot back, digging beyond Andre's comfort zone.

Andre stalled by looking back to the couple behind them, still at odds with one another. Then he bucked up, looked Karen in the eye, and said, "No, not in the library."

"And is that room so important to you?"

"The library is where we learn about the world and experience the universe. It's what we do when standing full height."

"So," Karen pushed a bit rascally, "you're not standing up?"

"I am today."

"And after spending day after day in the library, would you miss the kitchen, or want to redecorate the bedroom?"

"I'm sure of it."

"Sounds like a pickle to me."

"Or life. We're dynamic creatures," Andre said, totally satisfied with honesty. Subterfuge came slowly to him, and he was terrible at it. "What about you, Karen? What does your dollhouse look like? Michael is the smartest, most energetic, handsomest man I have ever met, but don't tell him so."

"You don't have to, Andre. He already knows, and it never goes to his head, and he stands tall in every room in the house."

"So, he's your perfect man. You must be very happy."

Karen softened her tone, remained mellow, but hinted at shades of dreary. "It's a strange thing, Andre. I love him, to be sure, and he loves me back, but he doesn't *need* me. He comes, goes, and lives every day in an island of solitude, graceful and kind to be certain; but with or without me, Michael is Michael."

"He says otherwise," replied Andre.

"Do you believe him?"

"No, I don't, and for the record, I need Michael too. I can't explain it man to man, but I do. And I also need you, which we both know is why I am here."

"So you need me more than you need Michael?"

"We both know the answer to that question; after all, we are in the library."

"That doesn't change, but we do."

"Your turn, Karen. What would Jesus say?"

"I believe he would look at you and me and Michael and Sarah and say, 'In all things use the measure of love.'"

Later they would tell the crew that they were just playing the part of man and wife, but the truth was that they both wanted to hold hands as they walked along.

Karen had a final question: "We know we change, Andre. Do you think God changes?"

"Wow—remind me to take you with me whenever I'm heading for the study. You're the only person I know, other than myself, who has ever asked that question."

Karen, serious and scholarly, said nothing, just waited for Andre to formulate.

"Well, let's see," he began. "Step one is data collection: we are one with God, who is one with the universe, which is loaded with lives not dissimilar to ours, which evolve in every direction of perception, each step heightening intelligence and broadening awareness."

"And laughing, and loving, and kissing."

"Yes, Karen … of course … and God is here with us riding along, for better or for worse, you might say."

"So we both agree?" Karen asked, knowing the answer was obvious.

"Yes, we do. I don't understand it, but it's logical to assume that God changes too."

"Then as we improve humanity, by magnifying love and certifying peace, God grins more, loves along with us, directs, and rides along."

"Works for me. Let's ask Jesus."

Dudley interrupted through ear tag channels: "Mayday! Mayday, you two. One half mile to the north, almost within sight of your heading, a patrol of Romans has a household surrounded. Scans show three families with numerous kids hiding inside. I recommend diverting south."

Andre and Karen waited until Leah and Elisha caught up. Without explaining why, they insisted that all four alter course. It was too late. A pillar of smoke appeared in the distance. The Romans were on the rampage. Elisha refused to budge.

16

Where There's Smoke

Avoid those who want to punish others; run from those who do. Elisha would do neither. When he caught up, Andre was standing with his left arm pointing.

"The Romans are that way," Andre said, raising his right arm as he turned his head in the opposite direction, "so we'll go this way."

Andre and Leah did. Elisha and Karen did not.

"Oh! No, no, no," sighed Andre. "Kar—Hannah—don't even think of it. 'Thou shalt not murder' also means 'thou shalt not let yourself be murdered.' Our time on Earth is limited. We must make the best of it. Remember why we're here!"

"And Elisha," Leah scolded, then lowering her voice for fear of being heard, "our child deserves a father. Get your ass over here!"

The closest Andre and Leah could get them was halfway, and the only reason they agreed to the next compromise was because Elisha and Karen promised to look but not touch.

A series of knolls separated the four from the smoke sighted. Elisha knew the terrain well. The land originally belonged to the Arenbergs. Hard times and marriage bonding had brought in the Gitelmans and the Javorskys. Uziel and Orpah were the only living grandparents. Of the nine children in the complex, the boy Asa was the youngest, barely two, and the oldest, Richael, age eleven, had just begun adult chores.

Andre, Elisha, Karen, and Leah squirmed forward on their elbows to reach the top of the last hill overlooking the farming complex. Three houses and one sandstone barn were well kept. Fields in every direction were doing well.

Elisha knew Sivan Gitelman, who was a hundred yards ahead of Elisha when the Romans had caught up with him. The only reason Sivan got away was because one kill satisfied the soldiers, and Sivan's speed outmatched them anyway; but they didn't forget his face and they knew where he lived.

The Romans didn't want to risk another sprint. A dozen soldiers, armed with swords and spears, herded the three families into the barn. Sivan, his wife Nizana, and their youngest daughter, four-year-old Akiva, were brought to the side of the barn. When trees were nowhere in sight, or the Romans didn't want to be late for dinner, nails held well in sandstone. The child was to be first.

Little Akiva shrieked when two soldiers pulled her away from her mom and dad, who were both clobbered unconscious when they went to her rescue. Their crucifixion would wait until they could feel every nail and have their children sobbing beside them.

"Here's the plan," Elisha said, not concerned about being heard over the lamentations of Akiva and the screams echoing from the doomed families inside the barn.

"Again—no!" commanded Andre with his most forceful voice. "We agreed on a plan. We look. You pray. We leave. There is nothing we can do."

Karen looked over with a squint. "Maybe there is, Adam?"

"No there isn't, Hannah. We run away now. We have no choice!"

"Or—" Elisha said.

"No!" added Leah with a punch to her husband's shoulder. "The Romans kill hundreds every day. Adding us four will do no good. We need to survive. Life will change. Elisha, we turn around and look for the Messiah. End of discussion!"

Andre and Leah crawled away low enough to escape detection. When they reached a rut twenty yards off, both stood to face Elisha and Karen. Neither had moved. Andre told Leah to stay put; he crawled back.

"Would it do any good to slug you in the arm, Hannah?" he hissed under his breath.

"You know better than that, Adam. Elisha has a plan."

"Does it include a side order of suicide?"

In 1939, if every Jew had opened their door and shot just one Nazi who had come for them, the entire Gestapo would have disappeared before a fraction of the Jewish population was lost. The deaths of fifty million people could have been prevented by the deaths of comparably few. Andre understood sacrifice and the history of violence combating violence on planet Earth, but he wasn't about to arm Palestine with tommy guns, and Karen knew it. She was playing dirty pool; they both knew it. A bond of trust was broken.

Elisha's strategy made as much sense as attacking crows with worms. There were twelve Roman soldiers down there. The three families with kids added up to seventeen Hebrews; adding their four made twenty. The Romans never chased alone. A single soldier was an easy kill for two or three Hebrews. The soldiers knew that. Pursuit was always a two- or three-man operation.

"If we can split up the twelve Romans into four groups, sixteen of us should get away," said Elisha.

"That's a 'maybe,' Elisha," Andre insisted. "When soldiers complete quick sword kills, they chase the next target."

"It worked in En Gedi last week," Elisha said. "And one of those who got away was Barabbas."

Andre collected his thoughts, calmed down, and turned to Karen.

"Hannah, there will be other times when bravery will have a higher probability of success. We are leaving now. Let's go."

Andre grabbed Karen's arm, not forcefully enough to actually pull her away, but firmly enough to communicate conviction. Leah walked ten feet from the three of them to make sure Elisha knew where she stood.

Elisha stepped forward. "Adam, you must do what you must do. I know what Sivan would do for me if the situation were reversed. I will not abandon my colleague, my country, or my God."

"Elisha," Andre said, "your God, that is to say our God, and Judea, need you to stay alive. Risking a life in combat is one thing, but throwing it away is quite another. I am sure Sivan wants the day's loss minimized. Let's go."

Elisha peeked over the mount. Nails were being laid out. Two hammers were already on the ground.

"I must do what I must do," said Elisha without apology. "Take Leah and Hannah and run for your lives. I will give you one minute before I charge in, and as soon as a group breaks off to pursue me, I will head away from you. If I make it, I will meet you at the base of Mt. Tabor."

"Adam," Karen said, "I train every day. There is no way a fat Roman carrying thirty pounds of crude armor can keep up with me. Elisha and I will spread out. It will be every man for himself. Don't worry about me. In three hours, I will be where you end up."

Andre's second attempt to physically remove Karen was intercepted by Elisha. Andre threw up his hands, turned his back with a scowl, and left to protect Leah.

"Grab a few rocks and walk slowly," Elisha said to Karen. "The Romans will have to lift their shields to keep from getting hit in the head. They will not be happy. As soon as their commander orders pursuit, you go north and I go south, and stay as far away from Adam and Leah as you can. Are you ready?"

"With the grace of God go I."

The Roman penchant for self-flattery was matched only by their conceit. It was inconceivable than anyone would walk into their swords. Karen and Elisha got halfway to the compound before they were noticed, and then they were ignored until the first rock hit the air. Karen and Elisha kept throwing. The Romans laughed at the pitiful display.

That's when the best plan of mice and men ran into trouble. The dozen soldiers were not alone. Four more heading in spotted Elisha and Karen launching projectiles. Finally, two soldiers next to the barn put on a show. They pretended to charge, then stopped. It was enough to turn Elisha and Karen around, which is when they discovered spears aimed at their chests. The two were marched to the wall. They would get the honor of crucifixion right after the children. Two more young ones were dragged out.

With desperation deeper than her soul had ever been dragged, Karen looked around. Andre was nowhere in sight as two screaming children were lifted to the wall.

There are times when children know better than adults. Hebrew after Hebrew accepted their fate, walked to a cross, and even lay down for the soldiers to do evil. The children knew better. One must fight to the end. They did.

The timbre of little Akiva's shrieking was a cumbersome annoyance to the Roman who held the little tyke six feet off the ground as he used a hammer to pound the first nail into the little girl's hand. To shut up the child, he bashed her over the head. The soldier knew she would regain consciousness in a few minutes. Akiva's parents would not be spared a single horror.

That's when Andre, alone, casually walked around the distant corner of the barn.

"Well, well now, what do we have here?" he said without an ounce of fear. "Is this baby shish kebab day? No one sent *me* an invitation."

A single unarmed Hebrew was the best joke of the day. Andre was happy to have made their day, but he was not alone.

In any era of the history of human civilization, there's nothing that will get a man's attention faster that a hot babe in a California bikini. Cindy obliged desire with just that, and she was carrying a bushel basket of fresh oranges.

She was also not alone. Dudley, forced into one of Cindy's swimsuits, wearing flip-flops with the cutest little hearts on top, appeared next.

"Pardon me, sir," Dudley said, facing Andre, "is this really necessary?"

"Dudley," Andre said enjoying the brazen contrast of it all, "the wilder the story, the less likely anyone will believe it."

"Roger that, professor. Now what?"

"Let's see," said Andre.

The commander, who had stopped laughing but was still riveted on Cindy's fine form, walked up to Andre.

"It seems to me," Andre went on, "the least you could do is get prettier-looking nails, you know, red for the boys and blue for the girls. And incidentally, I just love that skirt of yours. I hear it's all the rage in Paris this year. Is it a knock-off?"

"Knock off!" exclaimed the commander. "I'll knock you off. We are Romans. The world trembles before us."

"How's this?" said Andre as he bent his knees and moved his hands back and forth between them as they went in and out.

"Insolent and disrespectful!" shouted the Roman. "Kneel before me. Pray to the gods, beg mercy of Zeus, and I might spare your life. Your fruit and that woman will return with me. I can always use another slave."

"You might just regret that, metal head," Andre said with a smile. "Cindy does tricks you couldn't possibly keep up with."

"We'll see, now, won't we?" said the soldier, pulling his sword.

"Oh, there … now you've done it," said Andre. "And we were getting along so well."

"Silence, you senseless blockhead. I have changed my mind. You will be the next Hebrew we turn into wallpaper. Stand aside! I will start with your fruit and end with your woman."

"Whatever you think best," was Andre's answer. "But I wonder if this might change your mind."

Andre pulled a pouch of pure gold coins from his back pocket. Half he threw into the air for those behind the commander to scurry for, and the other half he handed over.

"I see," replied the commander. "How handsome indeed. That does change things."

"Fine. Are we good? You will let everyone go. Why kill today whom you can kill tomorrow?"

The commander's eyes lit up. Never had he seen so much perfect gold in one place.

"Well..." he said slowly, but with no less sinister intent, "I will change my plans. Instead of nailing you up first, I have decided to kill you last. You are an amusing little fellow."

That did it. Andre was not happy when anyone called him little, especially a soldier with the IQ of a cockroach. Andre stepped back.

"If that's the case," he said, "then what can I do? But perhaps you would like an orange or two first."

Andre did not lie. Cindy was holding fifty oranges, each one frozen solid. Later on, when they thawed out, the soldiers could either explain that they were knocked unconscious by a half-naked woman throwing fruit, or keep their mouths shut. Drinking on the job was strictly forbidden and punishable by death. Andre had it all figured out.

Major leaguers can throw pitches at one hundred miles per hour. Cindy and Dudley could throw at the speed of sound—but they held off. Not one cranium was fractured. And for dessert, Dudley walked around propping each solder up against the wall, naked, after IM sedation that would keep them out for two hours and crippled by vertigo for six more.

Andre was not without sympathy for the poor soldiers, whose life expectancy was short anyway. He did leave each a pair of long johns for the walk home. What Elisha couldn't figure out was how Cindy, a Twiggy look-alike, managed to trample five hundred pounds of armor to pieces.

"You know," Andre said, lifting Elisha off the ground, "I'm beginning to think Cindy might be the Messiah. What do you think?"

"I think the blow to my head has me hallucinating."

"I think you're right."

Karen had known Andre would not leave her, but she did have a moment of doubt, just long enough for Andre to make his point. She gave him a hug, treated the child coming off the wall, and sheepishly sat down beside the stunned Elisha.

"Don't let the others out of the barn until our friends and I disappear," Karen told Elisha. "We will meet you at the north foot of Mt. Tabor. Bring all three families. It's no longer safe for them here. And for God's sake, stay out of trouble."

Everyone has a breaking point. Elisha was overdue. He sat on the ground sobbing. Akiva, mended and feeling fine, stood beside him. Elisha buried his head in the little girl's chest.

Andre and Karen let Dudley and Cindy lead the way.

"That will do, Cindy," Karen said, when she noticed Cindy swinging her hips like the world's most limber stripper.

"Really?" Andre said, "And Dudley gets to keep flexing those puffed biceps of his?"

"Oh, I see," Karen said, flirty, "you don't want me to get excited? Are you afraid of what I might want to do?"

"Would that be the same thing I want to do?"

"There's one way to find out."

"And what would that be?" asked Andre, with eyes popping.

"Put on a Speedo."

"Yeah … okay … I'll pass on that one."

The shuttle was hidden a mile away. There was plenty of time to get back to the ship.

"So tomorrow?" Andre asked. "We're not heading for Mt. Tabor, are we?"

"No, absolutely not. I have a date."

"With me?"

"With Jesus, but you're welcome to tag along."

"How generous of you. I'll pick up Mary Magdalene. We can make it a foursome."

17

Jesus Night

A ndre and Karen made it back to the ship in time for dinner. Karen was hoping to have a selfie to show off, of her smiling next to Jesus. She wasn't sure about the pose. At first, she was certain a "V" for victory would be perfect. Later she came up with the idea of making a cross out of two fingers. Everyone has a trademark.

"Brad," Andre asked, as he sat down in the main ballroom next to Sarah, opposite Michael, Karen, and Janie, "you're Italian, right?"

"On my mother's side. We don't mention it."

"When people criticize Roman brutality, or the dictators of World War II, how come you guys get off without a dishonorable mention?"

"That's an easy one. It's because we throw good parties. I mean, really, what's more important? And is it my fault that your great-great-something ancestors weren't as good at making war as mine? They were all doing it."

"Sure—makes sense to me," Andre admitted. "More power to you. Did you also know that your ancestors held the award for having the immune system most resistant to tuberculosis?"

"It may surprise you that I do know that," replied Brad, "and my lung capacity is one reason I went to the head of my class in flight school."

"Yes," Janie said, laughing, "apparently your ancestors spent more time than anyone on earth sitting around coughing on each other."

Janie followed with a tough-guy imitation: "Hey, Vito, get me a cigar, and where's the Zabaglione?"

The crew had kept up with the day. They'd watched drone visuals all the way to the orange-throwing contest. When Dudley and Cindy walked onstage they got a standing ovation, complete with catcalls—not for Cindy but for Dudley's legs. It was a great day. No one got nailed.

Dudley objected, not heard above the applause, that the crew was wasting energy. Cindy loved it and raised the noise level by whipping off her skirt to model the bikini beneath. They were onstage to assemble Janie's request. She and Brad lived by the motto that there was no problem on Earth, the Milky Way, or the entire universe that couldn't be helped by a wild-ass shindig.

The instructions were simple. Male or female—come to the grand ballroom as Jesus Christ, Mary, or Mary Magdalene, which is to say, how they pictured Jesus or Mary in their minds. There were European Christs with blond hair and tiny noses, black Jesuses with Afros, and Asian Jesuses wearing meditation robes. All wore beards, and some earrings, especially the cross-dressers, who also made strong arguments for Jesus being gay. After all, who leaves home to hang out with guys for the rest of his life?

Janie was Mary Magdalene. She was a whiz on the computer, which within minutes directed the tailoring of an outfit exactly like the one Leah was wearing on earth, with two exceptions: the material was see-through all the way to her bikini, and just below her belly button was a fake tattoo that said "Jesus slept here."

Brad got more laughs. He was baby Jesus, six-foot-six-plus and all man, in diapers. A micro-drone imitating a star followed him wherever he went, and three robot wise men were next, carrying frankincense, myrrh, and government bonds.

Sarah showed up as "not Virgin Mary." She didn't want to set a bad example for modern women, as if any of them believed the story anyway, even though Mary was reported to have said no to the invisible ghost at least once. Later she amended her testimony to "No, not now, my husband is on his way. Come back later."

And, of course, gender rules did not apply. Karen was dressed as Jesus, but played up the bisexual angle, kissing men and women without prejudice. Andre was first in line. Janie was second smack and hard to beat.

Karen was elected either king or queen of the ball. She chose queen. King of the ball went to Michael. His green face was bearded. His robe was an authentic replica, but that's not what won the votes. He had a *mezuzah* and often quoted the Torah's command to "write the words of God on the gates and doorposts of your house," but instead of fixing it to a door for others to tap as they entered the room, he tied it to his pants zipper. It was the only mezuzah in the universe that came out to greet you and thanked the ladies for making contact.

Andre visualized the brain as a place with many empty parking spots. He added a detail that actually made sense. He went as teenager Jesus, with carpenter belt, level, and pencil in his ear. Andre wanted to experience the complete Jesus, a man who took pride and satisfaction in building a better life for others.

Andre also thought a canister of big nails might be funny. No one laughed. Apparently, it was too soon. Andre left the room to stash the spikes.

He returned with a second attempt at humor, something years ago he would never have dared. When he entered the ballroom, he was still dressed as Jesus the carpenter, but he also held up a poster on a stick. It read, "On strike for better working conditions." The party was off and funning.

After dessert was cleared, the houselights dimmed. A single spotlight lit center stage above the round black plate one quarter of an inch thick that Cindy and Dudley had installed. It was a gravity elevator. The spot marked where those who wished to do so could share their thoughts. The theme was "Jesus, the philosopher—Jesus, thoughts later."

Janie was the first to make her way to center stage; after all, it was her party, and she was the social director. She removed her shoes before stepping on the plate. The crowd hushed. With toes pointed beneath her and arms raised sideways, slightly elevated, palms facing forward, fingers cupped, she rose from the floor as the spotlight followed her up ten feet.

"Let the light so shine before them that they see your good works and glorify the father which is in heaven." Janie dropped her gaze from the heavens to those surrounding her. Her arms lowered to her sides as she finished. "The selfish suffer more from themselves than from what they refuse to share. We shall not repeat the errors of history. We all are equal. We all share. We all love." Janie finished just as her feet hit the floor. "We have grown the human spirit. Morality and philosophy are now one. But we must never forget that progress was bought by taking nothing for granted, by questioning everything and everybody, just as our children will do. The Golden Rule is an accomplishment of sanctity. It shall never tarnish."

Indistinct gospel humming accompanied Janie offstage. Those in attendance, with polite reserve and soft tones, repeated "amen" until she sat down.

Andre was next, but not by choice; Janie knew he had prepacked hot air all day, and the executive staff had heard it all. It was only fair that the rest of the crew, the few not within earshot for long, long periods of time, allow Andre to run out the recordings in his head.

He added a spin. Instead of hands up holy rising, Andre sat squatted down on the plate, took out a screwdriver from his carpenter's belt, and pretended to adjust the disk.

"Oh, yes," he said, still sitting, facing the audience. "They don't build them like they used to, and thank God."

He did comply with Janie's request for standardization. When the gravity waves had him at full elevation, he rose to his almost full height, opened his arms sideways, and spoke in the lofty breaths evangelists practice daily. "Our God is a God of Salvation, not revenge. Only through faith is there salvation, and only through love is there hope." Andre kept his arms out as he finished with words attributed to Jesus. "I desire mercy, not sacrifice. Believe, and you shall live forever. Walk with the glory of God in your heart."

After a deep breath, Andre lowered his arms and looked around. He paused when he got to the executive staff table. Janie, Michael, Sarah, Brad, and Karen were looking over attentively.

"Every personal conviction must be subject to reason," he said, "and consistent with two overriding principles. The first is that love is the measure of all things. The second is do unto others as you would have them do unto you, which translates into…" For his finish, Andre turned sideways and stuck his thumb out like he was hitchhiking. "Let's take love for a spin all the way to heaven."

"Best yet," said Brad, turning to Michael at his side.

"Couldn't agree more. I clocked thirty-four seconds, what do you have?"

"Thirty-five, but who's counting? Anything less than a minute of Andre preaching is perfect."

Sarah changed outfits for the final presentation. She walked onstage as Mary Magdalene, the mother. Since no historical data existed to prove or disprove the estimate, she arrived at two conclusions of her own, which in truth neither doubting Dudley nor silicon-head Andre could argue with, since neither side of the question owned a baseline.

Sarah's reasoning was straightforward and fit the age. Jewish men were required, as a duty to God and country, to marry and raise a family. Ergo—the cover-ups of history could have, and more than likely did, erase key factors, especially when the male-dominated Caesar behavior "Holy" Roman Empire went out of their way to blacken Mary Magdalene's image and swell the male ruler stuff.

So—Jesus was married. Jesus had sex, and liked it—a comment that Sarah got laughs with, even before the wink she added. And, the probabilities of procreation being what they are, they had children. No one disagreed. There was no need to, and it was a pleasant image.

It was also what Sarah cashed in on. Her Mary Magdalene outfit came with a mother's apron and three holographic children at her feet as she elevated. Halfway up, Sarah bent down and patted one of the youngsters on the head as she said, "Don't worry, Jesus junior, your dad will be home any minute now. He has a lot of work to do."

All three holographic children stood up, looked up, and joined their hands in prayer when Sarah began reciting from the Book of Matthew: "Therefore I say unto you, be not anxious for your life, what ye shall eat, or what ye shall drink; nor yet for your body, what ye shall put on. Is not the life more than food, and the body than the raiment? Behold the birds of the heaven, that they sow not, neither do they reap, nor gather into barns; and your heavenly Father feedeth them. Are not ye of much more value than they? And which of you by being anxious can add one cubit unto the measure of his life? And why are ye anxious concerning raiment? Consider the lilies of the field, how they grow; they toil not, neither do they spin: yet I say unto you, that even Solomon in all his glory was not arrayed like one of these. But if God doth so clothe the grass of the field, which to-day is, and to-morrow is cast into the oven, shall be not much more *clothe* you, O ye of little faith? Be not therefore anxious, saying, What shall we eat? or, What shall we drink? or, Wherewithal shall we be clothed? For after all these things do the Gentiles seek; for your heavenly Father knoweth that ye have need of all these things. But seek ye first his kingdom, and his righteousness; and all these things shall be added unto you. Be not therefore anxious for the morrow: for the morrow will be anxious for itself. Sufficient unto the day is the evil thereof." Adding dramatics of her own, Sarah finished by holding two of Jesus's children in her arms. "Knock and it shall be opened to you. Ask and it shall be given to you. Have faith, and you shall be made well. Believe, and you shall live forever. Walk with the glory of God in your heart. I am the Good Shepherd, and I know mine, and mine know me."

Sarah began the last sentence on the way back to the floor. One word at a time was heard:

"There … will … be … one … fold … and … one shepherd."

Dudley was standing offstage. He had asked Janie if it was proper for him to comb world literature for statements that were consistent with human history, completely political, not spiritual, not moral, not philosophic—more of an absolute truth thing. Janie wasn't certain what

Dudley meant by that, but the face Andre gave her when she told him she had given Dudley the green light had her worried.

"Janie," Andre said, leaning over at the table. "If I know Dudley, what he has to say will be accurate but will not fit the milieu of the evening. You might want to place him last."

There was only one more volunteer ahead of him anyway—Karen, of course. From the Book of John:

"I am the bread of life," she said. "He who comes to me shall not hunger, and he who believes in me shall never thirst."

She finished with her own mix, with arms reaching out to the entire room:

"Suffer he children to come unto me. While you have the light, walk in the light. While you have the light, put your faith in the light, that you may become sons and daughters of the light. No one who has faith shall go on living in the dark.

"The Lord is my shepherd. I will not want. Faith, hope, and love shall abide for all times. I will fear no evil, for thou art with me. And I will dwell in the house of the Lord for all times."

Approval was heard as Karen was lowered to the floor. Michael and Andre both nodded when she looked over to them.

After Karen had taken her place at the table, she looked up to see Dudley center stage, not on the disk, not rising, just outside of the limelight. He was wearing a charcoal gray knee-length 1850s frock jacket, a notched-collar white shirt, a vest, and a silk jacquard tie complete with diamond stick pin. He looked over to Karen.

"Commander."

"Yes, Dudley."

"Is it necessary to rise ten feet off the ground to make my words more believable?"

"It adds emotional depth, Dudley," she answered.

"But why, if you don't mind me asking, do you want to contaminate logic with emotional prejudice? I might as well be an actor, the most misleading fabricator on earth."

"The answer to that question," Karen got right out, "is that we don't wish to distort, but human beings more often *feel* something is right before they can prove it."

"My research supports the opposite contention," Dudley protested. "Most of what you feel has little to do with reality. You're off more often than you're on."

"Yes, Dudley," Andre said, who knew agreeing with consistency was the best way to shut him up. "But it's a start. We evolve from there."

"Oh, jolly ho … now I see …" Dudley said, straightening his shirt and turning to face the audience. "As philosophers, you are like children who fall on their faces over and over again before you learn how to walk on your own two feet."

"Yes, Dudley," said Andre, "we keep getting better, and closer to God."

"Okay, roger that. It must be just super to be one of you. And I just changed my mind. I was going to go with an Albert Schweitzer Mother Teresa binge, but instead I will quote a nineteenth century philosophy."

"Here comes Nietzsche," said Andre, who'd had a crush on the guy when he was eight.

Dudley did the trick one better. He did not rise straight up above the disk on stage. Instead, he floated himself twenty feet up, reflecting on rationality all the way:

"Man is a rope stretched between the animal and the Superman. I want to teach men the sense of their existence, which is the Superman, the lightning out of the dark cloud man."

Dudley looked around. Andre was correct. Everyone knew the author. There was great respect for the words of the son of a preacher.

"No one is such a liar as the indignant man. Nothing on earth consumes a man more quickly than the passion of resentment.

"This is the hardest of all: to close the open hand out of love, and keep modest as a giver. Is not life a hundred times too short for us to bore ourselves?

"My doctrine is: Live that thou mayest desire to live again—that is thy duty—for in any case thou wilt live again!"

Dudley had a strategy. He first laid out Nietzsche's philosophy, then added comments accurately describing the effects that organized religion had on his continent.

"I call Christianity the one great curse, the one enormous and innermost perversion, the one great instinct of revenge, for which no means are too venomous, too underhand, too underground and too petty—I call it the one immortal blemish of mankind."

The comment that followed bowled Andre over and left the crowd speechless. They all knew Dudley could not verbalize irrational associations without disclaiming them so—but he did not. He finished while looking down at his Nietzsche outfit.

"Apparently God does work in strange ways."

18

Jubilation

Silence hung for three long minutes as Dudley made his way offstage. He scanned the house looking for requests or conversation. There was none. No one disagreed with Dudley; the past was littered with abuse and stained with the seepage of selfishness hiding behind self-justification. It was just that it was yesterday's news; repeating it dampened today and contaminated tomorrow.

It was the Nietzsche thing that got to the crowd. In his day, the German philosopher was accused of being disrespectful, inappropriate, politically incorrect, and blasphemous. The Romans and Pharisees said the same things about Jesus, in several languages and with a handful of nails. Every truth begins as heresy.

The crew realized as much and had prepared their own existential theatre. They stood in silence to salute their Nietzsche stand-in. They expressed respect for one who resisted the black water of his day, just like Jesus did. Both men were up against misunderstood concepts of "free will" that had been distorted into totalitarianism.

Free will requires truth and logical perspectives. The ancient world had neither. That's their excuse. The modern world, Nietzsche and beyond, boasted both him and Charles Darwin, among many other intellectual giants, but for centuries preferred the arrogance that labeled clergy superior to others. Civilization suffered repeatedly at the hands of know-nothing do-gooders in the name of Jesus, or the fatherland, or anything else that came along.

Earth's past was a sad time. The lowest common denominator refused to rise. Freedom and genuine free will require opening one's eyes and cutting strings. Eternity has no need for puppet stormtroopers singing hymns. No one noticed the strings.

Nietzsche had good reason to resent the dark side of Christianity. For over a thousand years it forbade medical investigation. Every evil, every infection, every stillborn baby or dead mother was an act of their god, who must be appeased through them, at a cost. The cost was progress, depression, warfare, and millions of lives needlessly lost.

What Nietzsche didn't know is that Christianity cost him his life. He lost his mind to infection, one the diseases that would have been cured if the Vatican hadn't stepped in to execute every scientist they uprooted. Some got off easy, like Galileo, who was too famous to murder, and Copernicus, whose final work was held until he was dead. Even Darwin waited to make truth known for fear of being pelted with rotten tomatoes every Sunday.

Louis Pasteur barely escaped. In the year he was born, 1822, the Vatican was still killing those who disagreed with their stupidity. A church decree insisted that some sheep died of anthrax and some didn't because God determined which fields to bless and which ones not to. Pasteur disagreed, and he had a microscope to prove it.

The Catholics wanted to send out a hit man, but Isaac Newton's scientific revolution got in the way. It was a bummer for those pretending to be Good Samaritans. To their credit, they were very good at ignoring everything Jesus stood for, and they ended up well paid for causing trouble.

When he reached the edge of the dance floor, Dudley turned. He was confused by the goings-on that followed. Andre walked over to join him.

"Dudley, stay right here. I think you'll enjoy this."

"Enjoyment," Dudley said, stiff-necked, "is not one of my functions."

"Not yet, but your connecting Nietzsche to God a few minutes ago is something no robot has ever done. Your artificial consciousness may delve deeper than you think, or process, or analyze, or whatever you want to call it."

"Certainly, sir. What gives?"

Andre had Cindy send Dudley the complete text of Ionesco's play *Rhinoceros*. A single powerful beast is seen running down the main street. A luckless, unambitious youth spots the animal, notices how everyone gets out of its way, and wishes he had that power.

The next day he did. He turned into a rhinoceros. Two beasts stormed through town, then three, and before you knew it the entire country had turned into rhinoceroses, paralleling Nazi Germany, the Crusades, and self-righteous religions.

Instead of dressing up like rhinoceroses, the crew marched around the room two by two, arms elbow-linked, and bent over beside one another. They made animal sounds, crossed themselves, or "Heil Hitler" saluted.

Two laps followed before Karen stood in the middle of the room as Jesus Christ with arms open wide. When the train of followers got to Jesus, they let go, split in half, and became themselves again, smiling and hugging one another. The curse was broken.

"So, the message," Dudley guessed, turning to Andre, "is that Jesus can free human beings from the political or religious enslavement of their lives."

"Yeah, sure," Andre said. "Something like that. Every human being must be themselves. When one remains part of a war machine, economic factory, religious crusade, or a member of a certain political party I have no use for at home, one forfeits blessings."

"And adds abuse," Dudley concluded, "to oneself and to others."

Cindy had snuck up behind them. "Andre," she said, with uncharacteristic sincerity, "is there hope for this guy after all?"

"He's starting to think for himself," Andre said with a smile and a pat on the back for Dudley, "and he never wants to die, just like us."

"Yeah," she said, "I'll give you that. But how can we make him smile?"

Andre got everyone looking when he stepped forward and gave Cindy a kiss on the cheek.

"That's your job, sweetie. A tree falling in the forest that no one hears makes no sound. If it weren't for women, men would never smile."

There is no jubilation greater than hope, love, and charity. The ball was a ball. All slept well. Jesus smiled. So did Nietzsche.

—⚬—

The next morning Karen dressed in her Hebrew garb and went straight to the shuttle bay. She asked Andre, "Where is Jesus? And why aren't you dressed?"

Andre ignored her. He was standing in front of a panel of readouts, touch-typing the sixty second symphony in thirty seconds. Cindy was on his right, Dudley standing left; both had lights flashing at their stations.

Karen asked, "What the hell is going on?"

"It's gravity," said Andre.

"It's time," said Dudley.

"You're both wrong," said Cindy. "It's speed."

Neither Dudley nor Andre risked losing concentration. One false adjustment and the ship could snap distance, travel through time, or accelerate out of control.

"We're having a problem with energy containment and haven't a clue what to do," Cindy said in a matter-of-fact tone. "The ship might disintegrate and we all die, or you all die and Dudley and I float around somewhere."

Andre was wearing his one-piece leisure suit. The one he used when he stayed up all night tackling a problem. The previous night it was the problem that had tackled him at two in the morning.

"Why didn't you wake me?" Karen complained.

Andre didn't take his eyes off his screen, but he did reply, not at all pleasantly: "Because I have enough distractions as it is, that's why. And the three of us have been arguing all night."

"Yes," Dudley said with an attitude Karen had never witnessed before, "Andre called me 'bolt brain.' Should I be upset?"

"Dudley," Cindy added, "you called him dimwitted protoplasm first."

"That," Dudley said, "was accurate. Andre does not have my facility for calculating multiple relativities in time. Orbital space stations experience different time movement than those on the surface. A ship speeding by at light speed can cross the entire solar system before Earth's finest chronometer can detect time ticking. It's my forte."

"Yes," said Andre with obvious disdain, and frustrated that Dudley was still unwilling to add the variable Andre was working on, "but time is related to gravity, and more gravity means slower time, and gravity feeds through from the dimension that supports the entire universe outside of time."

"A variable, I must point out," Dudley said, "for which you don't have a single equation. There is no way to incorporate it in our trajectory."

"Duh!" said Andre, almost yelling. "What the hell do you think I'm doing over here?"

Cindy put her arm around Karen, who was not looking well. "It's been like this all night. And we're getting nowhere."

Andre was listening. "Speak for yourself. If I hadn't altered Dudley's equations twice, we would have blown up."

"Not blown up, my squishy friend," Dudley said. "Just blown away."

"Karen," Cindy asked, "does squishy qualify as an epithet? Is Dudley being a bad boy?"

Karen considered the question impertinent and was disturbed by Andre's snarled nerves. She proceeded slowly. "You can take any word in the English language and add emotional disdain or read insult into it if you want to bash someone over the head. That's what makes the funny word thing so ridiculous. It's like shooting at clouds to keep the rain from falling."

"So," said Cindy, "does Dudley get a time-out or not?"

"No," replied Karen, "and stop enjoying this so much."

"Perhaps—I've been trash-mouth troublemaker Cindy since I got out of my box. I think the two of them are hilarious."

"And wasting energy," Karen pointed out.

Suddenly, at the same second, both Dudley and Andre pulled away from their monitors. The ship had stabilized.

"My, how interesting!" said Cindy.

It was Karen's turn for words: "Again—what the hell is going on?"

As Andre and Dudley stood to the side, both with sheepish grins covering their retreat, Cindy explained. "Our physical dimensions are determined by gravity…"

"And I was right about that," insisted Andre.

"Yes, you were," said Cindy with a smile, then she added, "but time is what generates force in the gravity dimension, what was discovered after the boson particle led the way, and what Andre now names the fifth dimension, part of which is heavenspace."

"And my multiple time coordinates pointed that out," said Dudley with professorial pride.

"Yes, of course, bolt brain. Or was it grease monkey?" replied Cindy. "What is your latest nickname?"

"None of your business, Cindy," Dudley snapped back.

"My, my, how human you're becoming," Cindy retorted.

Neither Dudley nor Andre budged during the end of the story. Cindy pointed out that the energy bottled up to stop short was generated outside of time, so therefore it existed in stasis without a proper mooring to gravity, which meant it was able to penetrate at will.

Rebounding energy back and forth between external shields was no longer possible because the moon, where they had parked, was still spinning around the earth, and the sun around the black hole in the galaxy, and so on. That position, all relative speeds, had changed too much, and in so doing had altered the containment chamber.

Cindy crossed her arms and faced Andre to end the story. "So, Andre, what is the only way we have to reestablish containment, which I noticed you and Dudley just did?"

"By altering our speed relative to the Crunch-Bang photon field, the only reliable measure of time and gravity."

Karen looked out. The moon, the earth, the entire solar system—all were nowhere in sight. "Where did we go?"

Cindy explained that they hadn't gone anywhere. Dudley the bolt and Andre the aqueous solution had let everything else fly away. The ship was actually not moving at all, relative to the Crunch-Bang origins of time, space, and velocity.

"In case you missed the implication," Cindy said. "I was right. It was velocity we had to change to cool down."

"Not exactly," Andre huffed irritably. "Your solution was correct, but you had no markers to guide us. Dudley and I balanced the sheet."

"To-may-toes, to-mah-toes," Cindy added. "Are we done?"

"For now."

Dudley and Cindy stood guard in front of the monitors. All was well, although it looked like everything outside the ship was moving away. Andre and Karen walked to the clear hull to watch from there.

"So," Karen said, "back to my question. Where is Jesus?"

Andre pointed to a point of light in the inky blackness of space. "Right there."

"And when are we going back?"

"Not today. The ship needs to cool off and I need sleep."

"I've got that reading for you, Andre," said Dudley, returned to pleasantry. "It's 13,543,420,424."

"Oh, thank God," Andre exclaimed.

"Thank God for what?" Karen asked.

"We only lost a month."

"An entire month! Who knows what might have happened in Jerusalem since we left!"

"It could have been a thousand years," said Andre. "I'm beat raw, and you're welcome. Stand down—I'm in no mood."

"It's Dudley's fault," Cindy said. "Andre doesn't like fighting with robots. We always win."

Andre began to stomp out of the room but then realized how ridiculously he was acting. He criticized others for doing what they knew wasn't right, for making things worse, and for hurting others who were doing their best; and then he did the same thing. He returned to stand in front of two machines that were more than machines and one woman who was more than a woman.

"I guess I was wrong—a little—and misled you," he said. "And I should have been nicer. I apologize."

Cindy stepped beside Andre, rubbing her silicon-coated metal hand back and forth through his hair. "Don't you just love this little guy when he's human like this? High and mighty Andre crawls through life just like the rest of us."

"With less gravity," Andre joked with a laugh. Even Karen almost beat him on the scale.

"And," Dudley added, "thanks to me, all the time he needs."

"Oh, I see," said Cindy. "Now it's my turn to make a wisecrack about velocity. Okay, how about this: Andre, you'd better speed up if you ever want Karen back. She's way ahead of you."

"Cindy!" Karen said, then nothing as she slow-motion jogged out of the shuttle bay, at one point looking back at Andre long enough to wink.

19

Jesus Day

You can smile with your lips. You can smile with your eyes. You can smile with a hug. You can smile with your whole life. Karen shot the works. She jumped out of bed, literally. The night's plan had worked. Down from her window was Jerusalem. They were back on the moon.

When Sarah looked up she saw Mt. Washington, the peak in New Hampshire that had earned a reputation for having the worst weather on earth, blown by frantic, subzero north winds gusting over one hundred miles an hour. She and Michael were enjoying the view from the top of nearby Mt. Adams.

It was a great way to wake up, and they weren't alone. On many early mornings, a group of outdoor hiking enthusiasts met to tackle a mountain. They called themselves "the Sunrisers," since they could program the habitant recreational area's living wall to become an exact replica of sunrise in the White Mountains.

Cylinder gravity made it so. The looped repeating space they walked through felt like going uphill because the Sunrisers would hike inside a giant tube with floor gravity plates, making it feel just like the real thing.

And the view? Never better, especially since Sarah picked a warm, clear summer day.

"Wow," said Michael, plopping down on a rock to take it all in, "let's sit. We'll catch up with the others in a loop."

"Sure," said Sarah.

She looked over to Michael, who was watching two eagles in formation. He kept watching. Nothing else happened. He didn't shift to a flirty posture for a joke; he didn't stand to tell an outrageous story to keep Sarah entertained; he didn't spout philosophy to contemplate. No, he just kept looking.

Sarah knew him well. When he chose not to make contact with her suspicious eyes, she lightly tapped him on the shoulder.

"Yes," he said, pulling away nonchalantly. "What is it?"

"I don't know what it is. *You* know what it is. Michael, when you're like this, something is on your mind. Let's have it."

Michael swung one leg to the other side of the rock to face Sarah. "Do you like to party?"

"Yes, and so do you. If fact, the only person onboard who parties more than you is Janie. Everyone knows you're the man."

"That's true, Sarah, but's it's not all true." Michael hesitated and then looked around, not to find someone, just to remind Sarah they were in their own world. He stood, faced east, and pointed. "See that small mountain over there?"

"I do indeed."

"In the real world, my log cabin family home is in the valley on the other side. If we were in New Hampshire, we could start down."

"And six hours later…?"

"Six hours later, we'd be late for breakfast. But we'd be in a house that was perfect for raising a family. I didn't stay long the last time I visited. It felt empty. It needed life."

"I remember the story. Part of you wants to be there right now?"

"I think it's time. And the living room is gigantic, with three fireplaces and one old-fashioned wood-burning stove."

"That you'll have to put a fence around so the kids don't get burned."

"And a force field, and a dedicated robot butler whenever it's lit. I'm a great believer in security."

Sarah inched one foot closer. She did not make contact but did honestly bear truth. "You're not alone, Michael. I say a lot of things, but deep down I've known that I've been ready for years. I want to be surrounded by kids, my kids, the neighbor's kids, and all my relatives."

Michael dimpled two cheeks, smiling at the dream. "With family groups barbecuing outside on a warm summer's night, or sliding down cross-country trails to a cabin in the woods, with a fireplace, hot apple pie, and hot chocolate waiting."

Sarah raised her hands with palms out. "So, that's always been your plan. Why bring it up today? Tell me the truth. What's got into you?"

There was a limit to how far Michael wanted to soften up, so he stood and presented his conclusions more formally. "It's about Karen and Andre."

"Yes," Sarah said, turning her head sideways, still in the dark, suspicious about something she already expected.

"You know," Michael said, "when it comes to numbers and risks, Andre always lies."

"And Karen knows that. Go on."

"I ran the data by Dudley, who agreed that Andre's remote spatial field generator has less than a 50 percent chance of working. When the two of them leave for the surface this morning, we may never see them again."

"And Karen will never be down there?" Sarah said, pointing to the spot, as she challenged Michael by taking a step closer, near enough for him to bend forward and give her a kiss if he wanted to, which he did.

Michael understood the feedback. It was just what he was hoping to find. "Well, Sarah, you're right. Karen might never be there, but you and I could be."

Sarah did not gush or giggle like Michael thought she might. Her feelings were just as confused as his. Instead, she strutted back and forth like a sergeant inspecting the troops. Michael got the message. He felt the same way.

"There's just one problem with that, Michael."

"And that would be what?" asked Michael, hesitantly.

"What you're saying is that the great and desirable Michael would lower himself to marrying me. Your second choice, but still acceptable. How generous you are to the little people."

Michael hesitated wearily at the thought of coming off as being pretentious, and then he perked up, realizing Sarah returned his love. His denial poured passion.

"No, no…that's not it! I assure you that if it's within my power, I will beg the most astounding love of my life to join me in the woods."

"Okay, now I am confused. What are you getting at?"

"And you can stop playacting. You feel the same way, and we will never know just what is—Karen and Andre our special someones, or you and me the real thing—if they disappear."

"And," Sarah said, serious and worried, "they just might get left behind. We love them both, but we're not down there with them. If we join them at least it will be a foursome."

"Which would mean no New Hampshire ever," said Michael.

"Or Colorado's Rocky Mountains, or mom, or dad."

"Or my Minnesota folks and relatives."

So much for a lighthearted morning, which did bring honesty to light for both of them, and smiles all the way to Mt. Washington.

"So when do we tell them?" asked Sarah.

"Why don't we just show up at breakfast dressed and ready to go?"

Michael leapt, bent down, kissed Sarah on the lips, and got as sweet a smile back as he had laid on her.

"Dudley," Michael called, "front and center."

Voice projection brought Dudley to them. "Yes, Michael. I'm in the lab getting those gadgets ready for you. Were you successful with Sarah?"

"You're on speaker, and she's right here, Dudley."

Sarah tilted her head up to say, "Dudley, define 'successful.' What did Michael tell you?"

"You know better than that, Sarah. Besides, you already know he has the hots for you."

"Dudley," Sarah said, correcting, "Michael has the hots for everyone."

"Not Cindy," Dudley said, getting laughs he wasn't expecting.

—⟋⟍—

Karen and Andre had promised Michael and Sarah that they would wait for them to return from their morning hike before departing. Their plates were licked clean half an hour before the hikers walked in. Their patience was barely holding.

Clad in robes and sandals, without a word Michael and Sarah sat down next to them.

Andre puckered his lips and looked at Karen, who, inside, was happy ten ways she didn't show. She even managed a severe tone. "Don't even think of it, Michael. You and Sarah are staying here. There's too much at stake. Don't throw your lives away."

Michael was unfazed. "Right…" he said with a smirk. "Throw my life away? No. Not being with you and maybe even Andre for the rest of my life would be throwing my life away. If worse comes to worse, we get the best of all bests: the four of us will live out our lives in a tropical paradise. No European evil disturbs the South Pacific for over a thousand years."

Andre stood up, walked to the far chair next to Sarah, and said, "I'm not convinced that you want to risk leaving your family back home."

"I don't," said Sarah, certain of herself. "But we, the four of us, are also a family, with many years of happiness ahead. And I don't want you to be lonely. I brought your teddy bear."

—⟋⟍—

Step one was catching up with Elisha and Leah. Andre had stitched tracer threads to their robes. When Andre and Karen did not show up, Elisha and friends left for his uncle's town, a rundown soil-worn patch of disappointment near Jerusalem. There, soldiers were seldom seen. The town offered nothing worth stealing.

The main and only road was a dusty dirt path that ran through the middle of the settlement. West of it by half a mile was a ravine where large groups of people could assemble, unnoticed by the authorities.

Several citizens were strolling around town to make it look like a normal day. Michael noticed their patterns repeating. They weren't going anywhere; they were lookouts.

"Good morning, neighbor," he said to one. "I'm looking for Leah and Elisha. Can you help me?"

"No, I'm sorry. You should try Jerusalem. No one ever comes here."

Andre was on it. He knew just where they were and which houses their kids were hiding in.

Michael turned to the group with a wink. "We missed them. Let's keep going."

—⁂—

Thirty minutes later the four approached the hidden gully. Drone shots confirmed the presence of Elisha and Leah, along with one hundred forty-seven others. When the assembly caught sight of strangers approaching, the alarm spread.

"It's all right," said Elisha. "They're our friends, Adam and Hannah."

No fuss was made. The group returned to sitting. Elisha had said nothing to them about the strange day at the barn, and besides, he had found the Messiah.

"Please continue," he gestured to a robed man standing in their midst. The speaker was of average size and wore a knee-length tunic beneath a warm wool mantle. It was clear that he was descended from Judah—his dark skin, wide nose, and bold dark eyes gave it away. His curly black hair was cut short. His morning stubble wasn't noticed by Karen standing at the back.

"That's Jesus?" Karen whispered, with a gasp. Feeling woozy, she said, "But short hair, no beard, flat nose…"

"You don't approve of his DNA?" asked Michael.

"No… I… just… had another image in mind," said Karen.

"Along with every everyone else on the planet," added Andre.

"He looks just like the guy back in town who told us to scram," said Sarah, confused.

"And what were you expecting?" Andre asked.

"I don't know. A glow, or radiant light, or ..."

"Or an Oscar or two?" Michael said, stifling a laugh. "This is the ancient world, time of prophets and death. Everything down here is dull, drab, and exaggerated. A word of advice ... don't believe anything you hear from old men in Italy. The papacy is the ghost of the deceased Roman Empire, sitting crowned upon its grave."

"Shh, you two," said Sarah. "I can hardly hear Jesus from here."

What they heard came slowly, with conviction powered by joy: "The Spirit of God is upon us. I have come to announce good news to the poor, the downtrodden, and all those abused by Rome. This is the year of our Lord's favor. The blind shall see, the lame shall walk, and justice shall be delivered to the afflicted.

"God does not delight in the blood of bulls, lambs, or goats. You cannot buy yourself the favor of God, but clean hands and a pure heart are always welcome. All those who have not blackened their souls with vanity, nor sworn deceitfully, shall receive eternal favor. We are one family loved equally by the Lord our God."

Karen grabbed Andre's hand to bring him closer. She wanted him to take a scan. Halfway through the crowd she stopped when the speaker, known to them as "the Messiah," looked directly at her. Doubt turned to shame.

"The Lord our God is the one God," he said. "Thou shalt love the Lord thy God with all thy heart, and with all thy soul, and with all thy mind, and with all thy strength. Thou shalt also love thy neighbor as thyself. There is no greater commandment than these."

Sarah had to sit down. "I can't believe I'm here listening to him."

"Careful," Andre warned. "Good stories have a habit of repeating themselves from the mouths of many."

"My friends," the Messiah said loudly to all, "some of those among us say life is hard, and that an easy life is a sinful life. It is not so. I say to you, banish from your mind tales of black magic, evil spirits, and vengeful ghosts. Life must bring as many joys as we are able to bless it with. Everyone shares love. Perseverance and the reassurance of the Lord our God shall make it so."

Michael whispered over to Andre: "He's off script. What gives?"

"Possibly it's the real thing. Let's listen."

The Messiah paused to collect his thoughts before continuing, "Every man has the right to rebel against oppression or to raise his fist against fate; but no joy can bloom burdened by the stain of blood. The Romans' lust for gold betrays the will of God. One cannot serve two masters. We must not follow their example. Put down your weapons. There is another way."

Andre was contacted by Dudley. Under his breath Andre answered: "Roger that, give me five minutes. If nothing happens I'll come up with something."

The Messiah walked forward to stand dead center, close enough for Karen to comment on his dental care, and to feel strange about doing so, although she thought it brought a smile to his face even though he was still clearly beyond hearing distance. She smiled back through his final remarks:

"Every human being has the right to rebel against foul circumstances. We raise our fists against fate, but there is no joy down the path of blood and tears. The Romans and the Pharisees have let the lust for power betray them. One cannot serve God and man.

"Freedom is not just a word. It is the tranquility of sharing breakfast with those we love, working beside equals, and thanking God under the stars. We plant freedom on earth like we sow spring seed for fall's harvest."

The Messiah, considered by many to be no more than a wise rebel, raised his voice as he swept one arm over the crowd.

"The wind blows free across this land we love dearly. The most blessed gift is common joy. The best of days wakes from shared dreams. Fear not for yourself; God has left grain, fruit, and all we shall ever need.

"There is also sadness on our journey, but out of suffering and strife will come freedom. There is no greater pride than serving the Lord with our bodies and our souls.

"Someday the names of our oppressors will be forgotten, but what we begin here will follow mankind to the end of days. The future will dance beneath heaven. Let us pray."

The Messiah did not lower his head, but instead lifted his eyes even higher. "Dear God our Father, we give you thanks for all you have given us, and …"

"I'm really sorry to interrupt," Andre broke in, taking a step forward, "but I have it on reliable authority that a patrol of Roman soldiers is ten minutes away and closing in from the north."

The last to disappear to the south was the Messiah, who waved and smiled at Andre before he vanished.

Karen and Sarah sat on the ground swooning in ways Michael and Andre never understood. They knew drones and Michael's gadgets would keep them safe. What they couldn't figure out was how so much wisdom showed up so fast if it wasn't the real thing, which, as far as they were concerned, had just happened.

Andre sat down in front of Karen and, against his better judgment, crossed his legs meditation-style. He reached over for one of her hands.

"Karen, that was spectacular. You did it. We did it. Let's go home now."

Karen was overcome by determination. She did stand. She did walk west away from Roman spears, but she also turned to Michael and Andre:

"Jesus saved us. Now we save him. We *are* doing this, gentlemen. Lock and load."

20

Coffee, Tea, or Zealots

Onboard the ship, the next day wore a new face—relentless, stiff, and determined. Karen would be victorious. Defeat was not an option.

Cindy and Dudley were both summoned to the task. They stood beside her at Andre's science station. Karen was in his chair, operating his ship, doing whatever she damn well pleased.

Relay satellites were placed in stationary orbits one hundred eighty degrees apart. Continuous spy-drone feed was made possible. Karen sat analyzing data.

Michael's personal radar shouted, "Alert, something is rotten in Denmark!"

"Karen," he whispered, sneaking up behind her, "Why was half of our bed cold when I woke up this morning?"

Karen paid no heed and shot Michael a glassy look that let him know her opinion, "Sit down, Michael. Review readings from section seventeen. Hard copy printouts are also on the desk. Every conversation that mentions the Messiah, Jerusalem, or apostles has been tagged. We need coordinates. Find Jesus!"

Michael didn't buy it, but he did follow the wishes of his lady. Andre, right behind him, had other plans.

"Pardon me, please," opened his conversation, as he attentively slid between Karen and the displays she was working on. With one hand on each arm rest, Andre then gently rolled her chair back two feet and sat smack down on the flat keyboard she'd been using.

"What the hell are you doing? Oh, wait, let me rephrase that: what the Jesus are you doing?" Karen, who was acting not like herself in any way known to those who loved her, scowled as she rose, pushed Andre over with a wallop, and took one giant step backward to face her two favorite men, neither feeling so at that minute.

"What am I doing?" she complained to both with blatant disregard. "What am I doing? I'll tell you what I'm doing. Do you have any idea how many children—yes, boys as often as girls—fell asleep crying after they were told Jesus had nails driven through his hands and feet because of them? Do you have any idea how a five-year-old feels being dragged from one station of the cross to another while being scolded for his sins?

"Insults, whippings, a crown of thorns, crucifixion, hours of agony, and then a heart lanced with a blade. Oh, no, you don't remember! It's all in the past. That's what you both keep saying. But it's not in the past. It's going on down there right now. As God is my witness, no child will ever be abused like that again."

Andre and Michael looked at each other without expression. They said nothing. Each was dealing with the puzzle of how best to approach Karen, if at all. Neither volunteered. Both decided to wait for Karen to run out of gunpowder.

"I've been up half the night figuring it out," she continued. "Get ready, boys. Today we change history. Jesus the philosopher stays. Jesus the 'forgive your enemies and love your neighbor as yourself' stays. Jesus the martyr goes. Today we relocate Jesus to Tahiti! Any questions?"

"Only thirty-seven," said Andre, who hushed Dudley with a head shake before the robot got his mouth open. "But first, let's dine at the bow and wait for inspiration. Michael, will you pick up Sarah and join us?"

"Andre!" yelled Karen, shaking her finger, "You're not going to ignore me."

"Karen," Andre served back, right before kissing her outstretched finger, "I plan nothing of the sort. It's just that we both need food. Then we pod scan you to make sure you're not mentally or physically imbalanced, as determined by your own software. Then we talk."

Andre extended an elbow, offering to accompany Karen to breakfast. Michael was relieved to retreat; no one was a match for Karen. Andre would have been shaking in his boots if Cindy and Dudley weren't there to back him up.

Dudley offered Cindy his mechanical elbow. The two marched off right behind Karen and Andre. Except Cindy, overdoing disinhibition, couldn't help giggling at every other step. Suddenly she was "the good girl" and loved it but decided not to light up a holographic halo over her head.

Breakfast turned into a battle of wills. Andre didn't budge from "Look but don't touch."

Karen insisted, "Good things are better than bad things."

Sarah half backed her up with "We live for the good that we can do."

Michael cautioned with "Above all, do no harm."

Brad and Janie were the least emotional: "The past must deal with its own pick-up sticks, and remove just the right one, followed by number two. How are *we* to know? Leave well enough alone."

It also became clear that Jesus was far more than just an historical figure, more than a claimed Godhead, and much more than a political weapon. Everyone at the table, regardless of background, had a personal relationship with an individual who existed, and may have only ever existed, in the minds of those who brought him to life.

"I might be developing a sense of humor," Dudley said, standing behind Janie as he correctly served and cleared over her left shoulder. "Even the best parents occasionally rant against the world and pick fights with each other. And even though they regret it and make up later, they also, at times, come down too hard on the children. Brothers and sisters are also never perfect. They compete, get moody, and manipulate each other for favors. But not Jesus. Oh no, in your minds he remains the image of ultimate acceptance and eternal love, epitomizing what no living mortal could ever live up to.

"My conclusion," Dudley continued, sounding like a professor with tenure, "is that Jesus, to you, is not a person at all; he's a symbol. He's the one warm hand you can count on for the long cold night. He's the brother, sister, or lover who finally understands you. He's the one person you can always count on for a hug. Only there's one problem. He doesn't exist. He's a fabrication that replaced teddy bears and dolls when you grew up."

Cindy moved to Dudley's side to fire away. "The greatest story ever told," she said as scholastically as Andre ever pulled off, "is not a story at all. It's a *modus operandi* ... an imagined individual, with nothing documented, every trait assumed, and always on your side. Parents huff off, best friends steal your lover, and politicians lie through your ears, but Jesus? Oh, no, not ever Jesus. He is always there for you." Her sarcasm was obvious. "The only problem with that mind game is that he is *never* there for you. It is you who are there for yourself, for that part of you that holds on to your own personal Jesus."

"And what a story," Dudley added. "It worked so well in Egypt that the Greeks copied it, then Rome, and a dozen other cultures. Just as every plot of Shakespeare's was borrowed, every religion on earth is an example of plagiarism."

Andre looked around, amazed that the rest of the table took Dudley, the computer, so seriously.

"And," Dudley finished, "as long as you all keep up the charade, you all share responsibility for misguiding civilization."

Janie was less impressed by facts and more influenced by results, but she never confessed to being a pragmatist. "Big deal," she said. "Jesus the man, Jesus the God-man, Jesus the stand-in front man; who cares if what he says makes people happy and steers them in the right direction?"

"Objection," Andre said in legal tone. "Manipulation uses Jesus the image to mislead entire continents all the way to tyranny."

Sarah's mind lived close to the Bible Belt. Karen wasn't surprised when she spoke up: "Why can't Jesus be God? None of your arguments disprove that."

Karen lowered her voice to hand Sarah an answer. "Sarah, deep down inside, do you really believe Jesus, and Muhammad, and Buddha, and heaps of similar imitations, were each God? It's not easy to watch a hero drop from the clouds, but they all pick themselves up and walk away on two feet to do just as much good."

The concept chilled in ways they never understood. Perhaps it was the thought that at no time would the earth, then or ever, be under better management than oneself, a known imperfect commodity.

Dudley did his thing, adding data. If this individual did exist, an assumption he emphasized for the tenth time, fewer than one thousand people even knew about him when he died. And it was almost fifty years later that Saul the Jew got the ball rolling with the next installment, entitled "The Epistles of Paul."

Karen jumped on the concept. "So there you go. One way or another our few weeks here can't possibly make a difference. All we do is take the cross out of the picture."

Andre stiff-lipped a frown of disapproval. "You turned those facts upside down to push your cause, Karen. We all know your game."

"Andre," Karen said with a nasty looked that raised the stakes, "you're forgetting one thing: we saw Jesus yesterday. He exists and the world is changing."

"Correction," Andre said, holding the line, "we saw someone down there whom the crowd called the Messiah. And that's all we know."

"I'll tell you what I know," Cindy said with a wiggle dance. "You are all nuts! And your race fell for one of the oldest tricks in the book, called good cop, bad cop. Think about it. Big bad God wants to come down and punish you all with eternal incarceration complete with daily torture. Then the good cop shows up all sympathetic and sweet, promising to do what he can to help take the pressure off upstairs. 'Just cooperate with the dictators I left in charge. Do exactly what you're told and I will do my best to keep the heat off.' Ramrodded idiocy at its worst. And all that just to push people around to get more money and the power to boss the world around for fleeting seconds before each and every one of you dies and regrets your narrow perspectives for the duration of eternity. Grow up, mortals!"

"My vote," said Dudley the brain, "is that the story is an historical collection manipulated by Paul, which did, to his credit, take down the Roman Empire."

"Sure," Cindy agreed sarcastically, "and replaced it with one just as bad."

No one spoke. Cindy had them in the palm of her hand.

"My vote," she said, emoting irritability, "is that you all bore the hell out of me. So get off your damn asses, get back to Israel, and find out. If this wizard of yours sees right though you and says, 'Hello Karen, gotten any lately?' then we'll talk."

"Or," Dudley said without compromise, "come back with scans that show connections beyond time to the eternal dimension. If he's not connected, he's not God."

"I'll go for that," said Karen, knowing she would get her way.

Brad couldn't be bothered to interrupt his breakfast. With half a buttered and honeyed English muffin in his mouth, he added:

"Janie and I are staying up here one way or another. Someone must look after the ship and preserve sanity."

Andre, Michael, and Sarah hesitated, and then called Karen's bluff by heading for the door. Karen got the message. She spoke to their backs just as they were about to leave.

"I promise," she said obligingly, "to return at the drop of a dime the second two out of three of you vote to do so. And I additionally promise to take no overt action unless all three of you agree with me. Are my conditions acceptable?"

Andre held a hand to the side, asking Michael and Sarah to hesitate. "And," he said to Karen, "if you don't comply with our prudent recommendation to abort the mission, do you give Michael and me full permission to remove, by bodily force if necessary, your person from harm's way down there?"

"That won't be necessary, but yes."

Andre and Michael shook hands to seal that deal.

They located Elisha and Leah outside the gates of Jerusalem. The closest the group could land undetected was five miles away.

"I'm beginning to understand why all the old stories begin with Hebrews washing their feet. Open-top sandals, sweaty toes, and dusty roads are a bad combination," said Andre.

When they got to town, Elisha ran over to hug Andre. Leah held Karen's hand.

"Adam," Elisha said, "I'm so glad to see you. The meeting is about to start, and the Messiah is on his way."

Karen's eyes lit up as she looked around.

"Sure, Karen," Andre said, grinning, "like you can tell one Hebrew from another."

Rome's orders were specific: Groups of more than two individuals were not only suspicious, they were illegal congregations. The three couples would walk through the gates thirty yards apart and remain separated until Andre saw Elisha and Leah disappear into a rug shop. At the back of the rug shop they were to complain that the rug they'd bought last week was already unraveling. When the owner asked which part of the rug was defective, the answer would be "all five corners."

If the store were completely empty, they would be led to the large storage room in the back. If anyone came into the store before or while they were talking, they were to leave, and return no sooner than thirty minutes later. And of course, just two at a time.

Luck was with them. On the first try they were ushered to the back room. When the door cracked open, Andre and Karen heard not a sound. Behind a second door was the action—forty men and two women, crammed against the wall to listen to the speaker, who was standing in the middle.

"That's not the Messiah," Karen whispered to Leah.

"No. He's expected later. Most of these guys are from Elisha's old gang."

"Gang?" Andre questioned.

"Yes," Elisha said, "the man talking is Barabbas. I saved his life."

The subject was unjust laws. Dudley and Cindy monitored the proceedings from the ship, adding information, with their twist, to the stealth earplugs Andre, Karen, Michael, and Sarah wore.

Dudley began by pointing out that freedom was a modern phenomenon, and that in any era, only the educated are free. The ancient world had none of it. For example, before the Romans showed up, the Hebrews were not a free people. Past opportunists had left volumes of laws, all justified one way or another by the Torah, itself a product of ancient Pharisees taking advantage of their situation and, Dudley admitted, adding social stability to their mayhem and confusion. His first conclusion was that human beings could in no way ever handle their own ignorance. They threw out equations with unknowns to replace stories with laws that made absolutely no sense whatsoever.

"What kind of stories? And what kind of laws?" Sarah asked under her breath.

"What kind of laws?" Dudley retorted. "Well, there were laws that told them what they could not eat for breakfast. There were laws that told them what to wear, and whether or not, regardless of what was worn, it was respectable to go to town by yourself. There were laws that dictated how to cut their hair, to whom they could talk, and to what jobs their station in life allowed them to aspire.

"Generation after generation were even told that their own bodies didn't belong to them. Parents picked out the one person their children were allowed to kiss, usually for more land or better laundry service, which meant that whom you could get naked beside and have sex with was not a personal decision. Mom and dad insisted. Children obeyed. All, of course, a grand prostitution of God to serve the powers that be and manufactured stability needs.

"Even death did not end the restrictions. One's body was only allowed twenty-four hours of air space before it disappeared down under.

"To get the message across, again and again, once a week life came to a halt for everyone to sit around and agree to continue the farce, followed by one day a year that forced the entire country to sit around telling themselves, and others, what horrible sinful people they were. And that from a people who obeyed every law. Oy vey."

The Hebrews did get the last laugh, though. When one of their religious subsets renamed itself Christian, all the guilt stuff tagged along. Christians never knew what hit them. Just like in war, you don't hear the bullet that kills you.

Still, the Hebrews didn't complain. They knew no other way. The prison bars parents left behind were invisible. It takes a sharp mind, like Jesus, to feel them out.

And what good is a law without a stiff penalty, like blacklisted opportunities, social ostracism, and, of course, the always overused summary execution?

"I'll give you this," Dudley mouthed off to all before Andre instructed him to bug off, "limited resources do require social organization, and laws must prevent an individual from interfering with or harming another. But really ... a law-of-the-month club? Get bent."

Barabbas was a full-fledged hothead. He began with a prayer.

"In thee, O Lord, do we place our trust. Free us from the ungodly nation of Rome. Deliver us from the evil of unjust men. The meek shall join the Lord and the poor among men rejoice. The needy shall not be forgotten."

Life is an answer to a question. Barabbas hadn't gotten that far yet, for good reason. It takes the whole picture to focus a single day. The universe is not a thoughtless discharge. Not all space dust remains dust, and protoplasm is intended instability, so it's no surprise that metabolism, like Barabbas, is under zero obligation to legitimize what ends up somewhere between what can be and what should be.

"We will be revenged!" bellowed Barabbas. With a look around, he then lowered his voice, lest it be heard on the street. "The day of the Lord has arrived, and it is cruel with rage, fierce with anger, and ready for the desolation of the invaders. The Lord will punish Caiaphas and bury Pilate beside him.

"The Lord will also punish the world for its evil and the wicked for their iniquities. When we know a sinner, we must look upon him with horror and drive him from us. A righteous man turns away from evil, for the way of the weak may lead him astray. Our cause is just. We will arm ourselves this evening and attack tomorrow morning. The Messiah will assure victory!"

"Messiah?" Karen said, loud enough to attract attention. "Who? Where is he?"

Elisha had mentioned Andre and Karen to Barabbas, but since few women attended meetings, and none ever spoke, he looked worriedly in their direction. Only Roman women were so bold. Andre stepped in to draw attention and speak information meant for Karen.

"This Messiah you speak of," he said to Barabbas. "He is a leap of assumptions, is he not? Not one of your estimates is based on observation. Convictions are wonderful things, but reality speaks a different language. Reason is God's crowning gift to mankind. To abandon facts is to abandon freedom. If nothing you say can be proven true, then all is speculative. Call off your attack. Rethink your strategy."

Barabbas took the intrusion as a challenge to his authority.

"Well, will you look at that?" Michael said under his breath, as Barabbas raised his voice and stamped one foot, "the guy has an anger management problem. Remind me not to enlist in his army."

Dudley had the advantage of reviewing and remembering the masters of philosophy. He felt an obligation to secretly communicate to the group.

"Don't trust this guy. He's a time bomb who lights his own fuse. His emotions are preventing him from assessing the environment accurately, and the plan he is forcing down everyone's throat is corrupted by inaccurate data. I recommend you walk away."

"Andre," Cindy added to the mix, "you and I have known each other longer than anyone in this room. You know I can't deceive you without acknowledgment. I therefore suggest that the appropriate expression is that all profitable correction comes from a calm and peaceful mind. Barabbas has neither."

Dudley found no reason to soften his next entry: "Reality must govern thought to make truth the heart of life. Mediocre minds dismiss everything that reaches beyond their own understanding, and it would be a compliment to describe Barabbas as mediocre."

Cindy and Dudley knew Andre was not a fighter. Their words were needed to spur Andre on. He obliged, as Barabbas crossed his arms, prepared for confrontation.

"Barabbas," Andre began, direct and challenging, "your mood disturbs me. One needs to remain calm to properly identify with the environment. Self-possession leaves us at peace with others. In all of us there is surely a piece of divinity that owns no homage to those higher, or lower. Assemble a committee to evaluate options."

The blood on Barabbas's sandals never dried. If he wasn't killing, he was planning to do so. "I don't know who you are, Adam, but I sense a traitor. You are letting down God."

Andre had the advantage of Dudley tutoring in his ear. The certainty of his speech convinced all in attendance, except Barabbas. "Please don't misunderstand me, Barabbas. I do not attack fools, only foolishness. The windy stories of mysteries surrounding divinity are airy subtleties. Faith is a living thing. The Lord does not dwell in temples that men command. He lives in our hearts. His people are his temple. As rotten as the Romans are, they must also be helped."

Barabbas growled as he placed his hand on the butt of his sword and said, "It is the commandment of Moses, and the will of the one true God, that we make war on the Romans. You are an idiot, Adam. But worse than that, you have abandoned the will of God."

Karen tried to pull Andre back to sitting. She had to let go. Andre had stepped forward two paces.

"Again, please listen closely," he said. "Men never do evil so completely and cheerfully as when they follow religious convictions. If we begin with certainties, we end with doubts; but when we accept doubts, we end with certainties. Ask yourself this question: do you possess real faith, or are you just clinging to a set of beliefs?"

Barabbas marched across the room to stand in front of Andre, who tried not to smile at such a small brain trying to take him on.

"The law of Moses decrees it! The Torah guarantees it. Are you a coward? We will have nothing to do with little men like you."

There it was again. Not a day went by that somebody somewhere didn't call Andre a little man, only this time he took it well—which didn't mean he was about to let steam-brain off the hook or out of the frying pan, so to speak.

"The law of Moses," Andre said, sauntering back and forth as he spoke. "Do you mind if I add a few thoughts? And incidentally, if you ever combed your hair we would be the same height. Let me tell you what I think."

Michael leaned forward.

"Barabbas, don't say yes. Andr—I mean Adam will have us here all morning."

Barabbas didn't say yes. He just gestured to Andre to continue. Andre took a wide spin around him to the middle of the room.

Andre's next ten minutes of stall thanked them all for inviting him to the meeting. He commented on the weather and suggested that they consider hiring a fashion designer for next spring's robes.

Karen was not amused.

"Adam, my dear," she said with a totally false candy face, "there is no way you can delay until dusk. Get on with it. The Messiah is coming."

"All right, then," Andre announced, looking around. "Is anyone, or perhaps all of you, the Messiah we're expecting? What? No? Okay then . . . if he . . . or *she* . . ."—a word that triggered expressions from one corner to another—"comes in, do let us know, will you?"

Michael looked around at every door as if he was in charge of sentry duty. Andre waited until he had completed his inspection. Michael, getting into the hoax, flipped a hand in Andre's direction.

"Yes, now then, where were we? Oh yes, you were talking about the laws of Abraham, and the Torah, and the local tax, goat, and virgin collectors. Okay . . . laws . . . now don't get me wrong, the law is mankind's finest possession. Just laws make us free men in a free country. That is what you want, isn't it?"

"Why, of course," Barabbas barked, "and our Hebrew laws are just."

"Don't take this personally, fella," Andre said to Barabbas. "I mean, it's not like we're talking about your BO or anything."

"What's BO?"

"Oh, nothing, Barabbas, but would you mind stepping back a foot or two? Thank you."

Barabbas complied, and got a look from Sarah when he came within a foot of her.

"So here it is," said Andre. "We have a problem, and the only way to solve problems is to use reason, simple and pure. Every human need must be measured against the weight of multiple solutions."

"The solution," Barabbas exhorted, "is to strike swords between the ribs of Romans."

"Perhaps, but I must remind you that the entire ancient—I mean *modern*—world cries out for just laws, fair treatment, due process, and an end to tyranny. So, let's see if my friend Michaelosy has any news. Michaelosy, what is the score so far?"

"That would be Romans one hundred twenty-five battles won, and the world zero."

"So there you have it, Barabbas. You need a better plan, one that doesn't just swap one set of manipulating laws for another. Or you could attack tonight and die."

Sarah couldn't resist violating tradition by challenging Barabbas to match the wits of a woman. "Laws are more than just a set of rules written in funny language on parchment," she said, "something you recite and automatically assume justice will be done. This is true especially if the laws were written so long ago you can hardly read them, and you have no idea of the mental capacity of those who had nothing better to do that afternoon."

Karen stood next to Sarah to blow their minds good. With better diction and perfect sentences she added, "Laws, like our relationship with God, must be engraved on our hearts and practiced every minute of living, but not before we are certain they protect all equally and guarantee equal opportunity. The fact that your cutesy little group thinks you have all the answers you need, which aren't your answers in the first place, proves you have a long way to go."

The confused audience spent more time looking back and forth at one another than at the women.

Michael stepped in. "Your ambition and dedication are admirable. I also agree that just laws, when we find them, can't ever exist unless we are willing to dig in our heels, march through dust storms, and commit ourselves to suffer the fight for justice every day of our lives, for our neighbor as well as ourselves."

Michael sat down next to Andre, Sarah, and Karen. "That was fun, guys," he said. "We sure confused the hell out of them."

"We're not in Athens, Michael," Andre said. "And even if we were, their golden age has already passed, thanks again to the Romans. What troublemakers."

Karen never lost track. With a timbre as soothing as a mother feeding her child and as firm as Sunday's sermon, she demanded: "Where's the Messiah?"

From the back of the room a small voice was heard, not seen. "The Romans are back on the streets. I just got word. He's not coming."

"Where can we find him?" asked Karen.

The room went quiet. An outspoken woman who insisted on knowing the location of a wanted revolutionary? That spelled trouble. Spies were everywhere.

Andre, Sarah, and Michael all sat forward, placed one hand under their chins to hold up their gloating smiles, and looked over to Karen.

"All right ... all right. Tomorrow's another day," she said.

21

Last Lunch

Andre stood at the head of the table, arms stretched wide, head tilted back, eyes searching the heavens. "Dear Lord, we are gathered here in your presence to give thanks for the blessings of life, the love we share, and the beauty of Janie's booty."

Janie responded to the compliment by standing up and taking a bow. Andre continued: "But most of all, we your humble servants do lift our hearts to honor the greatest present of all—granulated sugar."

With that Andre tilted the chalice he held high and sprinkled glistening granules over four stacked pieces of French toast on his plate.

To complete the ceremony, he sat down, bent over his plate, and slurped a syrupy mix. Then Michael stood for the day's second benediction.

"Our mission has succeeded where so many have failed. Thanks to sports bras, athletic supporters, and the Grotto, we have not succumbed to the drag of lassitude or the long yawn of routine."

Karen had crossed her arms over her chest. She didn't budge an iota until Michael stopped talking.

"Are you two quite finished?" she said, sweet-temperedly scolding.

"Actually, yes," said Michael in a scruffy old-man's voice. "We are quite finished with quite a morning. If the real Jesus does exist, the least we can do is appeal to his sense of humor."

Karen was bubbling so much joy that nothing could tame her mood. Conversations recorded on the surface were played back to the group. Elisha was heard discussing a meeting on the side of a hill. The Messiah was the reason everyone was sneaking out of town. They were expecting a sermon at noon.

"Every time we come down here we have to walk farther," Andre said, shuffling in his sandals.

"We're lucky we got this close," Michael said, taking a deep breath of real air. "Half the country is headed for Jerusalem. There are camps everywhere."

Michael stopped to look around at rolling hills topped with vegetation surrounded by dazzling desert minerals. "It's funny," he said, "it's not that I don't feel right inside the ship, it's just that being on earth like this feels better."

"It's a mistake to sanctify emotions," Andre cautioned. "The opposite also applies; many aspects of life that don't feel right actually are."

Karen and Sarah locked elbows and lagged behind the men. That much fit the times; the men led the way, set the tone, and spent hours debating grandiose philosophic questions like "Just which shellfish are, and which are not, forbidden by God?" or "Which shade of depressing black serves God's purpose best?" or "Did Abraham really have a harem?"

The group actually had great respect for the Jewish religion and culture. Yes, their overpriced manuscripts did begin with burning bushes, rock slabs, and an ocean cut in half, but they were excusable. Lightning and spontaneous combustion start thousands of fires every day, climbing too high can cause altitude sickness, and Egyptian hieroglyphs do tell a story about a general who waited too long to pursue escaping Hebrews. A full month later, when he finally got it together, the rainy season had begun, and the dry riverbed had turned to quicksand interrupted by rapids.

Similar historical documentation points out that the oldest Egyptian child got the lowest bunk, the one that would be smothered in natural gas, methane, and volcanic burps when a nearby vent blew. Livestock outside would also die. Locusts can swarm and eat everything in sight anywhere on earth. It only takes one or two anecdotes to put a story together, especially when the teller ends up as the boss.

The Hebrews of Jerusalem, and those who followed, were at least honest with themselves and the rest of the world. The religion they constructed was man-made, and they admitted it. A typical service might be interrupted by every member arguing with whoever sat next to them, debating particulars, setting precedents, and not agreeing on dessert. The rabbi's job was to provide background music, hopefully on key, and muddle through vague suggestions from quotes void of direct interpretation, but mostly it was to act as umpire before getting invited to another dinner. Being well fed was the best part of the job.

"Less talk and more thinking—that's what I say," Andre volunteered as they passed a group debating an earth-shattering revelation, or so he assumed from fingers that kept pointing to the heavens. Everyone claimed a second opinion. No one ever produced one.

"Why bother?" was Michael's conclusion. The only full sentence he could make out insisted that "sunset" be used to begin prayers instead of "dusk." *Really?*

Information entered into computers remains long after it loses validity. The Torah had the same problem. Its input should have expired. Stacks remained long after making them tinder would have served a higher purpose, especially since no speck of evidence, thread of reality, or rational conclusion accompanied them.

"I was just thinking," Michael said, trying to add amusement to a strange day and a long, dry stroll. "What if—just what if, mind you—the Babylonian story that the Hebrews copied was written differently? What if a thousand years ago, when one guy, or maybe a gal in reverse drag, sat down and recorded the thought of the day—creation—what if he had left another story, one that got the job done in just four days, followed by God resting on the fifth, and maybe *with* a fifth. Who would know?"

Andre smiled at the implication. "So, instead of a seven-day week, there would be shorter five-day ones. Yes, I like that idea. Instead of just fifty-two Sundays per year, you'd have seventy-three. Less work, more play. And yes, it's totally arbitrary. I vote to eliminate Tuesday and Wednesday. They are the hardest to spell."

Karen and Sarah also fit the bill that morning. They side-tracked the "Is she God?" or "Is he not God?" question for more pressing curiosities, like "What kind of woman did Jesus like? Do you think he has a favorite dessert? I wish I had his number."

Karen popped her eyebrows, looking over to Sarah. "Do you think he will ask us to go for a walk?"

"We can hope," said Sarah, pulled away by her own fantasy.

"The other day he looked so cute. I would *so* do him," Karen said, breathing deeply.

"Oh, yes," Sarah replied, "me too." She lowered her voice. "Don't say anything to the guys."

"My lips are sealed. The ones above my waist, that is."

Andre and Michael looked back but didn't understand why laughter was all they heard.

"Shh," Karen said. "The boys are listening."

"So what?" Sarah said, "Yesterday I overheard them whispering nasty low-downs about Mary Magdalene. They are just as eager to know how they stand up, pun intended, to Jesus sex. Today we have an opportunity to set history."

Karen interrupted the laughter for a final zinger. "We will call our published memoirs *Jesus, X-rated and Love Tested*."

No sound pleased Andre and Michael more than their ladies having a good time. They were just never sure if they were laughing *about* them, *at* them, or at their next plan to trip them up.

"Perhaps," Michael said, looking back slyly, "we shouldn't tell the gals what we're talking about. They're too good at turning things around. Whoso would be a man must also be a nonconformist ... and really good at lying." He also added that the book that talks about the road coming up to greet you isn't correct. In Judea, the road just keeps stretching out in front of you, endlessly.

"To fill the time, I have another philosophical question for you, Andre," said Michael, tongue in cheek.

"Shoot."

"Everyone knows the character of Mr. Spock from the original *Star Trek*, which was copied twenty times all the way up to our era. Well, here's my question. If Spock were half Vulcan, with no emotions or feelings, and half human, yahoo and all, does that mean he only got half an orgasm?"

"Interesting question," Andre said, pretending to be overwhelmed by the shattering revelation. "We must convene another ecumenical council and put it to a vote."

"Of course, it would take six months to make a decision," Michael said most seriously, "and there would be a ninety-nine percent probability that they would be wrong."

"On the other hand," said Andre, "it would make the front page and draw a crowd, and we would have an infallible answer on Spock's sex life."

"And using up time would leave them with fewer hours to mess up the world," Michael concluded, sticking out his chest, proud of himself.

It was the ladies' turn to puzzle about what Michael and Andre were laughing about.

"Did you catch any of that?" asked Sarah.

"No," replied Karen, "but I'll bet it has something to do with sex."

"And that's okay … right?" Sarah asked hesitantly.

"That depends on what's in it for us. We know what's in it for *them*."

"Do you think they'll ever get wise to us?"

"Not a chance," said Karen. "Besides, they just want to have fun. Let's catch up, make it a party."

Karen asked Michael what was up. Michael lied. Andre asked Sarah what the two of them had been talking about. She lied. Two dull minutes followed. The road did not get shorter.

"I've got a story," Michael said, interrupting boredom.

"You're on," said Karen with a one-handed "get onstage" introduction.

"It's the year 1531. Copernicus is walking down the street with Pope Clement. The scientific revolution has not yet begun. Copernicus's *On the Revolutions of the Heavenly Spheres* has not yet been published, and it's one hundred years before Galileo is sentenced to life in his own prison, where he is forbidden to think and dies depressed."

"And," Andre interrupted, "two thousand years after Aristarchus of Samos proved the same thing."

"Yes, Andre, we know all that," said Karen, shutting him up.

"Well, anyway," Michael proceeded, "Copernicus turns to Giulio Clement and asks, 'Do you think the earth might just be round?'

"'That does not sound right, that doesn't feel right,' says the pope. 'Everyone knows the earth is flat and sits on the back of a giant turtle, and the flaming ball of fire we call the sun moves to the other side of a giant blue turtle shell that covers the sky, with cracks in it that let light shine through as stars. You're crazy, Nicolaus Copernicus.'"

Michael had no punch line, just more story.

"'But Giulio, look up at the sun. It is round. The moon is round. When we are offshore fishing, the tops of mountains are all that we see, because the curved ocean gets in the way.'

"'Absolutely not,' is the pope's insistence, under penalty of death."

Michael lifted a palm to bring Andre on.

"My guess, Karen, is that Michael is prepping you for an experience today that may not sound right or feel right, but will be right."

"Yeah, yeah," Karen said. "I'm not six years old. I know what might be, and I was hoping for a parable or two by now."

"Then I've got one for you," smiled Andre. "The pope..."

"Again, the pope," complained Karen with a twisted face.

"As I was saying, the pope, Muhammad, Buddha, and Jesus were walking down the street. The richest man on earth walks up and offers a billion dollars to the one who can get to heaven first. The pope rushes to his cathedral and downs one communion host after another. Muhammad makes a beeline to the nearest mosque to have himself proclaimed above all others on earth. Buddha joins a retreat, plops down on a cushion, and fasts for the rest of the day."

"And Jesus?" Sarah asked, flippant and frowning.

"Jesus joins a bunch of kids playing in a sandbox at the nearest preschool and says, 'The shortest way to get to heaven is to make heaven on earth.'"

They were the last to arrive. Over five hundred had gathered to hear the Messiah, who was still nowhere in sight.

"It's a shame mankind measures greatness by pageantry," Michael droned slowly.

The only space available was at the back. Andre filled the time with ruminations about earth's past and Judea's future.

"For better and for worse," he began, "human behavior is infinitely malleable. Civilizations are propelled along by reciprocating thrusts of cultural evolution and organized violence. Cultural changes end up the statistical product of the separate behavioral responses of large numbers of human beings, each coping the best they can with social existence within limited environmental offerings."

The thoughts, and the sight of so many confused and searching people, sobered Karen.

"Yes," she agreed, nodding her head and also sinking lower. "Someone must make sense out of all the nonsense. Goodness is a thing that must be done. No one is an island. We are all living rooms, like those stretched out here, looking for answers, dreaming of hope. But I disagree, Andre: the influence of a single individual can induce improved social behavior."

Sarah, the down-to-earth anthropologist, stood next to mouth her piece. "Mankind is not a dropping. You can pick your friends but not your atoms, and greed strains as a given. That cultural evolution you talk about... well, history confirms that beyond a specified brazenness, biologic evolution pulls cultural evolution back to itself. Human nature is stubborn. We breathe prejudiced appetites that cannot be denied without a cost."

"I would say," Michael added, sounding as sincere and intelligent as he was, "that freedom to live one's own life is requirement number one, and something no one sitting here is able to enjoy. But neither do the Romans, for that matter. Culture is the enemy. Holding on to your very own because it's the only life raft your parents used doesn't make sense when the luxury liner of truth is standing by."

"Nice metaphor, Michael," Andre conceded with a bow. "With your indulgence, I will repeat that all biologic necessities must be made not only respectable, but available on request—for example, ladies, tonight after dinner."

Karen and Sarah looked at each other knowing they held trump. Sarah couldn't resist.

"I suppose that might be fun, but you guys should know that Karen and I haven't ruled out the possibility of inviting Jesus to the ship for a nightcap. We reserved the Grotto before we left."

The crowd hushed. It was time.

"That's him!" blurted Karen. "The same little guy we met at the meeting. He must be Jesus!"

His speech was clear, the air silent. "Shine, Judea!" he began. "The light has come. The glory of God is upon us. He asks for steadfast love and not sacrifice. He brings knowledge and has no need for burnt offerings.

"Prepare thee the way of the Lord. Deliverance is at hand!"

The entire hill prayed "amen" to the clouds. The Messiah resumed when silence returned.

"Do not laden your heart with worry about what to eat or drink. The bread of God gives life to the world. Is there a man among you who by worry can add one minute to his span of life? The kingdom of God is at hand. All will be cared for.

"As you judge, so you will be judged. Their measure will also be yours. Therefore, forgive your enemies as they forgive you. No man of God provides reasons to hate others. All trails lead to love. I am the way to salvation, the unity of nature and souls."

The Messiah took several steps forward, and though fifty meters away, clearly looked Andre in the eye. "Every violation of truth violates the will of God, makes us less than what we are, and separates us from what we must be. When dealing with truth we are immortal.

"We must restrain ill-bred passion, unjust prejudice, and evil tendencies. Life is a dream within a dream. To understand it is wiser than to condemn it. To study the world is better than to shun it. To use the world for good is nobler than to abuse it. To love the public, to seek universal advancement, and to promote the interests of the entire world are the height of goodness. We shall do no less!"

Amens were not enough—open-mouthed cheering filled the sky. Then there was a lull. No one knew if he was finished.

Michael filled the gap. "You know, all that's just fine, but he sounds like a pacifist to me."

Michael got a chance to expand on his opinion when the Messiah resumed speaking: "Blessed are the meek; for they shall inherit the earth."

"As long as they run faster than the Romans."

"Blessed are they who do hunger and thirst after righteousness, for they shall be filled."

"Unless they die of malnutrition, like Muhammad's wife."

"Blessed are the merciful," proclaimed Jesus, "for they shall obtain mercy."

"In a few thousand years … maybe," quipped Michael.

"Blessed are the poor in spirit; for theirs is the kingdom of heaven."

"Is he saying that until then we can expect to be depressed?"

"Blessed are the pure of heart; for they shall see God."

"He left out schizophrenics."

"Refuse profane tales and old wives' fables. Be swift to hear, slow to speak, slow to wrath. God loveth a cheerful giver. By the grace of God, we are who we are. I have learned, in whatsoever state I am, therewith to be content."

"Content," Michael said. "I should say so. He gets free food, carried around, and waited on hand and foot."

"Beware of false prophets," continued Jesus, "which come to you in sheep's clothing, but inwardly they are raving wolves."

"Now that one," Michael said with a thumbs-up sign, "is a winner."

"That's enough, Michael," Karen said sternly. "Are you with him or against him?"

"You know I'm with him, Karen. I'm just not sure assembling targets for Roman soldiers is the best means to the desired end, and we still don't know if he is who you want him to be."

The outing was a grand success, if not bizarre. When the Messiah finished, two carts suddenly showed up. One was packed four feet high with loaves of bread; every mouth was fed, with one slight problem—over a dozen in attendance developed abdominal pain. Those with aching bellies got in line for the second cart, which held six wine barrels. That's when it got weird. There was no wine, which was great for the gluten-sensitive stomachaches. A rumor circulated that the Messiah had turned the wine to water.

"Now that does make sense," said Michael enthusiastically. "I never bought the story about Jesus the wholesale liquor salesman. Why would he turn something healthy like water into something that damages bodies?"

Someone said they thought they heard drums. Those in attendance looked around uneasily, and then dispersed in multiple directions in legal pairs. Elisha and a dozen of his comrades surrounded their Messiah on the top of the hill. Karen, Andre, Michael, and Sarah made their way to them.

The four stood respectfully off to the side. The most brilliant enigma in history breathed before them. Karen was speechless. The Messiah was not. He noticed the gang standing side by side. He walked over.

His pace was slow, his manner calm. For ten soothing seconds he looked face-to-face at them, smiling; he was greeted by grins brighter than Judea deserved. He approached Karen, lightly touched her robe, and said, "Nice material, and I love the stitching. Who's your tailor?"

The ice was broken. Michael played it up. "Mention Michaelosy you'll get such a deal."

"Are you who we think you are?" asked Sarah timidly.

Again, a pause, and glad looks for all: "Are any of us who we think we are?"

"All right," said Andre, respectful yet probing. "Would you mind answering a few questions?"

Elisha and two others nervously looked around and then stepped forward.

"Messiah, we must go. Romans have been sighted."

The Messiah began to turn away, saying, "I'm meeting friends for dinner, and the sun is not a safe place for Hebrews. We can talk another time. You must excuse me."

"Before you go," Andre pressed, "we've come a long way … and …"

"I know, everyone is talking about the two smart guys and independent women who suddenly showed up, with perfect teeth and healthy bodies. You must be careful. You are more obvious than you think."

"Yes," said Karen, "and we thank you for that, but we must know."

Karen, without thinking, dropped to her knees before the Messiah. He then did the same in front of her. "Is the view better down here, my dear?" he asked. "Otherwise, I see no reason to put our fragile knees through the ordeal. If you rise, I will answer one question from each of you. Then I really must go."

After helping Karen up, the Messiah approached Andre, and to his surprise reached out to hold both of his hands. "Adam … if that's your name today … what's on your mind?"

Andre flushed at the opportunity, if indeed it was so, to ask anything he wanted to know about the universe, so he did. "No mass energy equation has ever balanced speed–time variables. Is eternity a closed-system self-collecting perpetuation? And why are photons that leave not the same particles that return?"

There was no hesitation, just a more satisfying smile. "Are you the same person today that you were yesterday?"

"No," answered Andre.

"Then why would you expect energy, or energy quantums, to behave any differently? Every dot of time owns its own signature. Every star leaves itself behind."

"Okay," Andre said, becoming convinced, "but equations build from time up, that alters itself as I calculate."

"Not if you're calculating outside of time."

No one had ever before jumbled Andre's brain. He needed a moment to himself. He retreated, contemplating implications, and he already had Dudley and Cindy running numbers on the bridge.

Michael was the kind of guy who left no corner unturned. He was the first Junior Explorer Scout in his troop to circumnavigate the planet in a hang glider. His solemn manner let everyone know he was not, as yet, convinced.

"I never stop wondering what's ahead, down the street, over the next mountain," he said to Jesus. "No matter where I go there is always another horizon. Does existence span unlimited space? Are there multiple universes?"

The Messiah grinned less, took on a professorial tone, and answered in a manner that shared Michael's inquisitiveness. "I expected that question, and I do understand the dilemma. You see, neither the answer 'yes' nor the answer 'no' can be integrated into reality. Let me put it this way: If you did, say, leave this universe, travel great distances that you would have no way of measuring, and then discover another universe, how would you know that it was not the same one you left?"

"We wouldn't know," answered Michael.

"And nothing beyond knowledge exists, so therefore there is no other universe. And anyway, who needs one?"

Sarah stepped up. "We feed our bodies. We nourish our souls. What keeps the universe going?"

"That's an easy one," the Messiah said, looking into her eyes almost wantonly. "The purest and most rewarding of all sensations powers the engine of existence. Its accomplishments are trans-dimensional—it is love that transcends. You might think of a kiss, or a hug, or a family get-together as a puny event compared to endless time, but without these, time might come to an end. You are not letting God down. You are just warming up. Evolution is a thaw."

Elisha, with ten more just as tense behind him, interrupted. "Again, Romans are on the way. You have attracted a lot of attention. Pilate is getting nervous. He fears mobs. We must go!"

The Messiah heeded Elisha's warning. He turned to go. Karen was beside herself as never before. She jogged up next to the Messiah. Jesus looked over, pleased with the company.

"Please, one more question," she begged.

The Messiah, who appeared barely thirty years old, slowed his gait. "We can talk while we walk."

"All right ... Okay ..." Karen stammered, trying to get it together. "We walk, we talk, we learn, and, yes, we make love and share love ... and it's wonderful ... don't get me wrong ... but it's just that later on it's like something is missing, something very important that we don't grasp. What is 'the answer'?"

The Messiah tightened his lips, smile included, and almost appeared bewildered himself, but the question was not new to him. "If I were Socrates, and we had more time, I would draw one question after another out of you until the cupboard was bare and you saw the light. But life's moments are limited. So I'll repeat words you've already heard: 'From the day we arrive on the planet, and blinking step into the sun, there's more to be seen that can ever be seen, more to be done than can ever be done.' The entire universe is a wheel of fortune. It's a lift of faith. It's a band of hope. Your existence is eternal. Your home is the entire universe."

Andre said, "We know the song, but it's not what Karen wants to know."

"Or is it?" replied Jesus.

"How do you mean?" pressed Andre.

"Just this, plain and simple," replied Jesus. "You want the ultimate answer? Here it is. Life is the answer. All you need is love. And incidentally, I came up with it first."

That second, that hour, that day—was complete in ways the four never dreamed possible, and there was more. Urged by Elisha, the Messiah hurried away. Twenty yards down the hill he turned back and called to Andre: "Just so you know, Andre, if it's crispy enough, all you need is powdered sugar. And life, like French toast, doesn't require syrup."

22

Death

We paint pretty pictures and speak fancy words, but death remains horrible. The good news—it ends. The awakening following death cancels it out and adds sunshine.

The next day breakfast in the ballroom was a disaster. There was no joy in Shipville. It was a ghastly sight. Rows of crucified Hebrews stretched down one hill and up the next. Face after face was captured for all to see. Behind Karen and the gang, the entire crew sat eyeing full-screen shots sent from the surface. There were tears.

It was a tragedy of such proportion that sanity itself needed to be questioned. It accomplished nothing. It spoiled everything.

Life best played appreciates one sensational moment after another. Life played anyway, or life played every which way, doesn't escape a slap in the face when you least expect it. Hank and Sheila felt it first. They drew the graveyard shift on the bridge.

The action Hank and Sheila witnessed was frightening. When the soldiers broke down the door, Elisha sprang to defend the Messiah. One minute and two sword thrusts later, Elisha slumped against the wall. His eyes were wide open. He didn't want to go. His last sight was the image of Romans leading the Messiah away. For Elisha, violence extinguished hope and life in ten seconds.

Hank and Sheila kept the news to themselves. Through the night, Dudley and Cindy constantly stood by. They were curiously void of comment but did acknowledge the request to say nothing until the crew awoke, well rested.

The drone camera projected one crucified face after another. Each gasped for breath and moaned bleeding agony. One caught Dudley's attention. He maneuvered the drone for a close-up.

When life sours, human beings have a bad habit of speeding up just when they should slow down. Karen leapt out of her seat. Above the crucified young man was a scrap-wood sign. It read "King of the Jews." Karen didn't bother to look back as she made her way to the door.

"Andre, Michael, and Sarah … to the shuttle!"

"Karen," Andre asked as he got up, "don't we need a plan first … or perhaps … I don't know … reasonable cause?"

Karen stopped at the door and looked directly back at Andre. She pleasantly reminded her friends how resolute she was about the issue. "Andre, several options have been suggested. I am certain that on the way down we'll all agree on the best one."

"Well, now," Andre said, conceding minimal resistance, "I'm sure we will all agree. I'm just not certain it will be the right thing to do."

"Move over," Michael said to Karen when they got to the shuttle. "I'll drive. You and Andre sit in the back. You can review strategy on the way down."

"Did you pick up the medicine locker?" Karen asked.

"Yes," answered Andre immediately, still off balance, "and everything else you asked for."

And so began the boldest rescue plan in human history. Karen was overwhelmed by sympathy, convinced of need, and determined to have her way.

Andre was unable to define parameters. He began by pointing out that their rescue mission, in addition to an unspecified *whom*, had problems defining just what they were rescuing "may be" from. They may be, he pointed out, actually sabotaging a rescue plan already in progress, the end of which could have ramifications they were unable to estimate.

"The Czar we get may be worse than the Czar we got."

Karen successfully stumped him on the point. "There is nothing in God's universe that is purposeless, trivial, or unnecessary. Of all the dates, times, and events of history, only now do we have the opportunity, motive, and means save planet earth, and ourselves."

Sarah turned around to remind Andre that the same combination finds perpetrators guilty beyond a shadow of a doubt. So, therefore, they were doing the opposite, the *right* thing. She was brief and direct, and finished her sentence facing Michael at her side, whose face declined resistance as Sarah said, "If in the course of human life, one or many have the opportunity to help others, or even a single soul, the end result confirms its worth."

Michael listened attentively but did not stand down. "Sarah, your construction of logical steps is sound, but each level rests on assumptions and implications therefrom. It is also not uncommon in the course of human history for an act, even if properly motivated, to have just the opposite effect. In 1938, Neville Chamberlain signed a peace treaty to avert war with Germany."

"It also," added Andre, "ignores the adage, 'God works in mysterious ways.'"

Karen jumped on that one with devastating success. "Now look who's talking wishy-washy! Allow me to point out that 'God works in mysterious ways' is a bandage to hide confusion. The implication of accepting it is that God deliberately encourages events defeating ambition, corrupting happiness, and staining history. You're proposing that God does evil in order to get to good, a twisted strategy that allowed Neville's nemesis to slaughter millions and to order just as many to march off, or fly away, to kill others. Your suggestion betrays warped logic."

The shuttle went quiet. Neither Michael nor Andre had a handle on a single concept that didn't sound like a truck shifting into reverse to get up a mountain. The issue was dropped.

"I have a question," Andre said, less pressing. "Why is Dudley here? We have plenty of drone support. Why do we need him?"

Karen gave Andre the evil eye, then scowled to communicate irritability, but just as quickly realized that any message communicating emotional excess would alert Andre to the heightened probability of logic contamination. With substantial effort and some delay, she morphed her expression into one that was more pleasant.

"I want to minimize the suffering Jesus is going through," she said. "You no doubt have noticed that Dudley is dressed as a Roman general. We may need him to run off families mourning or soldiers standing guard."

Michael didn't buy it. "He is also capable of defeating the entire Roman army single-handedly. Don't forget that we have a deal. No overt action will be taken unless all four of us agree on the use of force."

"I know you think I'm cockeyed," said Karen. "Give me a chance. This will work."

As the shuttle entered the earth's atmosphere, everyone looked out the window at the most beautiful sight in the entire universe—Mother Earth, greener and bluer than ever.

"Listen up, everyone," Karen said, projecting to the front seat and interrupting a look Michael had for Sarah, "just so we are clear about step one … we get to Jesus as fast as we can, administer three micro-drone morphine analogues …"

"With respiratory stimulant," added Andre.

"Yes, of course, Andre. His pain will disappear and respiration will strengthen. His suffering will be minimized."

Michael couldn't resist sarcasm. "And what about all the other suffering human beings nailed to planks down there? Do we not care about them? Do we just leave them? How far are we supposed to go to feel good about ourselves?"

"And," Andre added, just as challenging, "do we include a respiratory stimulant to prolong their tortured goodbyes, or do we take them out with one wallop of pure heroin, which is arguably more humane? And you did not ask for a vote on the matter? You just issued an order."

"Okay, then," Karen said, standing down. "You're right. I vote we drug Jesus and send the rest on their way with an overdose. All those opposed, wiggle your noses."

Karen didn't bother to look around. She knew no one riding along had difficulty expressing themselves.

"Alrighty, then," Karen proceeded. "Step two is to substitute a lifeless organic doppelganger, and whisk Jesus away."

Step two raised six eyebrows. Andre asked Karen just how she planned to do it. Karen unconvincingly reminded them that clearing the road would be Dudley's job. She was also counting on him and just half a dozen drones to somehow manufacture a sandstorm to hide their tracks, and or perhaps a fog bank, the first the desert had ever seen.

Michael and Andre looked at each other like two astronauts taking off on their first mission to space, not at all certain where they would land.

Jerusalem came into view. Dudley had programmed the shuttle in the direction of the cross Karen pointed to on the ship.

"No, Michael, no!" Karen insisted when Michael began their descent. "Not here. I want to get closer."

"All right, all right," Michael said, followed by a phrase he otherwise had no use for: "Keep your pants on."

Less than one minute later, a compromise was reached.

"Karen, this is it," said Michael. "We'll wait sixty seconds for the drones to tell us the coast is clear, and as soon as we disembark, the shuttle will move to a more isolated position."

"Agreed," Karen said. "Then we run to Jesus."

"Not agreed," said Andre. "Running adds suspicion of culpability. We'll walk slowly, mourning our loss, just like everyone else. And tears will make it more believable."

Sarah was already depressed. "That won't be a problem, Andre."

On the ground, Karen's steps were slow but her strides long. The three lagging behind added an occasional skip. When the last hill was navigated, the cruel spectacle came into view. Karen waxed philosophic and slowed her pace to fit in. "I still don't get it. I know how human brains work. We respond with sympathy for those we witness suffering.

It's almost like we are sharing their pain. But look at those Romans. They're laughing and making jokes about the funny naked Hebrews who are too stupid to worship Zeus."

"I can answer that one," said Sarah, the anthropologist. "In our original behavioral settings, over eight million years of primate survival, when a male or female bully abused others, he or she had to do so in front of everyone. The entire troop would see it and reject the behavior. And if looks didn't put an end to it, a half dozen, or even the entire pack, would end it with clubs, possibly for good. Our lineage carries an innate sense of justice and fair play for all. But civilization changed the input parameters. Having collections of over thirty human beings separates those in authority from those governed. Caesar, Pilate, and the Pharisees can sit home eating grapes. They don't give a damn about the common man.

"And violence? Its appetite always grows and is never sated. The soldiers see so much of it that it becomes amusement. All the more reason never to let images of any violence, revenge included, justified or not, into our brains. What we allow ourselves to see can make us just as sick as eating rotten meat."

Dudley pointed to the cross Karen was looking for. She lost control, teared effusively, and ran forward. The possibility had been expected. Andre nodded to Dudley, who followed orders. He ran next to Karen to slow her down. She stopped, clutched Dudley, brought him close, and cried on his shoulder. As a therapist she rarely agreed with catharsis. That day she had no choice.

Dudley did his best to emulate human sympathy. He lowered his head, put it in contact with Karen's, and placed both arms around her. "Don't worry," he said. "It will be all right. We can fix this." Then with a jerk, he lifted his head up and responded to internal communication transmitted from drones, through Cindy onboard and back to him. "Yes, I see. Thank you, Cindy." Then he turned to the slowly advancing group. "Karen, there is no need to rush. Pulse and respirations have ceased. A life just ended. His pain is over."

Everyone heard. Everyone stopped. Michael, Andre, and Sarah all needed a moment. The men looked away at the sky. Karen moved over to embrace Sarah.

Andre and Michael weren't sure what pierced their hearts and dropped them to their knees. Was it the flagrant stupidity of their race, the sight of matter so preciously cared for and then wasted, or the earthly loss of an eternal spirit?

During the last hundred yards of their walk, sand was pushed forward by feet that had lost the desire to do their best. No one spoke. Everyone sniffled, and it was easier not to look one another in the face. It was too much to endure, but they were together. They were always there for one another, which turned into a thought most strange and yet in every way appropriate.

Michael, Karen, Sarah, and Andre were thrown together on a flight to everywhere and every time, where they faced the best and worst of humanity and the gifts and instabilities of God's grand universe. They did it together, as a family, which never wanted to say goodbye to a single member.

At the foot of the cross, no one raised their eyes. They were not ready. The four held hands boy-girl, looked into each other's eyes, saw only love, and then opened the circle to look.

Tears made their way to the ground. It was worse than they'd expected. Brutality had left marks. The face slumped over had a fractured orbital rim, a broken nose, and a scalp laceration that had crusted blood all the way to the chin.

Karen placed both arms around Andre's neck and collapsed. He held her up.

"Death," he pronounced with genuine conviction, "dies. It is already no longer. It has passed. The other side of death is God, and what more grand, what more joyful, what more loving feeling can there be?"

"And," Michael added when he and Sarah joined the two, making a tepee of heads sharing the moment, "death is also the birth of new life. We just don't hear the baby crying."

Sarah was the first to firm up. "We also know that this mortal dimension is only one of two vehicles that carry us through eternity. There is joy on both sides."

"Thanks, guys," said Karen. "You are absolutely right. And please do me a favor—none of you ever leave me."

Silence is soothing, but there was none. From all directions, dozens of bereaved family members, wives, parents and children included, were heard sobbing. Many had fallen to the ground overcome with remorse. Their loved ones groaned between screams of agony.

Andre looked in both directions. "Karen, we can help them."

"Yes, of course. Dudley, please do the honors."

A stealth drone darted pain relief combined with five minutes of respiratory support. Each suffering head raised itself on its own power, looked around at the blue bliss of earth, smiled at each relative, said goodbye, and then ended with a puckered kiss for each.

"The soldiers are beginning to confirm deaths at the other end of the line," said Michael, looking around. "They don't want to be late for lunch."

"I see," said Karen. "The relatives of the deceased will then be free to take the departed to the family tombs. Let the day play itself out. We'll sneak into the crypt tomorrow morning. There will be more than enough stem cells for us to bring Jesus back to life anytime we want."

23

The Loss

Karen, Andre, Michael, and Sarah dragged themselves back to the shuttle. The crew joined them for lunch in the grand ballroom. The motions of family dining were there, but it was frivolous. In silence all prayed for the loss. What hurt the most was knowing that it was a matter of ignorance. Of all the tragedies that beset mankind, the worst are those that persecute needlessly.

Crew members who had been thinking about getting back to painting, or sculpting, or that book they'd never started, sat up after lunch and went straight to it. Something must be made of life.

Brad worked on his golf game, which he considered an art form on the level of sculpting. Janie made life more colorful by designing new clothes. Karen and Sarah watched family movies. Both relived memories of mom and dad, and how much Jesus meant to both.

Andre was, in his way, also an artist. He took both his creations, Cindy and Dudley, for a walk. They amused him by insisting they were the ones taking *him* for the walk.

Dinner was morose. Conversation was infrequent. There was exhaustion beyond what the day had put them through. Everyone was haunted by what they too must go through someday, saying goodbye to life as they knew it.

Stories helped. Sarah told one about her grandmother, who lived to see her graduate from college. When Sarah was a child, grandma would sit on the porch every night and welcome all comers. She no longer hiked the hills, teased her husband, or traveled the galaxy; she didn't have to. Sarah would watch her body animate and her eyes sparkle just talking about her life.

Her favorite story was the day grandma met grandpa at the top of Mount Sneffels. He'd hiked up the north trail. She preferred the south. They shared the night's campsite. After sunrise on Lower Blue Lake, they left on her trail. Before leaving, granddad picked up a small rock, wrote the date on it, and stuck it in his pocket. Fifty more rocks from as many mountains lined grandma's flower garden.

When Sarah asked her why all the rocks were there, grandma said that they were the perfect size for scaring away rabbits eating her petunias. She also brought every one of them back to its special place. When she walked around the garden, she was never lonely.

Brad talked about his grandfather, of whom he was the spitting image. The man knew more people than the mayor, and got more respect. Everyone considered grampa's adventurism foolhardy, especially after he disappeared exploring the outer reaches of the galaxy. Only half of the territory had been searched for survivors.

Brad had had many conversations with Andre about assembling a fleet of drones, which he could afford to do, to search the remaining half. He was convinced his grandfather was still alive. His last transmission mentioned systems failure, but also a one hundred percent probability of making a safe landing on a blue-green planet.

Michael shared stories about riding the Canadian rapids with his dad. Janie recalled the joy of helping her grandmother decorate for parties. Karen had many stories, which of course included the most exquisite and expensive resorts on earth, which she took for granted, something her grandmother never did.

Andre, as usual, was the strangest of them all. He never knew his grandparents. His mom died young, and his dad was as obsessed with science as he was. But Andre did have his own little heaven, underground, in a lab, talking to the entity that made him what he turned out to be, minus all the human stuff that Karen added later.

Andre's nostalgic blather turned heads. He actually said he missed the peace and quiet of hiding out with Cindy, who then was just a computer. The world they constructed could be anything they wanted it to be. Needless to say, Karen reminded Andre that his world had everything a computer dreamed of—and that was all.

The evening ended on such a peculiar note that no one ever mentioned it again. A shuttle took them back to the surface. The Earth had rotated. North America was facing them. Each member of the executive staff mounted a sky sled to visit and hover over their hometown. There was no sign of human activity—no buildings, no roads—only tree-filled woods and a hidden Indian village or two. But they saw the same rivers, lakes, and mountains that they had grown up around, that were just as they remembered them.

That night Andre, Karen, Michael, Brad, Janie, and Sarah each fell asleep alone.

"It's time," Karen said the next morning at breakfast.

No one ventured a contrary viewpoint. Yes, they knew that the only way never to miss someone is never to love them in the first place—hardly a reasonable option, but they wanted Jesus back. No one wanted to be without Jesus, or what he was to them, to life, to himself. It was a strange concept that the gang no longer bothered to contemplate. They had the means, they had the will, and they were really good at building bungalows.

The conversation turned cheery on the way down.

"Naturally," Karen said, "Jesus will make up his own mind, but these pictures I brought along of the South Pacific should win him over."

"And," Sarah added, "I have videos of Antony and Cleopatra's family playing on the beach."

Andre was overcome by a vast hunger for life, one joy following another. "Now that we know the layout down here, it will be easy for us to sneak Mary Magdalene away. They can have a family, with a dugout canoe for every child."

Michael asked, "Do you think there is such a thing as having so much fun that you can't possibly have more fun?"

Sarah offered an opinion. She reached over and gently ran her hand up and down the inside of Michael's pant leg. "I stand corrected," he said. "What is will always remain a glimmer of what's to come. We look forward, never back."

Drones did the work. Dudley got the idea from watching a movie about a concentration camp escape, only they tunneled in instead of out. The crypt was on the side of a hill. They broke ground on the opposite slope, went down, under, then straight up to the trap door Dudley added.

The tunnel was wide enough to crouch through, and there was a ladder leading up at the end. When Karen opened the trap door, Dudley was standing between bone boxes and the melting dead. Nothing moved. All the medical equipment Karen had requested was also there.

The smell had been a prior consideration. A duct system brought in fresh air all the way from the other side of the hill. It helped, somewhat.

Dudley got the honors. He uncovered the corpse. The scars of brutal death left everyone horrified, except Dudley, who was busy calculating fluid loss, body temperature, and nanoprobe requirements.

Karen handled neuro-regeneration herself. A cerebral stimulator, basically a bushel basket mini-pod, was placed in position. Then they waited; nanoprobes take time.

"Systems check," said Karen, twenty minutes later.

"Cardiopulmonary circulation has been completely restored," Michael said with a cautious look.

"Intracranial temperature perfect, and micro-arterial circulation performing at maximum levels," Sarah reported, with excitement speeding her words.

Andre, at Karen's side, looked at her deadpan and said, "Is this really what you want to do?"

"Andre," she answered softly and soothingly, "this is what I *must* do."

"Then help yourself."

A last burst of radiation warming preceded electric arc activation of the neuro-cap. Dudley applied an ambu bag to jump-start respirations. When he stepped back, the lungs of the departed once again heaved fresh air. His eyes opened, and, to the surprise of everyone except Dudley, who had prepped the juice to do so, the corpse sat upright.

Confusion was an understatement. He looked around at the inside of the mausoleum, the hole in the floor, and the four standing before him. The nightmare of death also lingered.

But not for long. The man felt great, and smiled a wide one to let everyone know. "What ... who?" were his first words. "I mean, who are you?"

"You know me," Andre said. "I'm Adam, Elisha's friend. We spoke several times."

After looking again and swinging his legs off the table, the man slowly enunciated, with his dry mouth, "Nope, sorry. I got nothing." He then wiped blood from his face and coughed. "Boy, this place could use some ventilation."

Michael nodded in agreement and added, "You're the carpenter. Why don't you design a vent?"

"Carpenter?" the man said. "Where did you get that idea?"

"Well," said Andre, "we just assumed the man known as Jesus the carpenter was indeed a carpenter."

The young man looked around at every face. "Oh, now I get it. You think I'm Joshua, the messiah carpenter. Oh no, that's not me. I'm Sidney, the messiah plumber. But I will say, that carpenter guy is really something. He works the other side of the city. I've listened to him many times. Smart fellow. I repeat a lot of his material; works every time."

Karen stood next to Dudley with her hands on her hips.

"Well, Dudley, what do you have to say for yourself?"

"I believe the appropriate expression," he said, untroubled, "is you're welcome."

Sarah raised her voice. "You brought us to the wrong crypt, Dudley."

"Correction," he insisted, "Karen pointed to a cross and said take me to that messiah, and that is just what I did. Messiahs are a dime a dozen around here."

"He's right," agreed Sidney, the plumber.

"Yes, of course, young man," said Dudley. "Historical records document that Pontius Pilate executed over three hundred so-called messiahs during his reign. In fact, the very day our friend here was led to the hill, two others were also nailed up."

Andre was less understanding. "Dudley, you were briefed on the parameters of our search. Why did you withhold information?"

"What you really mean, Andre, is why would I assume it was logical to do so. That's an easy one. Karen jumped up, pointed, and gave me an order. It was therefore reasonable to conclude that she recognized the individual our search parameters described. Witness identification carries considerable weight."

Sidney kept feeling his body. It made him happy; being in Israel did not. "You'll have to excuse me. I have a bad taste of reality in my mouth. Does that tunnel lead out?"

"Yes, by all means, help yourself," Karen said, in that moment feeling grateful that she had helped the poor soul.

"Wonderful! I have relatives who live on their own farm in Egypt. When I hit sand, I plan to keep running until I get there. I don't know what just happened, but thank you all, and thank you, God!"

He wasted no time. Neither did Karen. Dudley showed her footage of the two other messiahs.

"That's him!" she yelped. "I am one hundred percent certain."

If at first you don't succeed…

After they packed up and covered their trail, Dudley began plan B. It was easier. The second mausoleum was more remote and was dug out of limestone, a quick grind.

Nanoprobes, fluid recycler, neuro-net, and Doctor Dudley stood to the side of death.

"That's him! That's the face!" exclaimed Karen. "I'm certain of it. And look, he didn't get beat up as much."

"No," Michael said with a twisted face, "just nailed to death."

"Let's do it," said Karen with childlike enthusiasm. She stood behind Jesus's head. Dudley had the nanoprobes unpacked and calculated.

Sarah walked over, put her arm around Karen, and looked down. "Karen," she said below a whisper, "may I speak with you for a minute?"

The two retreated to the back of the room, which did little good since every word echoed off the limestone, and Andre and Michael faced them to read their lips.

"What's on your mind, Sarah?" Karen asked, bewildered.

"It's about the resurrection."

Karen paused. She was past the need to know one way or another, and story similarities convincingly suggested that it was an add-on, which didn't affect her faith.

It was Sarah who had to ask. "Don't you really want to know, Karen?"

"Yes, I do. But I also know that it really doesn't matter," Karen whined back.

"Or you could ask yourself how much truth matters," said Andre without reprimand. "We have an opportunity here. Call it pure science if you wish."

"We could use plan C," Michael added. "One way or another Jesus walks away. It's just that with plan C we also learn something."

"Plan C?" Karen asked.

"We come back in three days."

"What if someone moves the body?"

"We'll leave a drone to guard the tomb," Andre said, obviously favoring the plan.

Sarah had her heart set on resurrection. She never let go, even when the odds kept sinking. "Karen, I'm not trying to settle a disagreement. I love you like a sister. I have no problem with the two of us looking at this differently. I'm not even sure why the issue matters. But we *can* find out if we want to."

Karen was definitely not onboard. In her mind, plan C was tossing a beach ball to Jesus. She walked to the far corner of the dank room, faced the wall, and closed her eyes. No one knew what she was doing. Two minutes elapsed before she returned to the bedside.

Karen placed the sheet back over the face of Jesus. Then she squirreled the boys' stomachs by bending over to hug him, head to head, through the cover. It lasted longer than anyone was comfortable with. Finally she stood up, dry-eyed and satisfied.

"Pack it up. We'll be back in three days."

24

Another Day

The next morning Karen floated to the breakfast buffet. No one knew just where her mind was, but wherever it was, she sure was happy. There were smiles and sparkling eyes for all.

"I felt something special yesterday," she announced, sitting down and speaking to midair, her head perfectly erect, her mood swoony.

"We felt a lot of things yesterday," Michael added, not lifting his head.

Andre interrupted loading calories. He was the only one. When she looked across the room, no one else looked back. Andre spoke in dulcet tones that alerted Karen.

"Karen, our inner limbic world brings up feelings of every sort."

"Oh…" she said, looking around. The entire room knew she was there, but they preferred to remain on the sidelines. "Andre, you also know when something is of this world or from another."

Andre nodded agreement and presented no further resistance. He also did not return to his plate of French toast, crispy fried, powdered sugar only. One look was all it took for either of them to reposition the other. Karen sat back. Her feet felt the floor for the first time since she had woken up.

"What is it, Andre?" she asked.

"I have something to show you."

He got up, walked to her side, and showed her a picture on his pad.

"That's the Tower of London," she said. "So what?"

"Drone 73 just returned from the surface with this shot."

"That's impossible," Karen said, who left her plate to run to the bow.

Andre followed. Dudley was standing by. Moving furthest forward, Karen ordered Dudley to project views from their telescope. He knew just what she was after, and there it was, in real time—the Tower of London.

"But that means …"

"Yes."

Michael, Brad, Janie, and Sarah had snuck it. They knew, and they knew what it meant to Karen. Breakfast could wait.

There was the beginning of a tear, then none, just a sniffle and a face that turned to stone.

"How?" Karen asked perplexed.

"We don't know," Andre answered.

"Dudley, Cindy …" were Karen's next words. She looked directly at them, and they answered in unison: "We don't know."

"Don't know? Don't know!" Karen projected, raising her voice. "You always know. You always have an answer, or alternatives."

"No answer. No alternatives," Cindy said in a sympathetic tone.

Andre offered a partial explanation. Bill and Lucy had bridge watch. It was three-thirty in the morning. Neither had fallen asleep on the job. Both had physiology readouts to prove it. They both also swore that one second was all it took. They just looked up and the earth had changed, and the time–date readout blinked "error." There was no error. Fifteen hundred years passed without so much as a single vibration.

"The first thing I did when I woke up this morning," Andre said, "was the usual—inspect and rebalance stored energy. That's when I knew. It was gone. Not a single joule left, and time travel is the only animal hungry enough to do that, only I don't know how it happened. It just happened."

"Andre," Karen said, combative, "you've played some dirty tricks in the past. This better not be one of them."

"It's not," said Cindy, genuinely hoping for peace in the valley. "Dudley and I reviewed the night's log. Nothing was touched. Andre slept."

"But how?" Karen asked, hurting inside.

Andre approached her with an air of timid sympathy. "Fail-safe protocols do contain override options in the event of power leaks, but both Dudley and Cindy must be notified and together agree that there is insufficient time to notify me. But they got nothing. It just happened."

"Andre," Karen began, "if you've told me once, you've—"

"Forty-three times, actually," interrupted Cindy.

"Okay, then …" Karen said, ignoring Cindy. "Forty-three times you have insisted that things don't 'just happen' in this universe; something must happen first to make them happen."

"Apparently something did. And the way you woke up this morning and walked into the dining room suggests that maybe during the night we had a visitor. Maybe that's what happened."

"Did you dream, or think you were dreaming, Karen?"

"Yes."

"About what?"

"I'd rather not say."

Karen was visibly stunned and a bit wobbly. "I … I … didn't get a chance to say goodbye."

Andre joined her at the bow, sat down against the hull, and faced her. "This is me, Andre. I know your life. I share your life. Every morning you say hello, and every night you say goodbye. Does one less time really make a difference?"

Karen shrugged off the comment with her eyebrows. "No, it's just …"

"Just what?" Andre said firmly. "Is your life just not good enough? Have you just not been lucky enough? Do you just not have enough friends? Do I just not love you enough?"

There was hurt in Andre's tone. There were tears in his eyes. He had arrayed the entire universe for Karen. He provided luxury, completed truth, and continued to offer adventure alongside endless love. And yet, it wasn't enough. He was forced to face the ultimate truth. He wasn't enough for Karen. He had failed to achieve his most cherished desire.

Michael and Sarah remained at the back of the room. When Sarah heard Karen and Andre trashing life, she reached over, took Michael by the hand, and walked all the way to the bow.

"Well, don't you two beat all," Sarah said. "Two little misfits who keep complicating life with bloated expectations, impossible goals, and needless disappointments we other mere mortals can't appreciate. Who do you think you are? What do you think you're supposed to be?

"And all the time both of you live right next to each other, with all the comfort, all the companionship, and all the hooty-tooty smart-stuff hypothesizing you want, all the way to overdose and self-pity. Smarten up! You have each other. You are all you need.

"Karen, you're depressed because you didn't get back to God. And Andre," she said, shaking her finger, "you're convinced that you've failed Karen because you're not God. Get real, guys! You're human beings. Give yourselves, and us, a break." Sarah looked over gravely, scowled, and then scolded without mercy. "You muttonheads. You might as well be blind! You both have been given more in this universe than anyone who has ever lived, but look at you, still wondering, doubting, and aching to come up with another angle, some ultimate truth or crap like that to overheat your brains. You don't know when to quit!"

"When to quit?" Michael added, at Sarah's side and as stern as she, "Andre and Karen, I'll tell you when to quit. It's right now. Neither one of you is perfect, and none of us is responsible for the universe. The answer? We know the answer. We've been given the answer. The answer is life. GO LIVE IT! The two of you, get off your asses and spend the day by yourselves in the habitat. Cindy has a private bungalow for you. I stocked it myself this morning. By dinner we will expect stories of paddle boarding, swimming, and a long nap together."

"Together?" Karen asked, looking directly at Sarah.

"Yes!" she replied. "Together. You can have Andre's brain. I'll take Michael's body any day."

Karen stood up, gave Sarah a long hug, and then headed for the door with her.

Andre and Michael were left alone at the bow.

"Michael," Andre asked, "when did we lose control?"

"You can't lose something you never had," Michael said, beginning a laugh that caught on from one corner of the bridge to the other.

Sarah opened the door, pulled it to the side, and planted herself on the spot. Karen took one step through by herself, then turned back to face Andre. "Well, Andre, are you coming?"

Under his breath Michael whispered sideways, "Andre, Karen just asked you if you're coming. Don't say 'not yet, but I will let you know.' Just say 'yes, dear.'"

"Yes, dear."

—m—

24 hours later

The crew of Explorer Seven had time-jumped past the terror of the Roman Empire, the terror of the Holy Roman Empire, and the pope's declaration of the Divine Right of Kings that turned an entire continent of white serfs into slaves.

On the other hand, you can call a saint the devil, and call Beelzebub a cherub, but you can't call a 5 a 4, and the universe communicates in numbers. Apparently, mathematics is God's first language. All mankind needed was for someone to invent calculus. Enter Sir Isaac Newton, on-screen, spy-drone-projected from the surface.

Andre walked onstage and stood in front of the picture to get as close to his hero as he could. After a few hecklers made themselves known, Cindy took Andre by the hand and moved him to the side.

"That's him, Cindy!" Andre exclaimed triumphantly. "That's the man who invented science. He never took 'no' or 'I don't know' for an answer. He was a mathematician, physicist, and astronomer."

A second picture split the screen. It was from another drone that Michael dispatched to the scene, which took no time at all since the ship had been moved to a stationary orbit above England. The crew were all in on it. After Michael's prank, they wagered on how long it would take Andre to shuttle down and shake Isaac Newton's hand.

Michael's drone caught the man, dressed in long coat, vest waistcoat, cravat, wig, and breeches, walking through the park with a friend, who appeared in parson's clothing. A debate was in progress. Newton led off: "We are certainly not to relinquish the evidence of experiments for the sake of dreams and vain fictions of our own devising; nor are we to recede from the analogy of nature, which is want to be simple and always consummate to itself."

"Do you really wish to embarrass yourself with such notions?" his frocked friend said. "We have all the answers we need. All is as God has made it so. We need know nothing more."

The two left the park. Dudley's research suggested they were heading for Newton's house.

"Why is there a third camera angle from a drone directly overhead, Michael?"

"Oh, nothing," Michael replied, so casually that Andre let it slide.

The discussion was heating up. Newton's friend was most specific: "It would be best if you would stop these experiments of yours, Isaac. Neither the king, the head bishop, nor the pope will tolerate disagreement. Their proclamations are all the information we need to know."

Newton lowered his head, shaking it in disappointment. "I can calculate the motion of heavenly bodies, but not the madness of mankind. And I don't know what I may appear to the world, but to myself I seem to be only a boy playing on the seashore, and diverting myself in now and then finding a smoother pebble or a prettier shell than ordinary, whilst the great ocean of truth lay all undiscovered before me."

Andre directed his drone to show him Michael's. It was a miniature drone holding an apple. Michael loved the story, but it had never been confirmed. As soon as Newton sat down under an apple tree, Michael planned to release the apple.

"Who knows," Michael said in his defense, with a grin, "maybe the apple I'm about to drop begins his formulating of gravity. Before Isaac Newton, civilization thought things fell down 'because they did.'"

The crowd shushed Michael and Andre onstage. They were there to listen.

There were apple trees in Newton's backyard. The men were headed toward one.

"Stand by, Dudley," Michael said.

Newton continued his discussion with the local representative of organized religion. "To me there has never been a higher source of earthly honor or distinction than that connected with the advancement in science."

The two sat down on a bench that, as luck would have it, was under an apple tree. Michael held Dudley off until the two finished talking. He wanted to find out how the conversation ended.

Newton's friend lowered his head to preach damnation. "Isaac, you must repent. Things happen on earth because God makes them happen. If you want to save your soul, you'll give up on this number nonsense of yours and embrace the will of God."

Michael chuckled before adding other thoughts from earth's past. "Titles are shadows, and crowns empty things. That minister has lost his way. To laugh at men of science is the privilege of fools."

Newton possessed a will that would not be shattered. "What you really want to say, my misdirected old friend, is that I should agree with you, and the bishop, and the king, and the pope, and everyone else speaking utter nonsense. The word 'God' signifies 'Lord,' but every lord is not God. It is the dominion of a spiritual being to be a true God or an imaginary God.

"Truth is ever to be found in simplicity, and certainly not in the multiplicity and confusion of things. Your rules and laws are absolutes based on nothing. You build walls. You never build bridges."

"Now," Michael announced.

The drone opened its claw. The apple dropped.

Newton looked up, confused. The rest of the tree hadn't ripened, and apples that red were nowhere to be found in all of Europe.

"Wait a minute," said Newton, "it is not just the apple that fell. The earth was also pulled up toward the apple. Or, better yet, at the moment of release, the apple responded to a force emanating from the larger mass of the planet, and the planet also was pulled up toward the apple. The two met somewhere in between. We just don't have instruments sensitive enough to measure the change in the earth's position. Gravity is the mutual force of attraction that governs the entire universe!"

Isaac Newton stood up and walked ten steps toward his lab before he remembered leaving the minister on the bench. "Pardon me, monsignor. I must get to my lab."

"You're wasting your time, Isaac. If you really want to help the world, go to church, sit in a pew, and repeat 'Hail Mary full of grace' ten thousand times. You are violating the will of God. I wash my hands of you."

"You know," Andre said to Michael, "you might have been right about that apple. It did distract Isaac from that narrow-brain God-nut."

"I see," Michael replied, satisfied; then with a look over to the crew checking their bets, he said, "So, when do we leave for the surface? The girls love to dress up. We can meet the king."

"Put it to a vote—I want to go home, Michael."

The tally was 240 to go home, zero to stay, unless you counted Dudley and Cindy, who were allowed one hour on the surface to meet the man who made them possible.

25

Twenty-Five Future Years Later

There is a reason a child's eyes pop wide open the second their feet begin to move—it is the earth, a resplendent bloom of enduring tones beneath blue that deserves heavenly praise. There's a reason youth dances to the romance of the eternal comedy of love—it is the earth, which fires passion one spring after another.

There are many reasons parents hold each other tight while watching their own play a day away; and there are even more reasons those who have seen more years look back on something so dear, so generous—the earth.

It was such a day on planet Earth that Andre, Michael, Karen, and Sarah shared the northern woods of Wisconsin with their families, and the sometimes dry, sometimes drenched challenging northern rapids in August.

"We're not going to make it, Michael," yelled Andre, barely heard from the front of their canoe as one giant rock after another flew past, funneling a deluge of river between pairs of boulders.

"It will work, Andre," Michael insisted. "If we have enough speed to plane out of the water, we'll make it through the gauntlets."

Andre was never without his pad. He picked it up to remind Michael that he had done the math. "Our weight displacement fraction leaves insufficient freeboard to prevent the wall-water waves from pouring over the gunwales … There! … Once again … at least fifty gallons … and all on me before it hit the floor, which now makes us even heavier."

"The automatic bailer is working," Michael added, not believing it himself.

"Right, Michael. At two gallons a minute, while we take on ten. Tell me again, why the hell aren't we in a covered kayak that can't be swamped?"

"You know why. It's because Karen and Sarah bet us that they could get down the rapids and we couldn't."

"They are one hundred and fifty pounds lighter than we are. Their canoe rides higher, and Karen's idea to put Sarah midship brings the bow up faster. My numbers prove we haven't a chance."

"Exactly! That's what makes it fun, Andre. And don't move to mid-thwart again. My weight back here is barely clearing the bottom."

Karen and Sarah had been given a head start. Time was not an issue; either you made it through or you didn't. Andre's three kids—Adam, Esmeralda, and Jesus—and Michael's triple play—Mary, Beverly, and little Michael—cast off last to amuse themselves with the spectacle of adults lowering themselves to child's play. All six were in whitewater kayaks. All six could barrel roll their way out of anything.

The speed of the kayaks, surfing a ledge drop, brought each kid to the side, and then by Andre and Michael struggling to stay afloat. Adam was the first. He back-paddled to stall for a second next to his papa.

"Father," the fifteen-year-old said, enjoying watching his smart dad do something really stupid, "your water line just dropped four centimeters. I predict you have two shoots left before you're swamped and must swim to shore. Would you like me to have Dudley gravity-extract your vessel?"

Andre didn't get a chance to answer. Michael beat him to it. "Absolutely not, Adam, and that is an order. Your dad's brain and my brawn never fail. We will do this!"

Adam hit a crest that sent him flying ahead. His eyes were on the game. He was heard calling out "Ya-hoo!"

The girls—Beverly, Mary, and Esmeralda—lowered their speed by dragging paddle, and took turns sending one ahead to scout the best water. As Esmeralda passed her dad, she pointed to the opposite side of the rapids, where she recommended Bev and Mary go through.

"Papa," she said, "mama told me you haven't a chance."

"What a coincidence," Andre said, pulling water sideways to almost miss the next boulder, which did indeed dent the front of their aluminum canoe. "That's the same thing she said to me the first time I tried to kiss her."

"Bye-bye, Papa! And just remember, there's no shame in losing to a woman."

"Of course," Andre said, not taking his eyes off the funnel ahead, "I tell that to myself as often as not, but not today. We are going to do this."

Beverly and Mary slid by them near the calmer left bank. Both giggled at the expressions and sweat on their dads' faces.

The next drop was half a waterfall. There was no family in sight. Michael and Andre were about to go down, literally.

"Michael!" Andre yelled back, placing his paddle sideways, with water halfway up his legs as he knelt on the bottom of the canoe, "Do you acknowledge the inevitable?"

Michael was having an impossible time steering. Whenever he placed his paddle out for a power stroke, the canoe let in so much water in that he had to jump to the other side to keep from tipping over.

"Andre! I admit defeat! All my muscle can't get this tub moving fast enough to top waves. Other than cheating, what do you have?"

"Pull over. I have an idea, and it is legal. We will get our canoe through this."

For Andre, the slogan "be prepared" always came in handy. The calculated probability of a thunderstorm was less than 10 percent, but it was not zero. Hence, Andre had packed a poncho.

In less than a minute, on the side of the foaming stream, Michael and Andre picked up and flipped their canoe bone dry. Andre next sat inside, one thwart back only, and put on his poncho. Following Andre's instruction, Michael secured the front of the poncho over the front of the canoe, and did similar roping behind where Andre sat.

Off they went. Andre sat inside, arms at his sides and only his head sticking out low at the bow. Michael did all the paddling.

"Hold your breath, Andre! We have a big one coming up."

"You don't have to tell me. It looks twice as big from where I'm sitting."

It was actually three times the size of anything they had come up against, so massive that Karen and Sarah ahead of them almost went under and barely made it to the shore to dump out before proceeding—something both agreed not to share with the guys. Beverly, the only straggler who caught the mishap, agreed to go along with the cover-up.

The hole beyond the rock funnel was ten feet deep. The front of their canoe, Andre included, disappeared completely, but the tarp held, and not a gallon made it over the top before the bow emerged from the froth. Andre took a deep breath, and Michael centered the boat.

"I'm sure glad I'm not an insect," Andre said, laughing at their triumph. "Now I know what a spider feels like when it gets flushed down the toilet."

Dudley and Cindy had dropped off camping gear on the wooded wilderness flats that followed. It was a perfect spot, northern pine surrounded and untouched by industry. Then, following orders, they disappeared to give both families a chance to be one with nature.

Andre told Michael to make straight for shore. His head sticking out opened every mouth laughing as soon as they rounded the bend. Michael stopped paddling to coast the last leg, something little Michael had never seen muscle dad do before.

The contest was declared a draw. Both sexes were successful.

Four hours later

Facing the river, two adult tents were flanked by two kids' tents, one for the boys and one for the girls. Andre, Karen, Michael, and Sarah sat warming themselves at the fire and finishing off a hot marshmallow or two.

"Which is harder to do," Sarah asked, "saying no to the kids or saying no to their grandparents?"

Michael's folks, Karen's folks, Sarah's folks, and Andre's dad had the kids at water's edge, trying to catch more trout. The ten they shared for dinner were well cooked, delicious, and examined by Andre with his portable electron microscope for pathogens.

"And we even told them that we wanted a private wilderness experience with the kids," said Karen. "They spoil them rotten."

"Well," Andre said, "at least they didn't park their shuttle next to our tents and invite the kids in for 3D gaming—"

"And disco dancing," Michael interrupted.

"Yes. Don't tell them, but I left instructions with Dudley to move their shuttle five miles away at sunset and to develop thrust and communication problems if they budge before ten tomorrow morning."

—⚒—

Five hours later

"Keep whispering," Karen requested, "I think the kids are sleeping."

"Uh-oh—do you see what I see?" said Andre. He tapped his pad. "C-D … front and center."

Cindy and Dudley responded, and were expecting as much, which is why the two of them, standing up and propelled by gravity belts, took less than ten seconds to fly in over the towering pines to the fireside. They held hands the entire way.

"I just found out myself," Cindy said, prepared to defend her behavior. "Brad and Janie arrived a day early. They contacted me ten minutes ago."

A space bullet, the latest high-speed shuttle, lit up the sky as it passed grandpas and grandmas, who couldn't figure out why they couldn't get off the ground. The side of the shuttle was easy to read: "Explorer Seven."

Brad didn't extend floats to anchor on the stream. He didn't put down stilts to disturb the beach. He just came to a complete stop six inches off the ground as the door opened and the gangplank extended.

Janie didn't wait for it to hit the ground. She ran full speed ahead, first hugging Karen, then pulling Andre in, and down the line from there. Brad's pace was slow and dignified; after all, he had just been elected the galaxy ambassador for planet Earth.

He and Janie had never left Explorer Seven. What started as a whirlwind honeymoon turned into a profession. He and Janie were the most well-known, respected, and honored couple alive.

"Where are the kids?" Karen asked.

"We put them to sleep before we left the ship."

"And your oldest?" Sarah asked.

"Is just eight, and never stops talking."

The camping kids weren't sleeping. Adam's pad was linked to planet ship scan. He knew Explorer Seven was on its way before Dudley did. All six ran out to hug uncle and auntie.

Three days later

Brad and Janie's fireside chat was brief. They had business to attend to, and banquets, and honorary diplomas, and retirement cookouts, and of course the grand ball hosted by none other than Janie, a consummate politician.

On the second day, all three families shared lunch aboard Explorer Seven. Time travel hardware was replaced by warp twenty slide-packs, but only after Earth's best couldn't get the ship to do what Andre accomplished, and twice almost lost her completely.

The third day, Brad declined an invitation to attend the grand opening of the latest orbiting space station. He, Andre, and Michael spent their time doing thirty minutes of each of their favorite sports on Explorer Seven. Brad, for the first time ever, actually beat Michael at squash. Michael said it was because he was rusty. Andre said it was because his stomach wasn't.

The girls played "dress-up-dare-you." Inside Andre's Lake Michigan mansion, each picked a period and style, like Earth revolutionary-simple, disco sequin-fancy, or future cotton-thin natural—a look that within two feet makes the wearer appear naked. The outfit that won had to be worn by all for lunch and all the way to Chicago for afternoon tea.

The nights were free to pursue private lives. Two days after Janie and Brad arrived, Karen reserved her usual habitat bungalow at Excelsior, a private club on the other side of what was once Canada. Cindy and Dudley were the only ones allowed to offer membership. Twelve months a year the indoor habitat, complete with personal cottage, was maintained at a pleasant seventy-six degrees, the private pond kept clean, with two robot maids standing by. Karen never activated them. She preferred peace and quiet.

The space was locked down. No one got in who was not invited. That's why Karen's clothes hit the floor on the other side of the door.

She looked down at herself. Nothing sagged. Her gravity implants made sure of that. In the dark or the light, she looked as if she hadn't aged a day since she married Andre.

"There is something about a naked swim," she said to herself, "that makes me feel *more* naked. Maybe it's the water rushing between my legs. Speaking of my legs, it's almost eight, and time to meet up in the cabin."

Two steps onto the beach she was warm-air dried by vents placed just for that purpose. Halfway up the stairs, nozzles on the sides of two palm trees sprayed invigorating skin cream below her neck.

When she got to the bedroom, she pulled the sheets back, placed two pillows, and lay down on her stomach.

"Oh … that's perfect … a little lower … I look forward to your back rubs all week, Michael."

"And I look forward to giving them," he replied, having skipped the dip and the spray to go straight to heaven.

"And now the front," Karen said as she rolled over, "and just your tongue will do. Oh my...oh my...would that every woman could have it so good."

Twenty minutes and one hundred decibels later, Karen rolled Michael over to ride on top.

"Oh...oh...oh..." she moaned. "Don't move, just breathe...that's all it takes."

That and again, and again, and again. The secret, they say, is never look back. Michael agreed. Every time he got up to go and looked back, the races started again, complete with home-stretch finish.

When at last he felt his legs wobble getting out of bed, he looked away and walked to the porch. Living wall constellations of planet Reptilia were playing. Clad in a robe, Karen joined him.

"A wonderful night as always, Michael."

"Every week I say to myself that there is no way it can get better. Then, the next week it does."

"Michael," Karen asked, "do you think Sarah has any idea you're my Friday night?"

"I'm sure she doesn't. And besides, she does her own thing once a week just like us. Everyone wins, no one loses."

"I still don't understand how you got Cindy on your side. She is such a blabbermouth troublemaker. I thought for sure she would blow our cover."

"If you promise not to leak the info, or technology, I will let you in on my secret."

"I've kept every one for the last twenty years."

"Okay," Michael said, laughing through his presentation. "I have, all by myself, designed an orgasm component that lets her get off on Dudley. She knows that if she so much as peeps a hint of us, it's gone. After the first night she begged to keep it. She's not a problem, and has confused Andre for us several times."

"Speaking of several times," Karen said, letting her robe fall to the floor before bending over the rail.

—◊—

Two hundred miles, or a ten-minute flight away

"I see," said Andre, "this is Indian night again. You actually want me to pick you up, throw you over my shoulder, take you into the tepee, rip your clothes off, and do you good?"

"Yeah, that's basically it," said Sarah, adjusting her beads, adding a feather, and pulling her dress down all the way to her feet. "But this time begin with kisses on the inner side of my right thigh all the way up, go in, and then down the other."

"Is all this really necessary?" asked Andre.

"Yes, including the drumbeat, which will start slow, once per second, then pick up slowly, as you follow with the same rhythm in me faster and faster."

"Okay," Andre said, sneaking a look by lifting Sarah's skirt for a preview. "Works for me. And I get second choice."

"Why, of course, my dear. What will it be? Upside-down cake again?"

"You know it's my favorite."

It took white man long time to make squaw squeal, and squeal, and sing to the spirits. Sarah said she wanted to wake her ancestors. She definitely did, but no one else, since the camp she owned, which Michael didn't know about, was miles from nowhere.

Sarah rolled over, panting. Andre just smiled, then giggled, then smiled, and smiled. Ten minutes later Sarah popped the question:

"Now, Andre?"

"Now would be just fine."

Andre laid back. It was Sarah's turn to stimulate Andre, two square millimeters at a time, which was the surface area of the tip of her tongue that made contact, up and down his most vertical, and growing, center of attention.

The rest was on autopilot. With perfect balance, Sarah welcomed Andre's crescendo, penetrating deeper than he imagined possible. Then, without losing the rhythm of her pumping, Sarah moved her body around, put both knees around Andre's head, and lowered her hips onto his waiting tongue.

A full spin was next. The tongues had it—hers around his, his in hers. One night they just held position "euphoria," their pet name for it, for twenty minutes. And Andre had the same problem Michael did. If, on retreating, he looked up or down or, heaven forbid, up and down—wow—it was back to the tepee.

Is sex the best there is? Or is it the moments that follow, when two have fulfilled more than both could hope for and then have each other to hold, closer, more intimate and more dear than love imagines possible?

Who cares? Best—better than best—could be—might have been. Hours of lust feel like days, and what a way to breathe them by.

"Sarah," Andre asked, "do you think Michael has any idea I'm your Friday night?"

"Absolutely not. Besides, he does his thing, we're all free. But I do worry about Dudley. How did you get him to keep his mouth shut? He and Michael spend half their time together."

"Remember years ago, when I told you I added another program to Dudley's interface?"

"Yeah, sure, a discipline thing, you said. As if he needs more, the dull blockhead."

"It was a little more complicated than that, and you might have noticed it was about the same time he and Cindy started holding hands."

"Oh, yeah, that still strikes me as a little strange."

"Okay … well … not entirely. You see, I added orgasms, and threatened to take them away if any news of us leaked out. Since then he monitors Karen to make sure our paths don't cross."

Sarah stretched luxuriously and sighed, "Great idea, and Michael does his own thing Friday night anyway" Sarah said. "Life is so grand it's hard to believe."

"Speaking of hard..."

It has been said that there is no such thing as bad sex, which is true. It has also been said that there is nothing in the universe better than good sex, which is also true.

26

Ever After

Lake Michigan's northern shore resembled Maine's Downeast coastline, except you could drink the water. That's where Karen and Andre had their vacation compound, which was another way of saying "Boy, are we rich." Karen's dad gave her brother an entire planet.

In addition to the post-and-beam central lodge, six private beachfront cabins dotted the compound's one mile of waterfront. Each had its own dock and several boats, and you could windsurf, paddle, or cruise, quietly solar powered and eco-pure.

The queen of the fleet was Explorer Eight, a two-hundred-ten-foot motor sailer docked in front of the main hall. It was Andre's second love, unless you counted Explorer Seven, and then it was his third. When fall arrived each year, as it had a habit of doing, robot sailors navigated the yacht through the St. Lawrence Seaway to the North Atlantic. Three days later the warm beaches of the eastern Mediterranean were reached, and the vessel was prepared for the arrival of the family at any time.

Andre never stopped looking up, and once a year he took a one-month sabbatical from teaching to visit an unexplored quadrant of the galaxy, always with Adam, and occasionally with the entire family.

There were times when Andre's off-planet excursions overlapped Karen's global psychology conference, when she, the head of the academy, would present pod scan results. Every year Karen and her staff absorbed accolades; never before had the entire planet slept better, ate heathier, exercised more completely, and made better love. "Input in—output out," was her favorite lead-in.

The compound also had a boathouse containing a host of craft, ranging from a fifty-two-foot lunch boat to a nine-foot wave surfer. Above the boathouse was a four-thousand-square-foot guest suite, where Brad, Janie, and their daughters Pricilla and Jacoline stayed, just for a night, to make the Sunday spiritual hootenanny before diplomatic need whisked them away.

"Dad, did you hear about the storm headed our way?" asked Pricilla while holding her dad's hand as they boarded Explorer Eight for the day's event.

There was only a 40 percent chance that the heat index would raise enough water vapor to precipitate a thundershower over the lake, but it was something Andre and his kids looked forward to.

Janie was the last up the gangplank to be greeted by Karen. The two hugged, and at Janie's request, Karen opened the present Janie had wrapped for her. It was a framed Arabic proverb, 60 percent original manuscript, 40 percent molecular reconstruction, that looked just like it had a thousand years ago when one of Janie's ancestors wrote it.

"Thank you so much, Janie," Karen said, getting emotional for no good reason, except perhaps the past. "I'll hang it on the wall of the main salon. I was hoping you would be guest master of ceremonies this evening."

Janie laughed and gave Karen a kiss on the cheek. "Karen, have you ever known me to pass up an invitation to go onstage?"

"No, and I like the idea of having your five-year-old Jacoline end the meeting with a poem."

"Yes, and thank you; it took her two days to memorize it. She also enjoys the spotlight. It must run in the family."

"So," Karen said, moving wrapping paper out of the way, "let's have a look at this ancient wisdom of yours."

"May I?" Janie asked, inviting herself. After a run-through in perfect Arabic, Janie translated: "Write the wrongs that are done to you in sand, but write the good things that happen to you on a piece of marble. Let go of all emotions such as resentment and retaliation, which diminish you, and hold on to the emotions, such as gratitude and joy, that increase you."

"How lovely," Karen said, with yet another hug for everyone within reach.

Michael and Brad cast off the bow line, the spring line, and the stern line. Then they met Andre on the bridge. Andre had two identical instrument panels, one inside-temperature-controlled, the other forward to feel the wind on his face. Both included electric sail trim, autopilot, and readouts from four drones hovering one quarter mile off the bow and stern.

A twelve-knot southwest blow heeled the sloop ten degrees, making fifteen knots over the water a perfect point of sail.

"Is that the electric output meter?" Brad asked.

"Yes," said Andre, "and only 60 percent of it is deck solar generated. The rest comes from the propellers."

"The propellers?" little Michael asked, who was forever holding his dad's coattails.

"Yes, Michaelette," as Andre called him. "When the electric motor is engaged, the propellers push us along. When we are sailing, and the motor is disconnected, the propellers spin from water moving by, which is free since the sails provide propulsion. That's when we connect the props to our generator. We use the speed through water to make electricity. We also cook and heat electrically. There is not an ounce of carbon-based fuel onboard."

"That's some battery pack you have there, Andre," Brad noticed.

"And placing juice deep in the keel means less lead for ballast."

The radar had everyone's attention. A towering chimney blackened the sky.

"The storm's bearing is one hundred and twenty degrees," Andre announced. "The center is moving north by northeast at a whopping thirty miles an hour. It's a beauty; might even be packing eighty-mile-an-hour winds."

Brad laughed at sailors taking their little toys across a dinky lake. However, the enormity of the approaching cloud bank sobered them and commanded respect.

"Even I can do the math here," he said to Andre. "Eighty-mile-an-hour winds and the square footage of the sail you have flying will knock this tub over. We'll all be standing on the port wall."

Andre explained that it could happen, but not for long, since the keel's center of water resistance was forward of the center of force felt above from the sails. A gust or storm automatically turned the boat into the wind, where it would luff safely until the sails were doused.

"But we won't wait. It's on its way. We'll take in sail now. Michaelette, would you like to do the honors?"

"Boy, would I," said the lad, coming to attention to salute the captain.

"Roger that," Andre responded in military fashion. "Reduce sail area by 60 percent. Keep it balanced and change course to one-fifty-nine. That's one, fiver, niner, sailor."

"Aye aye, sir."

Everyone gathered inside the safe pilothouse. The wind howled and the rain pelted with ungodly force. Lightning lit the sky in streaks connected cloud to cloud, so loud the kids put their hands over their ears. It was glorious. Michael, Brad, and Andre looked around at everyone having a wild adventure. All three were thinking about what they had gone through in outer space. Nothing was said, but Michael moved between Brad and Andre and put one arm around each.

To add thrill and personal amusement, the three dads added a chorus of "They built the ship Titanic, and when they had it done, they thought they had a ship that the water wouldn't go through. But the lord's almighty hand said that it would never stand. It was sad when that great ship went down … Oh, it was sad, so sad, it was sad, so sad …"

The storm passed, the sun came out, the wind dropped, the sails went up, and deck chair cocktail service resumed. Andre handed Dudley the wheel. Cindy, at his side, took over navigation and collision control, an easy assignment since nary a vessel was in sight.

Michael, Andre, and Brad walked to the bow. When you're exploring, one hundred feet farther does feel better.

"See that island over there off the Canadian coast?" Andre said, pointing.

"Let me guess," Brad said, "you own that, too."

"As a matter of fact, we do. There's a mooring ball waiting on the sheltered side, and nowhere in the universe can you beat the flavor of the wild blueberries on the shore."

Adam and little Michael went windsurfing. Esmeralda, Pricilla, and Beverly rowed to the island to pick and eat, and eat and pick, blueberries. Five-year-old Jacoline followed her mother around and brought her a Singapore sling she didn't order.

Without the influence of encouragement or disapproval, Karen's ten-year-old developed a thing for Michael's ten-year-old. They would walk off all by themselves for a quiet game of shuffleboard, or disappear into the woods hiking, or just hold hands. It brought a smile when someone would say, "There go Jesus and Mary."

Onshore, Michael dug a hole in the sand, and what a hole—three feet deep and ten feet square. The fire took two hours to burn down to coals. That's when Cindy layered it up, first with large leaf seaweed imported from Maine, then lobsters imported from Maine, then more seaweed, six inches of Maine clams, more lobsters, and a final layer of seaweed to steam it all perfectly.

"Really, Andre?" Janie asked. "Real butter?"

Andre's fingers were dripping. He was on his second lobster and ninth clam.

"It's from our own cow. This butter gives it purpose, and it makes me happy. And yes, there is a difference. I'll take the real thing any day."

You know it's time to sit when you can no longer stand. The overfed shore party all had the same idea: activate a gravity belt where they lay on the beach blanket, and the entire blanket, themselves included, would be lifted off the ground and onto the deck of Explorer Eight.

No one asked Dudley to do so; there are limits. And they were a family. They all groaned at the same time. The spiritual hootenanny was about to happen, and no one was to be late.

They decided to meet on the bow. The sun was setting. As always, Janie outdid herself, with a chiffon gown and jewels from planets no one could pronounce. She handed out duplicates on request, which cinched her as the "master of ceremonies of the year."

The kids picked songs, although the speech Karen had given the little ones about democracy in action backfired: There were six adults and eight children. The adults were outvoted when they wanted to delete rap numbers. Andre got around it by adding Dudley and Cindy, who obliged Karen and Andre on request and ran the surround sound.

The adults ended up going along with half of the kids' music requests. Their second wish the adults obliged completely. They wanted to see their parents, and each of their aunts and uncles, get up and say a few words. It was scheduled after the singing, which went well, and long, and ended with a special request to hear Cindy, the diva of North America.

So there they were, all six—Andre, Karen, Michael, Sarah, Brad, and Janie—standing at the bow, facing the stern, in front of all. Janie began:

"The proverb that Karen hung below deck is my saying of the day. Sarah will start things off."

Sarah stepped forward and smiled at so many happy, loving faces looking back. Her eyes came to rest on her oldest daughter, Beverly.

"When I was your age, a friend of mine from California reminded me that life is made up of many moments—of tenderness, of laughter, of devilishness, of hope, of insight, of success. They are all wonderful things, but there is something even more important. In the end, the quality of our lives is based on how much we live for now, on how many quality moments we allow ourselves to experience and appreciate.

"My advice," Sarah said, slowing down, "is to breathe, move, and express existence as a grand happiness, because that's what it is."

"Amen to that," was repeated, and heard loudest from baritone Michael, who was ushered forward.

"The teams I've coached have won more gold medals than any others in history. I know what it takes to get the job done. I work with young people who continue to astound me, who have taught me that you can't beat someone who never gives up. Persistence is the secret of success.

"Yes, of course ability counts, but so does courage, faith, pride, acceptance, effort, optimism, diligence, and commitment. Victory will prevail at all times when we make it so."

Michael ended his segment with an old-fashioned cheerleader's call: "Hip-hip-hurray!"

Brad was next up to ham it up. He spread both arms out wide and pretended to be an airplane coming in for a landing, right after almost crashing into three children giggling at his crazy face.

"Oh," he said, slanting his eyes off to the side, thinking. "I've got one for all you Buddha brains. When you are flying too high, aim down. When you are cruising too low, aim up. There is safety and clear skies in the middle, and all profitable correction comes from a calm, peaceful mind; so play it cool. Don't freak up, don't freak down, and don't freak out."

Karen got up next, and got sentimental again. It wasn't every day, or year, that her favorite people in the whole universe were all together. She gave each face a second, and then cleared her throat.

"I am a brain mechanic. I fix minds. Well, actually, I help them fix themselves. Step one is to acknowledge that biologic drives and biologic needs are nonnegotiable. Yes, sure, they can be denied. They can be repressed. They can be smothered to submission. But not without a cost, like happiness, fulfillment, and enthusiasm—not to mention a good night's sleep.

"Don't give adversity the satisfaction of getting you down. Suffer not self-pity. In the glamour of martyrdom you will only find regret. Conquer yourself, if nothing else. All we need do is make a conscious effort to cultivate positive qualities.

"In the whole of history there has never existed a single person whose conduct was always perfect. Do not let conflict possess your existence.

We need to give ourselves a break, to free ourselves from the unnecessary burden of artificial moral strictures.

"Be serene, forgiving, content, and self-controlled. The best response proceeds slowly with focused concentration. We will make it so. Happiness and optimism shall prevail."

"Amens" were back, and they lasted until Andre stepped forward to add final words. He began with a Tibetan proverb:

"Someone whose faith is not grounded in reason is like a stream of water that can be led anywhere. Science is a method of insistence, and truth is not an unstable variable. It is cold, indifferent, and engulfing and never bends under the burden of itself.

"Evolution comes with a price tag, and we must pay it. I mean, what the hell do we want from God, anyway? Give the guy a break—he knows when to stir the pot. God would not be here with us if everything wasn't going to keep getting better, and better, with an end, that is also today.

"But be wary, one and all. We must make sure others do not give way to greed, power, and personal gain. The forces of goodness must never lose their way. Those who scheme to enslave the mind and body of others can be dealt with. There is reason for being.

"And we—the human race—will move ahead; else tomorrow will be no different than today. Mankind's steps are paced by God himself. His completed goal is as yet beyond our understanding. Pay no heed. There is only one place we all meet God—in our hearts.

"We are never separated from the consciousness of God, and our lives are, will be, and ever shall be an endless dialogue with God."

One minute of silence followed.

Jacoline, Janie's five-year old, did not need to be led forward. She knew she followed Andre for the last spot. She was wearing her favorite character dress, Snow White and the Seven Dwarfs. It wasn't the sleeping thing that got her. She liked the idea of being surrounded by seven little friends.

"Hello, aunts and uncles… Hellooooo…"

She added the funny word and did a wiggle just like she'd practiced with mommy, and she got laughs and applause for her performance.

"My poem is called 'What I Live For.' It was written a long time ago by George Linnaeus Banks. If you've heard it, don't tell the ending. But I will give you a clue. It ends a lot like it starts."

She read:

> I live for those who love me,
> Whose hearts are kind and true,
> For heaven that smiles above me,
> And awaits my spirit too;
> For all human ties that bind me,
> For the task by God assigned me,
> For the bright hopes yet to find me,
> And the good that I can do.
>
> I live to learn their story
> Who suffered for my sake;
> To emulate their glory,
> And follow in their wake;
> Bards, patriots, martyrs, sages
> The heroic of all ages,
> Whose deeds crowd History's pages,
> And time's great volume make.
>
> I live to hold communion
> With all that is divine,
> To feel there is a union
> Twixt Nature's heart and mine;
> To profit by affliction,
> Reap truth from fields of fiction,
> Grow wiser from conviction,
> And fulfil God's grand design.
>
> I live to hail that season
> By gifted minds foretold,
> When men shall rule by reason,

And not alone by gold;
When man to man united,
And every wrong thing righted,
The whole world shall be lighted
As Eden was of old.

I live for those who love me,
For those who know me true,
For heaven that smiles above me
And awaits my spirit too;
For the cause that lacks assistance,
For the wrong that needs resistance,
For the future in the distance,
And the good that I can do.

—⁂—

And they all lived happily ever after.

www.ingramcontent.com/pod-product-compliance
Lightning Source LLC
Chambersburg PA
CBHW070521100726
47907CB00004B/927